Also available from Carla de Guzman

If the Dress Fits
The Queen's Game (Cincamarre Book 1)
Stealing Luna (Cincamarre Book 2)
Chasing Mindy
How She Likes It
Alta: A High School Romance Anthology
Make My Wish Come True:
A #romanceclass Christmas Anthology

Watch out for *Making A Scene*,
part of the #romanceclass Flair project,
coming soon!

SWEET ON YOU

CARLA DE GUZMAN

carina
press

carina
press®

Recycling programs
for this product may
not exist in your area.

ISBN-13: 978-1-335-65284-3

Sweet on You

Copyright © 2020 by Carla Marie Angela K. de Guzman

This edition published by arrangement with Harlequin Books S.A.

For questions and comments about the quality of this book, please contact us at CustomerService@Harlequin.com.

Carina Press
22 Adelaide St. West, 40th Floor
Toronto, Ontario M5H 4E3, Canada
www.CarinaPress.com

Printed in U.S.A.

To the #romanceclass community always, forever.

SWEET ON YOU

Chapter One

To Sari Tomas, finding the right café was like finding the perfect pair of jeans. She loved cafés that welcomed you inside like you walked into someone's inspiration board come to life, except the coffee was much better, the desserts were delicious, and the music was excellent. If you were extra lucky, there would be food, and that food would be good too.

After having spent her life in and out of cafés for studying, hanging out with friends, or just spending time with herself, Sari had always longed to open up a little place of her own. Somewhere she could always be useful and needed, somewhere that she could come to every day and work.

Their grandmother had run Tomas Coffee Co. for thirty-five years. She had done it all by herself, but when Sari, Sam and Selene took over, they decided on a different approach. They agreed to split the business according to the things they were good at, and the things they wanted.

Selene, the oldest, who loved the idea of running things and being in charge, ran the corporation from

Manila. She got the condo in Makati City, with room for her sisters when they needed it, of course. Sam, the youngest, who was only twenty-three then, had no idea what she wanted to do, and was willing to do anything. So she went down to Los Baños to learn agriculture and farming, and took over the Tomas Farm, growing their famous robusta beans.

And Sari, the middle child, who longed for a café of her own, learned the fine art of roasting coffee, creating signature blends for clients, got Café Cecilia. Named after their great, great grandmother who started the company, the café had been a side project that their grandmother put aside, until Sari picked up the lease from the Laneways and transformed it into her dream café.

The hundred-square-meter shop was everything she had ever wanted. It had a light, airy ambience thanks to the old warehouse windows that overlooked the Laneways, a carefully crafted mix of eclectic and comfortable furniture after scouting trips to Tagay-tay and Ermita, patterned Machuca floor tiles, a two-group espresso machine that gleamed in baby blue, and plants. A *lot* of plants that thrived in the sunlight that streamed in to the place, and made the café feel a little more welcoming. Sari wanted Café Cecilia to be the neighborhood place, much like the cafés she'd enjoyed in Manila and abroad.

Every day, Sari would go to the café and spend time on the floor, even when really, the place could run itself by now. But she enjoyed it, and couldn't bear to stay away for very long.

And for the next three years, it was perfect. Sure, her food selection wasn't the best, and her pastries were all pre-packaged from a factory, but it didn't really matter to customers who were here for the coffee and the vibe.

Until one day in November, when suddenly it mattered, *very* much. Sari was very calmly tasting a new coffee blend in her lab on the second floor when she was knocked off her feet by the dull, heavy sound of a hammer. A sharp sound of a drill had followed, then the acrid smell of welding, both coming from the then-empty shop next door.

A bakery, Ate Nessie had told her conspiratorially. *Some fancy boy from Manila is opening a bakery right next to you.*

Suddenly, the food in Café Cecilia was very important, and for the last month, Sari had felt like a headless chicken, running around and sourcing suppliers, only to be met by reasons like "we can't deliver outside Manila," "no way you can get it fresh every day," or "can't you just make it yourself?"

Now it was the first of December, and based on surreptitious, totally not constant peeking over the manila paper-covered windows, and the feigned ignorance of the deliveries being made to the shop, Sunday Bakery was ready to open their doors to the world. And Sari was not ready.

It was competition, after all, and if Sari couldn't be the best, what was the point?

"You're obsessing," her younger sister Sampaguita singsonged, her arms full of Christmas lights and ribbon as she caught Sari glaring at the bakery's window. Sari was aware that everyone was getting tired of it, but she couldn't help it. Every time she stood on the street outside the café and stared down at their doors, so close together they were practically one door, she just…didn't like it. It made her stomach flip in a bad way, made a sour taste swirl around in her mouth. She couldn't have that. Not when she made a living out of her own taste buds.

"It's Christmas, Ate. Lighten up." She held up a length of twinkle lights and shook it at her older sister like it was all the Christmas magic she needed. Sari huffed and shook her head.

"It's been Christmas since September," she pointed out. "And I wasn't obsessing. I was…observing. Scouting the competition."

Sunday Bakery looked innocent enough from outside. The aesthetic was half lab, half London Underground, made of all white subway tile on the walls, patterned mosaic floors, neon letters and phone camera-friendly lighting. They had half the seating capacity of Café Cecilia, and not as many plants. Sari was also definitely not always thinking about the fact that inside Sunday Bakery was a den of jewelled, sugary delights waiting for the innocent customer to try, test, taste. She'd smelled the butter on the pain au chocolat, seen the perfect frosting swirls on cupcakes, heard the snap of cookies. And while coffee was a jolt to the system, a great dessert was pure sin on a plate.

Therefore, it was the enemy.

Sari had no plans of interacting with Sunday Bakery next door. She'd seen the Mummy movies enough times to know that you couldn't just take jewels all willy-nilly. But the pastries and their other sinful siblings continued to tempt her, tuning her senses to locate them before they came too close. She could smell a baked good from a mile away.

"In short, you have an irrational dislike of the bakery

next door, because you want to try his baked goods."
Her younger sister shrugged, tugging at a tangled string
of lights.

"Sam, don't make it sound dirty." Sari frowned, taking the mess of twinkle lights from her sister and carefully untangling it. "All this sugar and sweetness in the
air is going to mess with my nose and my taste buds."

"I'm just saying. You've never liked change, or new
things, and this bakery is a new thing."

"Can we please focus on what we're supposed to
be doing?" Sari sighed in frustration. "The Christmas
decor is not going to put itself up."

Technically, Café Cecilia was already behind on
their Christmas decor. The other stores on the Laneways—Kira's chocolate shop, Meile's flower shop, Kris'
cookies, had all put up their Christmas decor around
the same time Sunday Bakery next door started construction. And even that was a little late, as the malls
put theirs up in September. One could argue that Halloween wasn't really a huge holiday in this country.
There was little fun in dressing up for Halloween when
the malls had already decked the halls with boughs of
Christmas sales.

But Sari was a stickler for tradition, and in the Tomas
family, decor was put up exactly on the first of December. While for her parents, that had been a simple, "put
up the decor," to their house help, Sari took a more
hands on approach, and naturally recruited her little sister to provide assistance. There were twinkle lights to
string across her storefront, deep red poinsettia plants
in pots to place in the window boxes, and candy cane
coffee to serve. The most serious of café owners would
have scoffed at Sari serving something so pedestrian,

but she didn't much care when it came to spreading the holiday cheer.

Now if only she could feel just as charitable for her neighbor.

"Parol coming through!"

For the grand finale of the decorating, Sari rounded up her staff, an electrician, and her sister Sam to make sure the parol was perfectly placed. The parol was a thing of beauty, a five-foot, star-shaped lantern made from capiz shells that cast a soft yellow glow when lit. It was their grandmother's, specially purchased in Pampanga as a gift from their grandfather. Making sure the parol hung in a place of prominence was one of the many traditions Sari took to heart. So they hung it by the window of Café Cecilia, year after year, guiding their guests into the café like a shimmering beacon.

Kylo, Sam's big black rescue who Sari believed was part horse, tilted his head to the side and barked, making Sari jump from her spot on the street where she'd been supervising.

"Really?" she asked the dog, who seemed to not care that he'd nearly killed his part-owner and flopped to the ground at her feet. Sari rolled her eyes and got back to the task at hand, supervising the perfect parol placement. "A little to the right. Forward. A little more. No, that's too much."

"How about this, ma'am?"

"That's perfect." Sari nodded, bending down and absently scratching behind Kylo's ears as she watched. "Sam?"

"Yup!" Her sister called from inside.

"Turn it on?"

The parol lit up and the rest of her staff started to

clap. Excited chatter filled the space, and people who were casually strolling the Laneways ended up stopping and watching too. Sari's staff were happily taking photos, posing with the giant parol to post on their social media. Some of them approached Sari joking about Christmas bonuses and how excited they were for the Christmas party happening in a couple of weeks.

"Relax, guys, it's just a parol," Sari laughed, but the sight of the bright star did make her heart feel fuzzy and grow three sizes. Memories of being a little girl looking up at this very same parol, clutching a little cup of tsokolate in her hands as her family sang Christmas carols by the tree filled her, and made her smile. They were old memories, ones that no longer rang true, but the joy she had was still there.

"We good?" Sam asked, poking her head out of Café Cecilia's door.

"Yup. We're good." Sari nodded. She was just about to herd the entire group inside, they had plenty of time to pose with the parol later, when "Noche Buena" started to play from unseen speakers. She turned her head in the direction of the music, and two staff members in specially embroidered aprons bearing the Sunday Bakery logos stood outside their shiny, new shop, holding a tray of soft little pillows of mamon that smelled absolutely heavenly and impossibly caramelly for sponge cake.

"Sunday Bakery's soft opening! Please try our browned butter mamon!"

"Oooh!" Sam actually exclaimed beside her sister, her eyes lighting up at the sight of free food. Even Kylo seemed to be sniffing his nose appreciatively in the direction of the baked goods. In her panic, Sari looped her arm around her sister's, then her free fingers through her dog's collar. She saw her staff starting to move in the direction of the bakery, and cleared her throat.

"Okay, everyone inside! Coffee isn't going to serve itself!" That got their attention. Ordinarily Sari wouldn't have minded her staff stepping out for a second when there was free food out, or when a huge parol was being put up, but not from next door. "Come on, Kylo."

The dog seemed to grumble, but followed Sari inside anyway, after a couple of tugs on his collar.

The rest of the staff were talking eagerly about Christmas plans, Secret Santa wishes, and possible dance numbers for the Christmas party. They had been like this since September rolled around, but Christmas was so close she could feel it in the air and taste it on her tongue.

With one last little scowl at the bakery and their mamon, she strode in to Café Cecilia. Now this, this was an area she knew to be absolutely *hers*. She knew which plants were growing where, which of their dining chairs had a slight wobble, which table got the best light in the afternoon. Sari knew every song on the playlist, every blend they used, remembered how she came up with each one in the coffee lab upstairs.

This café was home to her. Some days she felt it was the only home she would ever know.

Sari immediately went back to work, wiping down the countertops, checking the temperature of the pastry case, making sure that the gleam of the robin's egg blue coffee machine was pristine. As always, she had a peripheral view of Sam as she sat on her usual spot behind the counter. Even Kylo knew where he was supposed to be—at his corner of the café where he didn't get in anyone's way. Sari's regulars started to come in for their mid-morning brews, and everything was as it should be.

Except she could smell something in the air. A sweet, heavy scent, one that slid lazily across the space where it didn't belong. Sari wrinkled her nose. She had the sudden image of fluffy pancakes being drenched in golden syrup, imagined a little blob of butter melting with the syrup on the pancake's warm and fluffy surface. Her father knew how to make his pancakes extra fluffy and bouncy, and the memory of post-fight, post-drama family mornings with pancakes had no business being here.

"What is that?" Sari asked nobody in particular.

"It's probably from next door," Sam responded, not looking up from her phone.

"Ugh. It's making the café smell like pancake syrup."

"You're exaggerating."

"When have I ever exaggerated, Sampaguita?" Sari had spotted her sister moving behind the counter to raid the pastry case and handed her sister several napkins for whatever pastry she was about to get. Spillage was inevitable.

"I have to admit, it's not like you," Sam agreed. "I'm taking a cookie."

"It's that bakery next door," Sari closed the pastry case after her. "They're overpowering the neighborhood with sugar and gluten and sweetness."

"Eugh. This is awful." Sam swallowed the bit of cookie she already ate and wrapped the rest in the napkin, gently nudging it forward into a space where Sari knew Sam could conveniently pretend it didn't exist.

Being the older, more mature sister, Sari decided to

ignore the little dig at the pastry. Goodness knows she beat herself up about it more than her sister did. But she sniffed instead. Sari didn't open her café to peddle pastries, she was here to dispense legally allowable stimulants in proper dosages, sometimes with milk and sugar. She was *not* supposed to feel bad because her pastries were…average.

She was a coffee shop, and she was happy with being just that.

But as a responsible business owner, she really should have known better. This was the Philippines, after all, where market consumerism was driven by trends and the Hottest New Thing that someone copied from someone else. The food industry was a dog eat hot dog world, and when competition came in, the ones left behind were the ones who closed up shop first.

"Then stop stealing from me." Sari rolled her eyes. "Do you want coffee?"

"Always."

At least that, she could still do. Sari slipped a saucer underneath Sam's discarded cookie and handed it to one of her staff to take to the back. When she came back, Sam had just finished rummaging through her gigantic canvas bag for a tumbler, which she held up to her sister with a cute smile that only bunso kids could manage.

"Do I want to clean this before I put coffee in it?" Sari wrinkled her nose at the tumbler, which had definitely seen better days.

"A-*te*," Sam huffed, blowing stray strands of hair away from her tanned face. Ah, the long suffering sigh of being the youngest. Sari was not familiar. "That's clean, duh."

"I was kidding. Barako?"

"Hot as the devil, sweet as sin, and acidic like my heart, please."

Sari smiled, because Sam always said that, and Sari liked that she always said that. Some things, at least, she knew she could trust. Sam, a clean countertop, a good pull of espresso, and that a little bit of brow gel and great lipgloss could fix anything.

But as much as there were things she could trust, there were things she definitely couldn't. Her parents, who in their own ways never really grew past their teenage years, the guy who tried to sell her ice cold water for three euros when she'd been wandering the hot streets of Rome on vacation, and the bakery next door. The bakery next door where she could hear the slow cadence of "Thank God It's Christmas" clashing over the sweeter melodies of "Bibingka," and she hated it.

"And anyway, who opens a business just before Christmas?"

"Oh, we're still talking about the bakery?" Sam almost sounded bored from where she was sitting, and the thing was, Sari was aware that she was being boring. But she couldn't help herself. She was just so… perturbed. Perturbed by a bakery next door.

"It's bad business practice. I'm sure there's a feng shui rule against it."

"We're not Chinese, and Christmas doesn't count in feng shui."

"And yet you insist that the foot of your bed shouldn't point to your bedroom door."

Sari turned to the percolating coffee maker—barako was traditionally made on a stove, but she wasn't a traditionalist, and prioritized using a blend that had Liberica beans, instead of whatever alternatives other coffee brands were touting these days. Their grandmother, who had always been a scion of propriety and had banned the use of red lipstick among her granddaughters until they were married, had been known to drink heaping cups of the country's strongest, punchiest coffee. A bit too strong for Sari, but Sam's favorite. Sari held up the coffeepot, ready to pour, when it happened.

The bell to the shop rang, a bright, tinkling sound that cut through the music while Sari carefully poured Sam's coffee and stirred in a spoonful of brown sugar. Sari heard her staff politely greet the customer as they came up to the counter, heard the opening of a box as they studied the menu. Sunday Bakery, the box announced in big, bold, black and gold letters. Ugh. Their packaging was nice. Pretty enough to be eye-catching, enough for anyone who happened to see it to guess that there was some luxurious, sinful treat inside.

The customer was telling her cashier about the baked good she'd just purchased next door, looking for suggestions as to what she could drink with it. And the world moved in slow motion as she tore the hot pink sticker with a flick of her thumb and opened the box. Sari inhaled. She smelled the usual culprits—butter, sugar, chocolate, all deep and rich and much stronger than any baked good she'd ever smelled. But then there was an unexpected scent that lingered in the air. Was that…*banana*?

Her head shot up from where she was standing behind the counter. The scent had been subtle, but it came to her nonetheless, like a disturbance in the Force. Unexpected. But then again, did anyone ever really expect bananas?

Barako would go perfectly with the customer's cookies. A punch of strong coffee would cut through the sweetness, maybe a bit of milk to soften up the contrast between the cookie and the coffee. The combination reminded her of road trip snacks, ones they'd always had on hand when the drive from Manila to Lipa used to take four hours instead of two. Their mother had been on a health kick, so it was all banana chips for their girls, until their father gave up and got them Jollibee. Their mother had gotten angry and yelled, and their father yelled back, all the way to Lipa. It was the kind of yelling that made Sari press her hands to her ears and shut her eyes, wishing she could click her heels and just fly away somewhere else. Anywhere but where her parents were.

She shook her head, because she refused to feel anything about a baked good that wasn't even hers to begin with.

The customer smiled and ordered an iced Americano, which wasn't a bad choice either. Without prompting from her store manager, Sari got to work, using their finer, more floral Selene blend to match the scents in the air as the customer took her seat, smiling at Sam. Sari's hands were moving in sync with an invisible beat as she pulled the espresso, poured it into a mug with ice before adding the water to make the Americano. She knew this fruity blend would work well with the customer's pastry the same way she knew how to pull espresso from her beans.

She was about to put the coffees on the serving table when she heard the customer eat…whatever it was. *Crunch.*

Really, this was getting ridiculous. Sunday Bakery next door had been officially open for one day.

"Iced Americano for Leala," she called a little too loudly, placing the ceramic mug with her logo on the serving counter. She wanted to fight baked goods with coffee, even if it was all in her head. "Barako for Sampaguita Corazon Tomas!"

The customer was a little dazed as she looked up, and Sari could see the crumbs she brushed off her skirt. Tiny, innocent little things that were now in her territory. *Must remember to sweep the floor*, even if it wasn't her job, even if she didn't have to.

"What is that?" Sari asked the customer when she came to retrieve her coffee, and it sounded more like an interrogation than it did friendly conversation. Sam, who was reaching for her own coffee, flattened her lips into a thin line to stop herself from laughing. "In the box?"

"Banana chip and cacao cookies," the customer said hesitantly, clearly confused. "They're from the bakery next door."

"Of course they are," Sari grumbled, and turned her head to the wall she shared with Sunday Bakery, glaring at it like it was going to crumble if she glared hard enough. She certainly endeavored to try.

To her customer, (or to anyone else, really), it may have looked like she was seething, and she was, just a tiny bit. Give her a backwards baseball cap and a flannel shirt, and she was Luke the diner guy from *Gilmore Girls*. She was already dispensing the coffee anyway.

"Uh, can I have my coffee to-go instead?" her customer asked, edging slowly away from the counter and looking desperate for someone else, anyone else to attend to her needs. Sari opened her mouth to acquiesce to the request when Sam crossed the counter, took the customer's cup of iced Americano and deftly transferred the contents into one of the robin's egg blue paper cups, popping a biodegradable lid on and handing the customer her coffee.

"Here you go, have a great day, and merry Christmas!" Sam chirped, giving the customer a polite but unnecessary bow. She smiled back, taking the cookie and its scent away with her.

Sari felt her shoulders drop, and she hated that they did. She briefly wondered if her great, great grandmother, Cecilia Tomas, had ever felt like this. She was the one who started the Tomas Coffee Co. right here in Lipa, seeing herself, her farm and her staff through wars and natural disasters to make sure it was passed on to her granddaughters. Cecilia had had her husband at her side to help her learn how to properly cultivate and care for the coffee, the side Sam had taken to like a fish to water. Sari's grandmother Rosario had their grandfather to help her learn how to truly expand the business, selling to big chains and groceries in Manila and Batangas, the part of the business that Selene now looked after.

The specialty coffee blends and the café? They were all new, all Sari's. Sure, they used to have the café across from the Cathedral, but that was mostly just because Lola Rosario's friend had owned the building and needed a renter when they fell on tough times. The first version of Café Cecilia had been an afterthought, until Sari told her sisters definitively that it was the part of the business she wanted.

Selene still said that it was one of the few times she'd ever seen Sari so decisive.

She was supposed to be better than this. She'd owned

this place for three years, with coffee that her family has been serving for generations, but with decor and blends that were all her own. Sari wasn't going to fail just because a bakery opened next door.

"Do you...do you want to talk about it, Ate?" Sam asked, always the most sensitive among the three Tomas sisters.

Sari wanted nothing more than to curl into a little ball and tell her baby sister that she was a little worried about it, but quickly decided against it.

"No," she said primly before she grabbed a tray and started to load it with mugs and a little jug of locally produced fresh milk, a rarity in the Philippines. It was one of the reasons why Sari had loved the idea of opening her café here, where she had access to fresh, local ingredients without having to think about the logistical nightmare it would have been if she were in Manila. "I'm all right."

"You're always all right," Sam muttered under her breath, and Sari pretended not to hear.

"I have to go upstairs and prep for barista class."

"Need help with that?"

"No."

"Cool." Sam shrugged as she and Kylo followed Sari up the stairs to the coffee lab/her office on the second floor. Juggling a tray of coffee mugs and milk, Sari nearly fell back when Kylo wriggled between them and reared up on his hind legs to scratch at the door.

"Oh my God, Sam, your beast—"

Sam pulled Kylo's collar back and opened the door for Sari. The big black dog squeezed between the sisters and bounded into the room with zero regard for the expensive things inside and flopped on the daybed by the window, a throw pillow between his paws to drool on. Sari watched the dog resume his nap with a wistful sigh before she walked over to her work station and placed her precarious tray of things on the counter.

"Your dog is too big," she told her sister.

"You love him." Sam closed the door behind her.

"Don't you have a farm to tend to?"

"The coffee beans literally grow on trees, Ate. There's not much to do at the moment." She shrugged, and Sari frowned, immediately going into big sister mode. Sure, Sam was in the café most days, but the way she said it made Sari wonder if her sister was trying to say something else. The thing with being an older sister was that over the years, Sari had learned to read her siblings as easily as she could a list of instructions, even when they tried to be inscrutable.

"Are you excited about the Christmas party?" Sam asked, getting up from the table to walk around Sari's space, picking up the mister and misting the plants. "I mean, I know you and Ate Selene dominate the karaoke contest every year, but you really have to give me and Kira a chance, she's super determined to win."

"I make no promises." Sari grinned, because her Christmases had fallen into a familiar and comforting pattern, and winning the Annual Christmas Party Karaoke Contest was just par for the course.

She briefly wondered how the Sunday Bakery's attendance at the party would change up the dynamic. Not much, if she had anything to say about it. She was determined not to let her new neighbor mess up her Christmas joy, no matter how good their browned butter mamon had smelled.

Chapter Two

If the café was like Sari's living room, the lab here on the second floor was her bedroom. Not exactly the best way to describe one's office, but it brought that same feeling of safety and comfort to her. Sari liked that she could leave a window open and let the cool air from outside waft in. Liked that she knew where everything was, and where it had to be.

There was a wide assortment of manual coffee makers, gleaming and waiting for her to use and play with. There was a sink for cleanup, a tiny office, and a daybed by the window, her favorite spot, with shelves overflowing with books and an assortment of plants in jars. Coffee books on the left, historical romance novels on the right. She had a tabletop coffee roaster to bring out delicious flavors from the beans, where she worked out how to make the tricky, tougher robusta bean into something that blended perfectly with the lighter arabica. Then there was a bigger roaster in the back for when she roasted beans for the café every Thursday, and for specialty clients of Tomas Coffee Co. The bigger roasters were over on the farm in Sta. Cruz, where they also packed the beans before shipping to Manila.

There was the grinder, ready and waiting with today's blend—the Rosabaya Robusta, perfect for the basic barista class scheduled for that afternoon. A single-group machine, bright and gleaming in the middle of the room, still in that pale blue she loved, with red letters showing off its fancy Italian name. The whole space only smelled slightly of coffee, just a barest hint of the many flavors Sari had been able to pull here.

With practiced hands, Sari flipped switches, and the station came to life, whirring softly and humming in anticipation. With a press of a button, perfectly roasted beans were ground into her waiting receiver, and Sari started to move through the motions that every barista knew within their soul. It was a dance, one she could lose herself in easily, fueled by knowing exactly what came next, when to turn, when to wait, when to hum.

This, she couldn't mess up, or fail, or lose.

Deep liquid gold poured from the spout and into the espresso glass waiting below. Grabbing one of the now warm mugs that she'd placed top down on the machine, Sari poured her newly extracted espresso into it, taking a quick sniff of the Rosabaya's fruity notes, the way the addition of their family's robusta beans punched through. Arabica snobs would scoff at the Tomas family's dedication to bringing fine robusta beans and blends to the masses, but they had been in business across three generations. They were doing just fine.

Sari added milk to a little jug and plunged the steamer wand into it, letting hot steam rise like a witch's brew. Then she poured the frothed milk into her mug, tilting, swirling, coaxing until she had a pretty tulip pattern in milk and foam.

Behind her, Sam snorted as she leaned against the countertop.

"Show-off."

"Not my fault you never learned," Sari pointed out.

But this was the agreement the siblings had forged very early on, when Sari needed it. One of the things Sari had always been grateful for was an older sister like Selene, who saw that her grandmother's business was failing at the negligent hands of their parents, and spoke to her sisters, asking if they were willing to take over. After Lola Rosario died five years ago, Selene had become the head of the family, taking charge when she needed to, taking over, the operations, the marketing, the…other things (Sari honestly had no idea). Selene's determination and her belief in her siblings had been what eventually convinced Sari and Sam to pick up their roles and responsibilities. And one of the main reasons why the business worked out was because their jobs were so separate yet intrinsic to the whole thing, and one sister knew better than to overstep the other.

Well, at least, Sari and Sam did. With Selene, it remained to be seen.

"Ate," Sam said very suddenly, her voice serious as she sat facing Sari on the bench, and Sari felt her sister's gaze fixed on her. Sari's heart thumped in her chest irrationally, the way only an older sister's would whenever the baby of the family had something serious to say. "I need to talk to you."

"Aren't we already talking?"

"Ate."

"Sam."

The look on her sister's face made Sari pause. Sam was the family's baby, the least serious of the Tomas sisters, and when she was, something was wrong. Sari's sister instincts went into overdrive, and started to think of all the things that could come out of Sam's mouth. Knowing her sister, it could be anything from "Kylo is dying" to "I need a haircut."

"I'm moving out."

Sari's heart immediately dropped into her stomach, so sudden and so quickly that she was surprised that she was still standing. She opened her mouth, closed it again, and words just absolutely refused to come out.

Selene had always joked that Sam was going to be the death of her two older sisters, but Sari never thought that could literally be possible until she pulled the rug out from under her. It hit her all at once, and ugh, it made her stomach hurt. She hated it when her stomach hurt. It reminded her of overroasted beans on a rainy day. Reminded her of her seventh birthday, when her mother had showed up with the perfect cake, caramel with buttercream roses that looked like a basket of flowers, days after she'd been nowhere to be found. *I needed a break from you, darlings,* she'd said. Was that why Sam was moving?

"Where…where are you moving to?" Sari managed to keep it together long enough to ask.

"To the farm," Sam said, wringing her hands the way she did whenever she was nervous. "You…you remember when I took over, I told you guys there was still a lot of land that we weren't using?"

"Yes," Sari said slowly, wondering what this had to do with the rest of the conversation. The Tomas farm was in Sta. Cruz, not too far from the heart of Lipa City. Her grandfather had purchased that land after the original family lands were lost in the shuffle of Lipa relocating from one place to the other over the years, and that was where the new Tomas Coffee Co. set up their farmland and processing facility.

When Sam took over, she told her sisters that the land was actually much bigger than they thought, and explained that she wanted to start growing their own food—vegetables, fruits, maybe even a dairy farm. Apparently all of those expansion plans were in motion already.

"I was walking through the property with some of the farm hands, and we found *cacao*," her sister continued, her eyes sparkling like they'd stumbled upon treasure. "Trees and trees of it. I mean, masukal pa rin, it'll take some time to clear it up. But I want to be there to supervise all of it. I want to set up a training department, keep my head farmers in tip top shape, make sure the interplanting is going well. I keep thinking about all the things I have to do, and I lie in bed at our house and I feel…trapped. Stuck, which is nuts, because the farm is only fifteen minutes away if there's no traffic."

As happy as Sari was to see how excited her sister was, she couldn't help but feel her heart break. Did she feel stuck because of Sari? Because of the house?

"And living on your own is going to help?" She asked, hating that she sounded so testy and mistrusting of her little sister. She tried to channel Selene on the day she asked if they wanted to take over the business, tried and miserably failed.

"I mean, I'm already twenty-six. If I don't do it now, I don't think I ever will, and—oh, please don't be mad, Ate."

Sari was trying to keep her own emotions in check, but that was a lot like saying she was trying to hold her organs up after they had been pulled out of her body.

"Ate?" Sam was giving Sari that look. That classic "I'm the bunso and my cuteness will make you submit" face that Sam always used on her sisters. "Are you...?"

"I'm fine," Sari frowned, crossing her arms over her chest. "You want to move out to the farm?"

Sam nodded.

"And you know how to look after yourself, to get food, to clean up after Kylo?"

"Look at me, Ate. I'm not a child anymore. I can take care of myself." Sam crossed her arms over her chest and huffed, which she had been doing since she was a child and was really annoyed. And Sari couldn't unsee it. Sam at six years old, with dirt on her knees, scrapes and bumps every time she went out to play.

"Jollibee doesn't deliver to that part of Lipa."

Sam huffed, looking up at the ceiling to gather strength, and Sari immediately knew that she was crossing a line. Her sisters had always accused her that the more Sari was backed into a corner, the more vicious she became. It was a defense mechanism, one her grandmother used to tut and say she inherited from her mother. Her mother who had tried so hard to keep the family together, until one day she just...let go. It was hard to reconcile the woman who used to meticulously go through her daughters' homework to the woman who was now #livingherbestlife somewhere else, even more so knowing that she and Sari shared the same character of lashing out.

So she took a break, tried to calm herself and remember that this wasn't about her, or her mother. This was about Sam, and what she wanted, and as the older sister she had to be the one to keep it together. She could do that for her.

"Where are you going to live? There isn't really a house in the farm."

"Well, there's Lola and Lolo's old house," she explained. "The one they lived in when they first got married. It's pretty big, and it's really beautiful still. Lolo planted bamboo trees outside, and maaliwalas siya. Mang Vic and I checked the water and electricity, they're still good. It needs a bit of work, a lot of cleaning. But I want to move right away, so I'll be in the new house by January. And could celebrate your birthday there, Ate, you would love it."

"What is this really about?" Sari's heart, which was already lodged in her stomach, twisted around and thrashed. The same angry emotion bubbled up in her, and she blurted out the question before properly considering her sister's feelings. She was really bad at this.

"It's..." Sam started, and Sari braced herself for impact. "I love living with you, Ate. I mean it. You bring out ice for Kylo in the summer, and I always have deodorant and shampoo on hand. But I want my own life. Make my own mistakes, forget my own deodorant, and everything that goes with it. I feel like I've relied on you and Ate Selene for too long. Now that you guys gave me the farm to take care of, I *really* want to take care of it. So I have to be there for that to happen."

Immediately Sari envied her sister's confidence in the answer. Here was her twenty-six-year-old Sampaguita, who knew exactly how to fill her own life, how to make her days better, and how to help the family. And whatever that life was, it didn't include living with Sari.

So pardon her for feeling just a tad betrayed. She shook off the horrible feeling that was attempting to crush her. Sam walked around the counter and did what every good little sister did whenever they realized they had nothing else to say. She hugged her. A bone crushing hug, as if she was forcing Sari to forgive her, not to be mad anymore.

"I think it will be good for you too, Ate," Sam reassured her, and Sari actually felt her sister petting the top of her head, like *she* was the younger one. "We're still in the same city, technically, fifteen minutes away."

"I know, but…"

"And you'll finally have Kylo out of your way! Weren't you always saying that the house is too small for him?"

"That's true, but…"

"You prefer doing things yourself anyway, it'll be easier when I'm not there. Plus, you'll get to do all the things you want to do when you live alone!"

"Such as?" Sari asked incredulously.

"Walk around the living room naked? Bring a boy home? Walk around the kitchen naked?"

"I do not have a secret desire to walk around the house naked, thanks." Sari shook her head, but couldn't help but chuckle at her sister's ridiculous suggestion.

The Tomases lived in a two-floor house in a narrow street two blocks from the Cathedral, and lived as bayan as the bayan could be. The land, and the house had been with the family for a long time, but it was a teeny tiny place compared to the size of the house in the farm, she was sure. It was small, and not incredibly private when the house next door could hear when you played music a little too loud, but it was manageable, and, Sari thought, the right size for the two of them.

"I dunno, Ate. Repression does that to a person. Closes up their vagina."

"Oh God."

"I'm just saying! It's been three years. It's getting all dusty down there."

"*Sampaguita Tomas*," So she was twenty-nine now, with no romantic prospects, and no *plans* for romantic prospects. The lack of a man wasn't a big gap in Sari's life, not when she had a vibrator and a healthy imagination to keep things…not dusty.

But she certainly wasn't going to tell her sister that. "Ate Selene was right. You're going to be the death of me."

"Okay, but even Lola Rosario always said how much she relied on Lolo Marco when he was alive," Sam pointed out, making Sari frown.

Lola Rosario was Sari's namesake, and the person she always thought of as the one who had raised her and her sisters. When their father decided he was no longer interested in being a father, and her mother had nowhere else to go, Lola Rosario had taken in the three girls and showered them with as much love and affection as she could afford. Sari never met her grandfather, but Lola Rosario kept him alive with stories of her and Lolo Marco working to reopen Tomas Coffee Co., stories of how they ran it as a team, like their granddaughters did now.

"I thought that it was you and me," Sari said, and she hated that her voice was so small when she did. Because never mind that moving in the middle of the holidays was a *bad* idea, never mind that Sari didn't want to be alone in their house. Her younger sister was a force of nature who was always going to do what she wanted, even if her sisters didn't agree.

"Hay, Ate," Sam sighed, squeezing her again. "Don't you want to fall in love with someone, have a family?"

We had a family, Sam. Look what happened to them, Sari wanted to say, but kept her mouth shut. There was no need to get into that with her sister, not now, and hopefully, not ever.

"I suppose there's nothing I can do," she finally said. Sam loosened her grip on her to look at her face.

"What do you mean," she said.

"It means I can't stop you," Sari said almost grudgingly, when deep inside, she would have said yes to anything Sam asked, even if it meant her being left behind.

"Oh, Ate, thank you SO MUCH, I really—"

Whatever else she had to say was immediately cut off by music. Loud music, the kind that was belted out by neighbors on karaoke machines on the weekends. Sari knew this song, too. Because who didn't fall in love when they heard *the* boyband Christmas anthem of the early 2000s, "Merry Christmas, Happy Holidays"?

The manila paper that had been placed against the window, the one that separated the café from the blasted bakery next door was ripped off to reveal a shiny, gleaming, chrome and white kitchen, with huge machines that would not be out of place next to her big batch roaster. Whoever it was on the other side of the window had strung up twinkle lights, which were now casting a little glow in Sari's space. From where she and Sam were standing, she could see open shelves with sprinkles with every size, shape and color, meticulously arranged like candy in a store.

Ohhh she hated Sunday Bakery. She felt her blood boiling under her skin, a little scowl on her face. She might have growled, because she saw Sam glance at her oddly and take a very wise step to the side.

And still, the music played like it was mocking her. Thanks to Sam's announcements, Sari's holidays were sure to be miserable, and now here was this happy, poppy song trying to hammer the point home.

"He's dancing," Sam said, as mesmerized as Sari as the sisters stared at the window. And just as Sari was about to ask what she meant, she saw him. A man was dancing in the shiny, gleaming kitchen with a kind of reckless abandon that was sure to end in disaster. He was singing too, hitting every note perfectly as he shimmied his shoulders, and threw his head back. Dark curls flew back with it, struggling for freedom under a bandana that was exactly the color of Sari's espresso machine. His mouth was covered by a face mask, clearly the man needed it if he was planning on singing that loud the entire time he worked.

He did a spin, extended an arm, and just like that, a stick of butter and a heap of sugar went into a mixer. He was *baking*. How incredibly unprofessional. Not that Sari didn't have a tendency to enjoy music while she worked, but this was one step above what was acceptable, surely?

With movements that looked professionally choreographed and a little bit of a shimmy, he added flour to the mixing bowl, some which flew up and billowed like the clouds from a witch's cauldron.

Double, double, this guy is trouble.

See, this was why Sari preferred the men from romance novels. The men in her books were serious, and proper, and certainly didn't *dance* while baking. Although, to be honest, she wouldn't mind reading about a duke who made a mean blancmange. Just the other day, reading a hero who knew how to make roti and dal had her mouth watering. But this was a completely different situation altogether. The man was flagrantly happy, like he had the world on a string, even if he was being inconsiderately loud, just like the entire store had been the whole month they were in construction. The bass notes of the song were starting to pound in her skull.

"I'm going to talk to him," she said, whipping off her apron, practically slamming it on the counter, making Sam jump in surprise. "Stay here."

"Where else would I go?"

To the farm, and as far away from me as you could go, Sari thought darkly, walking to the fire escape they shared and closing the door behind her. The moment she did, the music dulled, and Sari knew that there was a teeny, tiny part of her that had needed to escape the room. She'd never had that need before, and she hated that Sam had been the cause.

But she was here, still boiling mad and annoyed at the store next door that had been a tiny thorn on her side for the last month, so she rapped the heel of her palm against the heavy metal door. The music played on. Sari growled and repeated the action. Still nothing.

Do I have to kick down this door? Sari wondered as she pounded again. Her head was swimming with anger and annoyance, and it all built up inside her already rollicking insides. The music's volume lowered about three decibels, and Sari heard the fire escape door unlatch, then finally open.

She'd once read a book where someone had described any strong emotion—anger, sadness, melancholy—as waves. It came and receded, sometimes weak enough just to touch your toes, other times so strong it threatened to overwhelm you. But just because the emotion had abated didn't mean it disappeared altogether, and that was exactly how Sari felt when she first laid eyes on her new neighbor.

The fancy Manila boy had a pretty face. It was all sharp angles and softened features, warm brown eyes and the kindest face Sari had ever come across in a human. He immediately pulled off the bandana, showing off a head full of big, bouncy curls. His entire face changed when he smiled, it lit up everything that came even a little bit too close. He had dimples and smile lines so deep he had to be younger than her. He looked like he had never been hurt, never experienced sadness or any kind of unhappiness, and needed protecting at all cost.

But then Sari heard the music again, and her anger came back in a huge wave, spilling over any kind of initial fondness she felt for him.

"Hi," he yelled over the music like people knocked on his fire escape every day, and suddenly the entire world resumed its regular course, and music blasted from inside the kitchen. Sari hadn't even been aware that it had stopped. "Can I help you?"

"Yes!" she managed to yell back. "You're very loud!"

"Oh, thanks!"

"No, that's not a good thing," she exclaimed, shaking her head. "I'm Sari Tomas. I own Café Cecilia next door."

"I know!"

He said it like being Sari Tomas was the most brilliant thing that he'd ever heard in his entire life, as if Sari being next door to him actually meant something. Sari's frown returned in full force, even if she could hear her mother berating her that she would never find a man if she frowned like that.

"In case you haven't noticed, we share a window," she told him, momentarily distracted by the arm that was holding up the door. The baker had rolled his sleeves up at some point in the baking process, and veins and corded muscle tensed against the strain of the door. It was hard not to miss the darkened patches of skin that came from old burns, little scars and cuts from accidents past. Sari pretended not to see that. She was good at pretending that she didn't see things, didn't notice. And she'd had plenty of experience pretending not to see Sunday Bakery. "And you play your music way too loud. And your construction guys were loud too, and I sent complaints to Ate Nessie, but you never did anything about it, and why is this the first time I've ever seen you in the bakery?"

"Can I interest you in a dalandan muffin?" he yelled over the music.

"What?" she asked, completely caught off guard. Damn this guy, this baker, this, whatever his name was, who had wormed his way under her skin for the last month without actually showing his face, and now he was here and burrowing himself deeper. She hated it. Hated him, too.

"Well, not dalandan, it's actually sinturis. I'd never heard of sinturis before, but it's apparently a local variety. I got these from Blossom Farms in Bolbok," he continued like he didn't give much of a shit for Sari's annoyance, or her quiet. "Have you ever been? It's totally amazing, I was there for their pineapple planting the other day. They harvested sinturis recently, and they gave me a basket since I just moved in. I'm still tweaking the recipe, so it's not going to be perfect, but anyway. Muffin?"

"Sari," she corrected him behind gritted teeth. "Not *muffin*."

"No," he said, and the guy had the utter gall to chuckle like it was adorable that she could barely hear him over the sounds of "Araw-Araw". Not a Christmas song, but a good one, still. "Do you want a muffin, Sari?"

He looked at her like he was fully expecting her to leap into his arms and say yes. And really, who would say no to a free muffin? It would go perfectly with the sweet jammy notes of the coffee already waiting for her in the lab.

But this was Sari's territory, her space. She was already losing enough as it was, she was not going to let this man with the pretty brown eyes and taut muscles and annoyingly adorable smile invade her space without her permission.

"Not interested!" she said, hoping she sounded equal parts firm and clear. "Turn down the music, I can hear it through our window!"

Oh, she was calling it *our* window now?

"Yeah, I was wondering about that too. Why do we have a window?"

"We share the same warehouse," Sari sighed, unsure of why she was explaining all of this to him. Surely this was one of the reasons why he rented a space in the Laneways in the first place? Because it was cool, because it was a great use of old space, because it was a tourist destination?

The Laneways were what remained of an old row of warehouses in Lima, just on the edges of Lipa. From the Tomases' house to the Laneways was a quick fifteen minutes if you passed through J.P. Laurel Highway, which Sari rarely did because she knew the traffic was always bad on a good day. The Luz family, who owned the warehouses, converted the best of them into rows of commercial space, each warehouse cut in half to accommodate two lessors, and a brick lane in the middle for customers to move around in. Kira Luz, who owned the chocolate shop, said that her family had gotten the idea from seeing an old beer factory in Taiwan that was converted into an art space.

In a country where public parks were synonymous to closed, air-conditioned malls, and every family enjoyed a nice stroll on the weekends, the Laneways, with their brick roads, bougainvillea-clad walls, cool spaces and ample parking, was unique, the kind of place that, hopefully, never went out of style.

"This is an old garage that had a second-floor office. I think we're the only ones with second floors, too. The owners just cut everything up into rentable retail spaces."

"Aaah, the Luzes, right?" he asked. "Everyone keeps telling me they're like, a Big Deal here, no? This place is so…kakaiba. I mean, not too different. I've heard Lipa's the closest you can get to being in Manila without actually going there."

Sari narrowed her eyes at him, because she wasn't sure if he meant to say that as an insult or a compliment.

"Kira Luz was actually the one who helped get me this space," he continued, steamrolling right over any retort Sari might have to the contrary. "We were classmates in Ateneo. In Manila."

Because of course, he was.

Who did this guy think he was, just showing up in the Laneways, opening up a store, with a fancy Ateneo education, perfect English, cringey Taglish, blasting his music loud enough like he had the right to all of it, and offering Sari *muffins* of all things. *E di ikaw na yung magaling! Buwiset.*

"I know where Ateneo is," she said, rolling her eyes. "I went to UP. Diliman."

"Oh, a smart girl," he said, and she wanted to wipe that little grin on his face, because it wasn't fair that she was the one getting all riled up, and he had yet to take the bait. "Have you met her?"

"Who?" Sari asked, and God, these tangents. Stick to one conversation topic, sir!

"Kira Luz?"

"Yes, I know her. I know her better than you do. We grew up together, went to high school in Manila together." Sari shrugged. "If you think the Luzes are a big deal, both our families have been in Lipa for as long as Lipa has been a city."

A fact that she had found out very late in life, when she and Kira were old enough to do a little digging on their family histories. While the Tomases had been here since the Spanish priests brought coffee to Lipa in 1740, the Luzes had lived in Lipa long before that. Legacies like Kira's and Sari's were rooted in the land, and Sari had thought more than once that it was her legacy that saved her.

"My apologies, Big Deal," he said, humoring her with a little bow, and Sari's frown deepened even further. They were getting off-topic again, and the man clearly wasn't respecting her authority.

"Just keep the music down."

"What?"

"Music!" Sari made a gesture like she was either telling him to lower the volume, or trying to pet a very small dog. Clearly he was thinking the same thing, because he suddenly pressed his lips together and looked away like he was trying very hard not to laugh in her face. "All I Want for Christmas Is You" was really not helping Sari's mood.

The timer that she hadn't realized was attached to the front of his apron beeped, and he frowned and pressed a button on it.

"Hold that thought, muffin," he said, giving her a little wink before he turned and left the door, making Sari scramble forward to hold it open. She was just about to barge in to his space, invade him a little bit (not innuendo) when he came back with the music volume a little lower, and a tray of freshly baked muffins that he placed on the counter near the fire escape.

"You sure you don't want my muffins?" he asked using his pouting lips to point at the muffins before he walked back to the door and held up his side. Sari could just smell the sweetness of him, the little bit of citrus and flora from the sinturis that he must have been hand-squeezing. It was an intoxicating smell, mixing in with the coffee still lingering in her own clothes. If she closed her eyes she could remember being a kid lying on the grass, with sunlight filtering through the trees as she sipped sinturis juice from a glass. Her grandmother would be inside, calling the kids to merienda, tired after trying to convince her daughter-in-law not to leave her son.

Sari immediately knew getting this guy's muffins was a bad idea.

"My mother taught me not to take baked goods from strangers," she managed to say without fluttering her eyelashes.

"Lucky I'm not a stranger, then. Gabriel Capras," he said, holding out a hand for her to shake. One look at his long, tapered, sugar-splattered fingers and the veins on the back of his hand made Sari's knees feel slightly weak. She pushed that thought to the furthest recesses of her mind, in a box labelled DO NOT OPEN. "I just moved from Manila, and I'm not a Big Deal like you or Kira, but…this is my bakery."

Did she just imagine that little catch in his voice when he said that? If she hadn't, then he covered it up quickly, picking up a steaming mug of coffee that he raised to his lips.

Sari couldn't help it—her nose wrinkled.

"Is that…3-in-1?" She couldn't help but ask. Yes, her voice had A Tone. She was totally aware that the instant three-in-one mixes were popular, convenient, and sugary sweet. But why have that when she was right next door?

I smell a hypocrite, Sari heard her conscience whisper. But she was way too deep in the waters of her annoyance to really try to process that, so she stayed in it, glaring at the mug. It was almost insulting, really, that he would *dare* put that stuff anywhere near her café.

"Yes it is," Gabriel said, lifting his mug, which said, "I've got big buns." "You sure you don't want a sinturis muffin?"

"Yes," Sari said decisively. Clearly having as little interaction as possible to her neighbor was going to be the right course of action here.

"Yes?"

"Yes, I'm sure I don't want one," and because she was her grandmother's granddaughter, she struggled to find a polite reason to decline perfectly baked, fresh muffins that were, just as importantly, free. "I'm...on a diet. No carbs, no sugar, no muffin."

"Why are you on a diet, though? You're gorgeous."

Sari nearly let go of her side of the door as her knees buckled. He said that like it was a fact. *The sky is blue, grass is green, and you're gorgeous.* Had anyone ever said that about her?

Sari didn't really want to think about it at the moment. Between this and her upcoming Naked Dance Parties after Sam left, she was having one of those days when nothing made sense. And for someone who needed her entire world to make sense, she absolutely hated this, hated *him*.

"It's gorgeous because I haven't touched a carb in two years," was the least caustic of the replies she came up with. "I'm going back to my lab. Keep the music down."

"Only if you can resist dancing to it." Gabriel smiled again.

Her cheeks burned hot, and she knew from experience that Gabriel could see it. She preferred when she didn't know her competition was this flirty, and had a smile that betrayed how...bastos he was.

"You sure I can't tempt you, Sari Tomas?"

Seriously. Sweet face, but the things he chose to say with that mouth? Ka bastos.

"I'm sure."

"How about a date, then?"

Now, Sari knew when she was being teased. It had happened to her often enough in other places. And she knew better than to trust anything this guy said to her, especially after she'd been so rude to him.

He probably didn't think she was gorgeous at all. Her mother was right. Boys didn't like girls with big thighs. *You know it's wrong when you start thinking your mother was right*, Sari told herself.

She decided then and there that one, she disliked the bakery owner as much as she disliked the things he baked. Two, she was putting a ban on all his products in her shop, and three, she was never, *ever* eating anything this guy made.

"Music down. No muffins. And drink better coffee, my God," she summarized and exited the fire escape to head back to the safety of the coffee house, where Sam had patiently waited for her.

She could have sworn she heard him laugh as she closed the door behind her.

"Don't look at me like that," Sari grumbled at her sister, making a beeline for her abandoned coffee cup, the foam now dissolved, turning the coffee into a sad, cool mess. But she didn't like to waste things, so with a few motions, a bit of tinkering, and a gigantic pour, she was now drinking an iced latte.

It was no sinturis muffin, but Sari had her pride to keep her cool at night.

"I was just about to leave," Sam said with her trademark innocence. "Lots to do, things to plant, muffins to eat…"

"Sam, it was a fire door, how on Earth did you even hear…"

"I have my ways! Anyway, I'm heading back to the farm to talk to the construction team," she said, and the reminder that her sister was moving away sent pangs flying right back into Sari's heart. Sam kissed her on the cheek. "Oh, did I tell you? Your used coffee grounds worked really well in the vermi-compost."

"I told you it would."

"I know. The worms love your coffee."

"Lovely," Sari said drily before she took a sip of her latte.

When the three Tomas sisters inherited the Tomas Coffee Co. from their grandmother, Sari and Selene were surprised when their younger sister announced she was taking over the hectares of farmlands that the family owned just outside Lipa. But it seemed that Sam loved it more than they thought she would, and now she was going to move.

She was going to move, and Sari was going to be alone.

"Ate?"

"Hm?" Sari acted like she wasn't paying attention, busying herself with prep for the beginner's barista class later. She didn't have to do this, her people knew how to prep these things for her, but she wanted to. She needed to, really.

"The baker guy," Sam said gently. "Why didn't you say yes?"

"We are not talking about that," Sari said a little too quickly, setting the tray down a little too hard on the table, making the mugs rattle.

"Whatever you say, Rosario," Sam's voice was too light and singsongy when she said that, before she headed out to the door of the coffee lab. "Although you've always been partial to the pirate look!"

"*Sampaguita*," Sari yelled back at her sister, just to make sure she had the last word.

"Merry early Christmas, Sari!"

Sam closed the door behind her, and Sari's heart gave a little jump when she realized that this was going to be a familiar scene. Sam would come into her café, come into her space, flip it around, mess it up, and then leave everything a little less bright, a little quieter. Sari looked around the place that had been her comfort when she was starting out, and suddenly felt it was too big, too open, too quiet. The music next door had finally stopped, but instead of being a comfort, only made her feel more alone.

This is what your life is going to be like, she thought as she released a shuddering breath. *Get used to it.*

She was about to busy herself with work again when Kylo barked behind her, blinking expectantly at Sari and making her jump fifty feet in the air, spilling coffee on her clothes, because she'd been so dramatic about taking off her apron just minutes ago.

"Sam!" she yelled. "Come back here and get your horse!"

Kylo barked again, as if in protest.

It was going to be a *long* day.

Chapter Three

To Gabriel Capras, Christmas meant lengua de gato. So when he baked a test batch this morning, it took a lot of his inner strength not to stuff the biscuits into an old ice cream tub and munch on them all day.

The paper thin pieces of biscuit perfection snapped like nobody's business, but were so creamy and delicious on the tongue that you had to have more. Kira Luz's mom knew how to make the biscuits by hand and had sent a whole tub to the Capras family every year that she and Gabriel were blockmates. And every year, Gab would go down to the Christmas tree and sneak a piece or two without anyone seeing. Sure, once or twice he needed a sibling accomplice, but there was nothing a little piece of the prize couldn't do to keep them quiet about their heist.

He hadn't thought about Tita Alice's lengua de gato until he was in Australia. Years since the last tub of lengua de gato arrived in his house, working late into the night, so lonely he wanted to sob, and all he craved was a sliver of lengua de gato with his coffee. Gab had felt pathetic, thousands of miles away from home, years left in training, with nothing to his name but a staggering lease, burns and cuts. He wanted lengua de gato, and he didn't know how to make it.

He decided that one, that was ridiculous. He was a Filipino baker, he should know how to bake Filipino things. Two, it was time to stop wandering. If he was going to make something of himself, he was going to stay in one place and make it happen.

When he'd told his younger sisters, two halves of a responsible whole, of his plans, they both gaped at him through the screen of the video call. Gabriel was only a year older than Lily, two years older than Daisy, but to them, their kuya might as well have been a wanderer all his life. Four different courses in all four years of college, until he'd finally managed to stick to culinary school long enough to get a degree. Then there was the whole Kelly phase, when he thought he was in love enough to wait for her, to marry her, but…well, that didn't happen.

After that, he'd literally wandered, finding work in Hong Kong, then Japan, Bali for a while before he went to Singapore, then Melbourne, learning how to bake breads and mille-feuilles, croissants, desserts and puddings of all kinds. He could make a perfect caramel, had a sourdough starter that was at least five months old, and even if chocolate tempering still eluded him, he'd known he was armed with enough knowledge to *finally* do something worthy of his father's approval.

"Kuya," Daisy, the third in the family, the sweeter of the two, had said excitedly. "You're coming back to Manila, that's great!"

"Oh no, not Manila," he'd scoffed, shaking his head. "Too many chances of me running into people. I was thinking Lipa. Kira Luz just called me, said she had an open place. The rent's not too bad, and if I get a business partner, it'll be even better."

"What do you mean not Manila?" Daisy looked crestfallen, but Lily had always been the faster one of the two of them to catch on to things.

"Kuya, aren't we too old to still be emotionally scarred by the things Dad told us when we were younger?" Lily shook her head with the same kind of disapproval Gab was used to getting from his father.

He hated to say this, but the girls didn't understand. None of his eight siblings could, even Angelo and Mikael, the only other boys. His father had expectations of his oldest son. The onus was on the oldest to be the most successful, the most impressive, to blaze the trail for the younger ones to follow in his footsteps. Even more so for the oldest son, to be the head of the household, the one everyone deferred to or consulted, and Gabriel, with his wandering heart, didn't meet that criteria.

How do you expect to raise a family of your own on a baker's earnings? I raised nine kids on a VP's salary, and even that was extremely hard!

Not that he'd ever had any plans to have that many kids. Gab knew his limits. But clearly that hadn't mattered to Hunter Capras, who expected nothing but excellence from his failure of a son. *Unless you had a whole chain of bakeries, and I don't think you can focus long enough to do that.*

And because while Gabriel was a failure, he was obedient, so he'd decided that he would follow his father's suggestion exactly—open a shop that he could turn into a whole empire, make enough money to comfortably allow at least nine kids to have the same kind of life he had. And he would do it all without telling his father a single thing.

Challenge accepted.

Lily and Daisy had been gobsmacked at the plan, and he *knew* they were full of reasons why it was a bad idea. But because they were good sisters, they agreed to help him carry it out, swearing to tell nobody else in the family. Let them think he was still in Australia, or maybe even Japan. It didn't matter.

He had just pulled the freshly baked lengua from the oven, the scent of butter and sugar filling the warm air, when his phone chimed with a message. Trust Santi to text as early as six in the morning. The man never seemed to sleep.

Any chance you'll reconsider your chocolate supplier? I really think we'll have an easier time when our supplier doesn't make chocolate based on mood.

Kira's chocolate is the best out there, Gabriel texted back with one hand while he placed the hot baking pan on the counter to cool. Better than some of the other local variants I've tried. I've never been disappointed. And Gemini Chocolates is just across the street so we save on delivery. Also I thought we agreed that I was the baker here?

Fine, Santi replied. Gabriel chuckled and tucked his phone back into the front pocket of his apron. Lily did always say that Santi was very particular, both in and out of business.

Anton Santillan was a classmate of Lily's from grad school, with an MBA to his name, had his own restaurant in Lipa and was in need of a supplier for his baked goods. Gabriel knew the difference between a sfogiatelle and a biscotti, so they set up a meeting.

With his sisters' help, Gab created a business plan in Melbourne, then flew in to Manila and drove straight to Lipa to talk to Santi. He made his sisters swear not to tell the rest of the family where he was, and secured the partnership. Santi liked Gabriel's ambition, and six months later, the one-year lease was signed, and the bakery began construction.

It felt like a perfect first step, and Gabriel was locked in on this path, for once. And while he missed his siblings dearly, he didn't regret his decision not to tell his father about it. He was never the kind to look back, so he didn't.

"You and I are going to do good business together," Santi had said, clapping him on the shoulder like they weren't the same age. "Run the shop well, and I'll talk to the malls. I'm sure we can get a space in the next couple of years."

And while Gabriel's ultimate goal was to get to the malls, he enjoyed being in the Laneways for now. He really liked the Laneways. It was quaint, the way things in Manila were rarely allowed to be, nowadays. All the little alleys were still paved with concrete, with greenery growing in between them. The walls had so much bougainvillea growing that it looked like someone had poured them on in greens and magentas. Gabriel liked that every single shop in the Laneways was specialty— masters of crafts that they had picked up or had been passed on to them and revived in this hipster village. He liked that the street was lit up by strings of Christmas lights that moved from one store to the other, like a pretty web of twinkle lights. He liked that Lipa got light jacket cold when Christmas rolled around, so cool that he didn't need air conditioning some nights.

His siblings would love it here. They used to go to places like this, rent a big house that they didn't fit in and hang out like the internet didn't exist. Lily and Daisy would organize some kind of game, and Gabriel would lose his head trying to make sure nobody got injured. Ivy and Rose would complain the most, but would play along anyway. Angelo would scrape his knee, because he always scraped his knee. Mikael's face would go all red whenever Mindy started getting competitive (which was all the time), Iris would try to make peace, but would never be heard.

Nothing like being alone to remind him how used to chaos he was. He'd grown up around it, and in the midst of all his wandering, he always knew that coming home would mean at least three people ready to welcome him, that there would always be somebody begging him to bake them something.

But he'd pushed that anchor aside when he left, and he missed it very much. So when he felt his saddest, or his loneliest, he turned up the volume of his music and pretended that he didn't feel that way. With the first batch of lengua de gato done cooling, and the second already in the oven, Gabriel's finger hovered over the volume control on his phone, ready to turn it up, but he hesitated. Normally he would love to blast Sugarfree while pity baking, but today he hesitated because Sari Tomas had shown up at his fire escape.

He grinned at the memory, because it really was a little bit funny how mad at him she was. He'd clearly missed something, but the way she'd barged in only to summarily reject his attempts at kindness was different, and funny, and the kind of hijinks he didn't expect he would run in to in Lipa. It wasn't every day that he had a beautiful woman fuming at him in his fire escape, rejecting his muffins.

It still made him smile whenever he thought about her.

No, not her. It. The muffin incident in the fire escape. He wasn't thinking of Sari Tomas. Thinking of Sari Tomas when she clearly didn't like him was a foolish thing to do.

Be serious, Gabriel, his father always told him. *Be serious.* He couldn't afford to be distracted by women in his fire escape, certainly not a woman with bright blazing eyes.

But Gabriel liked the Laneways, liked the city. It continued to surprise him, how like Manila and unlike Manila Lipa could be. Yes, it was getting more and more crowded by the day, and he was a prime example of that, but it still managed to keep the things that made it unique, an obstinate stubbornness to the old traditions that he was quickly finding out was uniquely Batangueño.

"Hijo, ka tag-al naman niyan," Ate Nessie said as she walked up to his kitchen, a frown on her face and her arms crossed over her chest. She was carrying a now familiar paper bag, and the heady scent of fried bread filled the room. Gabriel grinned. Bonete time. "Dali. We have to talk about those common area dues you asked me about."

"Almost done po," he told her, just as the timer on the second batch of lengua de gato ran out. He quickly left the new batch on the cooling rack and headed downstairs, stopping momentarily to pick up two paper cups of coffee. He found Ate Nessie sitting on the bench outside Sunday Bakery, where she was already waiting with the bag of bonete to split between them. When he first met Ate Nessie, she'd scrutinized him from the top of his head to the tips of his toes, and said he was going to do well in Lipa.

As long as, he was promptly told, he didn't attempt to make bonete, he would be fine.

"I would never dare, Ate Nessie," Gab had declared, taking a bite off the little bonnet-shaped roll, so small he could cradle it in his palm. He loved the way the bread smelled savory but left a hint of sweetness on the tongue. The roll was crumbly, filling and was delicious at any time of the day.

Ate Nessie had a way of baking the bread to create a sort of crust at the bottom, his favorite part. It would always remind him of the day he and Santi had come to the Laneways to check out the space for the first time, and Ate Nessie showed up on his doorstep—calling herself the steward of the Laneways, faithful employee to the Luz family—and offered him bonete.

Gab had fallen head over heels in love right then and there.

With the bonete, not Ate Nessie.

Now it was a week after his soft opening, here he was, settling in to a new routine of morning bonete with Ate Nessie as they talked rent details, finishing up his construction, last minute turnovers and the like. Then, as a way to introduce him to the neighborhood, she segued into gossip—who sold what, who their suppliers were, who they were married to or related to. Ate Nessie knew everything that went on in the Laneways, and whether Gab liked it or not, he was going to get to know his new little neighborhood, every morning on the bench in front of his shop. She brought the bonete, he supplied the 3-in-1 coffee.

"You make the best bonete in Lipa," he announced again, reaching into the bag for another piece. He could finish a whole bag by himself, and right now, he had zero competition from his siblings, one of the perks of living away from the family home.

"And you are full of shit," Nessie said, squeezing his cheek and leaving a little oily stain on it. "Pretty eyes, but full of shit."

Then she flicked crumbs off her lap, standing up to her full four-eleven height. "Do you attend Simbang Gabi?"

"No…?" And instantly he knew it was the wrong answer. "Isn't that still two weeks away?"

"Oh, hijo. No. It starts in seven days. But really, you're not planning to?" Ate Nessie looked surprised. "You, who just started a business, just moved to a new city and have no girlfriend? You have *nothing* to ask the Lord for?"

"Am I…supposed to?"

He didn't particularly want to. He usually woke up at the ungodly hour of four in the morning to prep for the day's bakes anyway, and if he attended the dawn masses before Christmas, he would end up behind on his schedule. And while his family was Catholic, Simbang Gabi was low on the Caprases' list of traditions and priorities during the Christmas season.

But then again, Simbang Gabi meant freshly baked, fluffy bibingka with burnt sugar and cheese on top, warm and sweet puto bumbong, or maybe even sapin-sapin. If he was lucky (and he usually was), there would be sweet suman rice cakes topped with coconutty latik, or maybe even chocolate.

"I would if I were you." Ate Nessie shrugged. "Anyway, I'm off. I'm going to the Cathedral to light a candle for Kira. That girl relies so much on horoscopes and other witch voodoo, it's sure to send her straight to hell."

Gab bit into his bonete to refrain from saying anything. Kira ran Gemini Chocolates, one of the most popular chocolatiers south of Manila, and the biggest draw of the Laneways. People had told him on more than one occasion that Kira had the ability to choose flavors for their customers without having to ask what they wanted. She also had a penchant for matchmaking and astrology. And while Gabriel wasn't *quite* convinced of her matchmaking skills, he loved her chocolate, and had zero doubt that magic was involved somehow.

"Well, she did say that Geminis have two personalities."

"Like I said, witchcraft." Ate Nessie said like it was a done deal. "Are you sure you're not planning on going to Simbang Gabi? You get a wish if you attend all nine masses, you know. Some people wish for more money, good business, a love life, that kind of thing."

That's the stupidest thing I've ever heard, Gab could almost hear his sister Rose say. Had his eight other siblings been part of this conversation, he could imagine how very easily they would spiral into a discussion on theology and belief systems, and then eventually go back to astrology, because Mindy's favorite response was always, "you're only saying that because you're a Virgo!"

He squirmed in his seat. Manila was eighty kilometers away from Lipa, but it may as well be thousands for how much he missed his family. But he was the oldest son trying to make a point, and he owed it to his younger siblings to prove that point and have his father shove it.

Said like a real kuya. He could just see Lily rolling her eyes at him. Whatever. Gabriel was here, he was motivated and he was going to prove to his father that he could do this, and do this well.

"I think you need the wish," Ate Nessie announced with all the authority of a wise woman who made excellent bonete. That was all it took to interrupt his thoughts.

"For my love life?"

"For your business!" Nessie sighed in exasperation and downed the last of her coffee, and frowned down at the now empty cup, like she did every morning. "Ano ga ire?"

"3-in-1...?"

"Why do we have this crap when Sari serves perfect coffee next door?"

"Sari next door doesn't like me," Gab pointed out, standing up and folding the now empty paper bag into a neat rectangle. He hadn't told Ate Nessie about what had happened in the fire escape a week ago, but he'd seen Sari occasionally through their shared window, through the shared frontage.

"How do you know that, aber?"

"She told me, aber," he said with the same sarcasm that would have gotten his ear pulled if he was in touchable distance of his mother. "Okay, fine, she didn't exactly *tell* me, but the glares she gives me every time she sees me are more than enough."

Sari Tomas. His neighbor, master coffee maker was

an enigma wrapped in a mystery with brown eyes that haunted his dreams and thighs that made his fingers twitch. He caught himself wondering about her lips more times than he had any right to. And if he wasn't busy smoothing out the kinks that had popped up since their soft opening, or prepping for his grand opening after Christmas, he would have flirted a little harder, or made more of an effort to make her not like him a little less.

But then again, it had been a week, and he was marginally less busy now than he was a week before. Should he do something to be a little more nice? Drop by her café maybe, extend the proverbial olive branch? He could probably to that.

"Mmmmm. And I heard that she banned your pastries from her café." Ate Nessie apparently decided to stir the teapot, because why not? "Other food, she's fine with, but as soon as she sees your logo on those white boxes, she apparently flies into a rage and asks the people to leave."

"That does not sound like good business practice," Gab said, half amused and half wary of the café owner next door. Like he said. An enigma wrapped in a mystery, wrapped up in a pretty package.

No, wait. Not pretty. It would be a lie to look into her gorgeous face and not think *beautiful*, at least. He could easily imagine himself kissing her lush lips, tracing his hands down her curves, gripping thighs so thick she could snap him in half in a good way. She seemed to be ten leagues of cool above him, every tiny detail of her seemed perfect, and genetically engineered to make Gabriel swoon.

But that didn't change the fact that she hated him.

Well, Gabriel was no stranger to mind tricks and psych-outs. He'd been to culinary school, after all. And he didn't care. Really, he didn't. He didn't care that he'd been nothing but nice and neighborly, and she'd said no to his muffins. No. To. *His*. Muffins. Nobody could resist free food. Especially not in the country where sharing food was required for every two-person conversation.

"I should change my boxes, make them logo-less to throw her off the scent."

"I doubt that will work. She has these heightened senses from all her barista training and certification. She'll know if you try anything sneaky," Ate Nessie pointed out, tapping the side of her nose just to make extra sure Gab got the point. "And I wouldn't mess with Sari Tomas if I were you. Batangueño blood runs through that girl's veins. She's tough as nails and bitter as barako. Did you know she and her sisters kicked their parents out of the family business? It was a huge scandal when Doña Rosario died, her son tried to take the business, but Sari and her sisters muscled him out after he lost their biggest client."

"Your point?"

"Don't mess with Batangueños, Manila boy."

"I've never backed down from a challenge, Ate Nessie, and I do not intend to start now."

Ate Nessie gave him an assessing look, and he wondered what she saw. A guy in an apron playing bakery? A serious man, trying to make his business work in a new place? It was hard to tell. But whatever she saw, he had a feeling it wasn't good.

Must stop trying to project your father's opinions on other adults, he reminded himself.

"Hmm," she said finally. "You should reconsider Simbang Gabi, hijo."

"For my business?"

"No, to pray to God that you survive the wrath of Sari Tomas." Ate Nessie shook her head and brushed the bonete crumbs off her lap. "Have a good day."

"Thank you for the concern, but I'll be fine." Gab gave her a saucy little wink. "Happy candle-lighting."

Nessie rolled her eyes one last time for good effect, and then proceeded to make her way to the end of the Laneways. From there, it was easy for Ate Nessie to hail a tricycle and go to Lipa's famous San Sebastian Cathedral in the heart of the city.

He once heard that if you threw a rock at any point in Lipa, chances were you would hit a church or a chapel. Some of the older folks called Lipa Little Rome for that reason, and that was just the kind of place Lipa was. Steeped in tradition and history, but knew well enough when to make room for new things.

They must really do Simbang Gabi big here. Maybe he should do something too, like Jollibee did every time they released their tuna pie, or McDo with their fish fillet meal. Like offer grilled ensaymada with queso de bola? Was that appropriate Simbang Gabi fare? He really didn't know enough about these things to make a decision, and he didn't like that.

He walked back into his shop and took a quick look around the place. The kinks they ran into during their soft opening were hopefully as smooth as he could make them, and with the Christmas season coming in, there was a special nip in the air that gave him a spring in his step.

Armed with steely determination, a hand for hand-lettering and a lot of 3-in-1 coffee sachets, Gabriel spent the rest of the morning crafting a sign on the specials board he had outside his bakery, right next to Sari's window.

FREE 3-IN-1 COFFEE WITH ANY PASTRY PURCHASE!

To be fair, he was just thinking of a Simbang Gabi special, but he realized that this little plan had the extra side bonus of making Sari really, really mad. And he kind of wanted to see that.

Chapter Four

Gabriel was a good kuya. The best kuya, really. He was always volunteering to drive his siblings around when they needed him. He was the one the older girls called when they were too drunk to get home by themselves, the one the little kids confided in when they weren't sure how to tell their parents something. Gabriel was his siblings' champion when it came to their parents. So much so that when it was his turn to go to war, he knew there was no way he could involve his siblings in it.

Anyway. Gab was a great kuya. The best kuya. Except he was also the naughtiest. The number one pranker in the Capras family. Who could forget the time he changed his mother's keyboard to spell 'gaga' instead of 'Gabriel,' which meant she could only text him change this right now, gaga! Or the time he switched all the clothes in his sisters' closets? Everyone still talked about that one summer he gave everyone water guns with instructions to blast Mindy when she came home, which was only fair because she'd been the one to initiate the prank war by pretending it was his birthday at their usual Sunday restaurant.

Here, now, in Lipa, he knew he'd started a war. He had a feeling Sari wasn't going to take his free coffee lying down. But he didn't expect it would be this much…fun.

Gabriel was practically skipping into his kitchen the next day, while his staff downstairs was busy dispensing vats of 3-in-1 with every pastry purchase in his shop. He actually had a line. A line, on soft opening! It was brilliant, so brilliant in fact, that they needed him upstairs and baking more ensaymada because they were running out. Having recognized that traditional Filipino bakes were not his lane (he had a ready list of recommendations every time someone asked), he tried to make his ensaymada with the tangzhong method, the same method they used to make pillowy, fluffy Hokkaido milk bread when he worked in Hong Kong. Topped with queso de bola buttercream, Gabriel was happy to sell his "not quite ensaymada" to the crowds.

"I got it!"

That was when he heard the shout that had definitely come from Sari's side of their shared space. Edging close to the window, just enough that he could peek and not be noticed, he saw Sari from behind in a pair of jeans that really…accentuated certain assets he had never noticed before. He swallowed thickly and forced himself to listen in on the conversation.

"They were a little more expensive than you expected, they really couldn't give us the wholesale price since it was already in-store, but I think there's enough for the whole day," the person said, handing Sari a bright blue box that was patterned to look like a woven basket. Gabriel may not have been a Lipa resident for very long, but he knew exactly where the box was from. South Mart, the grocery on J.P. Laurel Highway, had a bakery attached that sold cheap bakes. In fairness to them, he really enjoyed their sugar cookies and sponge cake rolls with yema inside.

But why was Sari suddenly buying up the whole lot? On *retail* prices?

Gabriel was just backing away from the window when the person Sari was talking to spotted him, and Sari herself whirled around and fixed her laser beam gaze on him. Oh shit.

"Hi," he said, wiggling his fingers at her.

Sari jerked her thumb in the direction of their shared fire escape, and he knew there was no way out of it. He stood up and opened the door, where she leaned against the railing, glaring at him and holding a cup of coffee. She'd put something on her lips to make them look all shiny and a little thicker, and Gabriel found himself needing to clear his throat as he shoved those thoughts aside. He should have brought something, like a cookie or a cupcake. *The Art of War* probably said something about not going to negotiations empty-handed.

"Is that coffee for me?" he asked, leaning against the railing beside her.

Sari looked down at the cup in her hand, and there was a moment where he legitimately thought she would throw it in his face. She wouldn't. Would she?

"No," she said instead, lifting the mug to her lips, leaving a shiny, pinkish red lip print on the rim of the pure white mug. Gabriel inhaled. The coffee smelled delicious. "Clearly you have enough going around in your shop."

"To what do I owe the pleasure of this weirdly intimate assembly?" he asked. The moment he'd seen Sari do a double take at his little piece of chalkboard art the day before, Gabriel had felt all of his cells rise and his competitive streak kick in. It was hard not to have one, not in a family where if you didn't stake your claim at something, you got nothing. Plus, he was the oldest, he had to be the most competitive so his sisters didn't walk all over him.

Not that he thought of Sari as his sister. Oh no. Sari was the enemy, the evil witch behind the extremely tempting coffee that wafted into his nose every time he walked by Café Cecilia. He knew a good brew when he smelled it, and the café didn't seem to have a bad coffee day in its life.

"This is just an acknowledgement." She shrugged, her lashes fluttering as she looked up at him from her coffee mug. "I see your declaration of war, and I return it with one of my own."

"Giving away the coffee is a Simbang Gabi promo," he argued.

"Simbang Gabi is at four in the morning, and is six days away," she pointed out, which, to be fair, was true. She saw right through the little lie he told himself. "Is this because I didn't agree to go on a date with you?"

"No, it's because you didn't eat my muffin," he said, and he made it sound very dirty, even if it wasn't because he figured that if there were any buttons to press, it was the fact that Sari had not stopped staring at his face. "What are you planning on doing with all of those sugar cookies from South Mart?"

"Oh, I'm testing a theory," she said breezily. "Are people more willing to pay 150 pesos for a good coffee and a free cookie, or 150 pesos for a sugary sweet and a free bad coffee?"

"That sounds like a false analogy." He frowned, because of course his old debate team skills still came up to him in the least convenient moments.

He was a model kid in high school, getting good grades, captaining the debate team, joining the student council. Back then there had only been one path to pursue—good grades so he could get into a good college. But the moment Gabriel stepped into the hallowed halls of the Ateneo, he realized just how *huge* the world could be. Since then, he never could seem to stick to anything, to commit to anything.

He was determined not to let that happen. Not to Sunday Bakery, not to this little rivalry he had with Sari. He was going to do it because it was here, and he was serious about this being his life now.

"Hm. We'll see about that," she said, and he didn't miss the little smile that was playing on the corners of her lips. Then she pushed herself off the railing and opened the fire exit door, keeping it propped open with a weight that she'd placed by the hinge. Gabriel saw into her coffee lab, but didn't make a move as she put her mug aside and started to make another espresso. It was mesmerizing, seeing her work. She had a deft hand with the machine, and worked like there was nothing about the process that surprised her anymore, and that was a good thing.

He was still watching her when his side of the fire escape opened to reveal Ransom, his manager, looking at him with slight panic on his face. Gabriel had worked with Ransom for a little over a month now, bringing him in just before construction started. He was a good employee, but had a tendency to panic when it wasn't needed, Gabriel was just learning.

"Boss, have you started on the ensaymada?" Ransom asked. "We're out, and Faye isn't here yet, so we could really use some help in the storefront."

"Ransom, it's *not* ensaymada."

"Whatever, boss, we need it!"

"Okay, I'm coming in," Gabriel said, reluctantly pulling himself off the railing as well. He was about to take one last peek at Sari's lab when he realized she was walking toward them with a beatific smile on her face, holding a paper cup with Café Cecilia's logo on it. The coffee smelled so incredible that Gab could almost see it—the curls of deep and dark scents, twisting with the sweetness he brought to the table.

"Why thank you," Gabriel said, smiling as he reached for it, but Sari moved right past him to place the coffee in Ransom's hands. Both he and Gabriel looked at Sari in surprise, as she smiled sweetly at *his* manager.

"For you," she said to Ransom, giving him the most stunning smile Gab had ever seen grace her face, all sweetness and light. Even Ransom looked momentarily stunned, accepting the cup. "I know your boss works you really hard. You deserve a little break."

Gab narrowed his eyes. He knew tactics when he saw them, and he was sure this was part of Sari's ploy to get under his skin. The coffee was just too tempting, strong and seductive, it was the kind of smell that both lulled you to sleep and jolted you awake, depending on what you needed.

But no. Gabriel wasn't about to let her win. It wasn't that kind of Christmas.

"I need a little help here!" one of his shopkeepers from downstairs yelled, probably standing at the bottom of the stairs. Clearly their new wave of 3-in-1 customers had come to claim free coffee with their purchases.

"Ransom, put that coffee down and get to work," Gabriel said, holding his hand out for her cup.

"But Miss Sari…"

"Is not your boss, remember? I am," he said, and he meant it to sound threatening, but it only came out as a little exhausted and pleading, and he heard Sari stifle a laugh next to him. Ransom was glaring murder at Gab as he handed over the coffee, threw up his hands in surrender and marched back into the kitchen, muttering something about Gab not making the not-ensaymada and this being way above his pay grade.

"Oh great, you've turned him against me." Gabriel narrowed his eyes at Sari before he took a sip of the as-of-yet untouched coffee. It was sweet but didn't have a bit of sugar in it, and it was actually warm and comforting, perfect against the cool, overcast day. Gabriel pressed his mouth shut so he wouldn't accidentally moan, it was so good. Way better than his 3-in-1 for sure, but he wasn't about to tell her that.

"Good?" Sari asked, and there was a look on her face that made him wonder if him drinking her coffee had been the plan all along.

"Mm, it's…okay," he said. He stopped drinking and shrugged. "I guess."

"You are such a liar." Sari rolled her eyes and walked back to her coffee lab, but not before he noticed that she was smiling. "I look forward to our next encounter, nemesis."

"See you then, Big Deal," he said, giving her a little mock salute and watching the way her hips swayed as she walked in to her lab.

One batch of the freshly baked not-ensaymada later, Gabriel had just come back downstairs to the shop floor when he heard the sounds of a ringing bell. Every single head inside his store turned to the direction of one of Sari's baristas standing outside, holding up a sign that had much prettier hand lettering than his chalkboard had.

"Free yema roll with every coffee purchase! Get your free yema roll with every coffee purchase here at Café Cecilia! Only 150 pesos for a coffee *and* a cookie!"

"What the—" he began, but remembered Sari had told him that this was exactly her plan. Apparently, despite the false analogy, her little idea worked out in her favor.

If there was anything Filipinos loved more than a reason for snacks, it was free snacks that came with good coffee. Gabriel's crowd cleared the bakery faster than kids on Christmas morning.

"I've got to hand it to her, boss," Ransom said, shaking his head as he served the last cup of 3-in-1 to the customer who was already at the counter. "She's really smart. And really pretty. You sure you can handle being her nemesis?"

"Why does nobody in this city think I can handle a little friendly competition with Sari Tomas?" he asked out loud.

"Because clearly, you don't know Sari Tomas," Ransom commented, slinging a bimpo over his shoulder. "I'm taking my break! Do you have a 50, boss, I think I'd like coffee and a cookie."

"Traitor!" Gab yelled over his shoulder as Ransom kicked himself out of the running for employee of the month by laughing as he headed to the café next door.

Chapter Five

December 11

If I were the one running this prank war, what would I be doing? Sari asked herself, kneeling on the daybed and glaring out at the street below like it was going to provide her with the insight she needed. Despite being an excellent strategist for agawan base, and being well-versed in Pokémon battles (she made the Elite Four several times over, fact), she didn't feel she was equipped to handle this. But she was sure as hell going to pretend that she was. Sari found it twice as exhausting to keep herself sharp in case of a prank than to actually execute one, but she was going to do it anyway.

Executing a prank was easy, especially now that Gabriel's bakery manager had basically defected and could be found at Café Cecilia on his breaks, sipping a free cup of coffee that Sari was only too happy to provide. And while Sari wasn't familiar with prank war tactics, she did know that there were three tour buses of a religious group stopping at the Laneways today for a pasalubong run before they resumed their local pilgrimage tour, and that was an optimum time to pull a prank. So she stood by her window, watching menacingly and trying her hardest not to blink. "Don't even blink. Blink and you're dead," at least according to Doctor Who.

"Anyway, Ate, I'm picking out bedsheets today, I could really use some help," Sam was telling her over the phone, but Sari was not ashamed to admit that she was only half-listening to her sister.

"Mhm," she said, squinting through her window when she saw movement by the entrance of Sunday Bakery. "Good for you."

"Are you not coming? I'm in the department store, the salesladies are going to get me and I will come out with three plates but no bedsheets! Help me!"

"You're a grownup now, remember? You can doitI-believeinyou," Sari said quickly, hanging up on her sister because Gabriel was dragging something to the front of his bakery. She found herself sprinting down the stairs, nearly tripping over her feet as she did so. Her staff jumped in surprise when they saw her, and as Sari was about to open her mouth and explain that things were Totally Under Control, "Take A Chance On Me" blared out from a set of luggage-sized speakers that someone had rolled out to the street. Gabriel was peeking inside Café Cecilia with zero subtlety whatso-ever; Sari didn't move, didn't breathe, didn't dare blink.

"M'am Sari, nililigawan ka ba?" one of her baris-tas asked her, and she tsk-ed and denied it right away, marching outside to a group of slightly bewildered titas in varying states of amusement that someone Gabriel's age was playing an ABBA song.

"Oh, there you are!" Gabriel exclaimed, his entire face lighting up with glee as the music filled the air. Then he smugly looked over his shoulder. "Ransom, bring out the brazo."

Sari gasped as Ransom came out of the shop carrying the bounty. Immediately Sari seethed, and she could almost feel steam coming out of her ears at the sight of the perfect, bouncy, caramelized log of sugar and eggs.

"You *traitor*," she exclaimed at Ransom like they were caught in the middle of a telenovela, but she didn't care. "I told you about my favorite cake in confidence!"

"Ransom knows who his boss is at the end of the day," Gabriel said, whipping out a knife as Ransom placed the cake on a previously unnoticed table that had a tablecloth and a small stack of paper platitos and those biodegradable forks.

"Please leave me out of this," Ransom begged them both politely. "I literally did not sign up for this."

"In for a penny, in for a pound, Rans," Gabriel said, patting his manager on the back, even though it was clear from the confusion from Ransom's face that he had no idea what the very English expression meant. "Now who wants a free slice of brazo de mercedes?"

"I need a raise," Ransom said miserably, and Sari was treated to the sight of her customers leaving her store, literally dropping bags of coffee beans back into the little outdoor selling area she'd set up, to exclaim over Gabriel's cake. She could see it from where she was standing too—frothy, slightly toasted marshmallowy meringue with a just runny enough, sticky and sweet custard center. The cake looked absolutely perfect, with a lovely crust of sugar on the outside. Sari's stomach growled, and she could almost *taste* the brazo de mercedes in her mouth, only to be sorely disappointed because her pride was in the way.

"You cheat." She narrowed her eyes at him. "You dirty, rotten cheat."

"All's fair, muffin," he teased, winking as he took a bite of his own slice of cake. "Now are you sure you don't want a taste of my…brazo?"

He made a show of holding out his arm, twisting it and flexing it for maximum muscle exposure. And Sari would never, ever admit this to anyone (who would she admit it to, really?), but Gabriel had a very nice braso. It was the kind that could carry things, formed by the work of his own hands.

She gulped. Sure, most of the aunties eating cake were utterly confused as to what was going on, but still, Sari knew she had to retreat. So she huffed, and flounced back into her café without a slice of her favorite cake.

"I'm going to kill him," she announced to her staff as she passed them on her way back up to her coffee lab. "I'm really going to kill him!"

"We think he's nice, m'am!"

"Sagutin mo niyo na kasi, m'am Sari!"

Chapter Six

Thanks to Gabriel's brilliant tactic, he was sold out of the brazo de mercedes, the not-ensaymadas and all his cookies by the end of the day. The fact that he'd managed to do that was actually a lovely bonus, he didn't even know the consortium of titas would be walking through the Laneways. Who knew that the combination of ABBA and cake would be the perfect marketing strategy for the bakery?

God, he was really good at this pranking business.

"I'm exhausted," Ransom groaned as he and Gabriel closed up the café for the evening. The rest of his staff had gone home with still bright and happy faces, which told Gab that Ransom was groaning and grumbling because he could.

"You should be happy we're doing well, Ransom," Gabriel pointed out, throwing on his cardigan as Ransom dragged down the metal sheet that kept the store locked and safe. "I never thought we would do this well on our soft opening."

"You didn't?" Ransom asked, slightly confused. "Why not?"

"Oh, I don't know," Gabriel said, although thinking about it now, it probably wasn't a good thing that he hadn't thought that way. If he was aiming for an optimum level of success, he should expect optimum levels of success, shouldn't he? "I could have forgotten to put butter in something. Or used confectioner's sugar instead of granulated, and turned the cookies into dry polvoron. Any number of things."

"Yeah, that's funny, boss," Ransom chuckled, shaking his head. "You're a really good baker."

That made Gabriel stop. Had anyone ever told him that before? Sure, hearing his customers go "mmmm" every time they bit into something he made was validation, but it wasn't quite the same as being told that he was good at this. Like it was just right that he was exactly where he was at this moment.

"Even if you did engage in the most immature prank war I've ever seen," Ransom grumbled. "Look, Miss Sari's even glaring at you."

Gabriel turned just in time to see Sari looking down at him from her coffee lab. He gave her a smile and a little wave. She fumed and huffed, immediately abandoning her post. Gabriel was sure he hadn't imagined the blush that colored her cheeks before she'd left earlier that afternoon.

And that made all of this worth it.

"Sorry, Ransom," he said, his determination stronger than ever. "I need all the help I can get."

"Sir, I really like you, but I really don't want to be your go-between just because you managed to guess which cake was Miss Sari's favorite. Now I'll never get free coffee again."

What Ransom didn't know, and Gab never told him, was that talking back to your boss, rolling your eyes and protesting everything he did was akin to insubordination. Had he done any of this back in New York where he trained, he would have found his ass on the street faster than a flipping pancake.

It was one of the reasons why he loved being here. Here, he didn't have to be tough, he didn't have to pretend to be the smartest guy in the room, didn't have to have a huge ego that he couldn't pull off. He didn't have to shove anyone aside or step on anyone else's toes.

Here, being exactly who he was, was enough. Which was a nice change, after everything his father had told him.

But this isn't a mall spot, or a franchise, he reminded himself, snapping himself out of his own feelings. *This isn't going to be enough to satisfy Dad, and you know it.*

He shouldn't get too comfortable. If all went well, he would only be here for a year.

"Goodnight, M'am Sari!" Ransom's voice cut through Gab's thoughts just in time, as Sari walked past them, a swirl of dark hair and soft pink fabric as her skirt swished. She gave Ransom a smile, but fixed Gabriel with a look that could kill dragons dead.

"Sleep with one eye open, Baker Boy," she said, her middle and pointer fingers in a V pointed at him in a universal gesture of *I'm watching you*.

"I'll do it with two eyes open thanks to my 3-in-1, Coffee Girl," he breezily replied, leaning against his doorway with his arms crossed. He was ignoring the fact that Ransom was rolling his eyes behind him, so exaggerated he could almost hear it.

Sari huffed again, and her dark hair fanned around her face as she and her pretty pink skirt walked down the Laneways, heading to the direction of Kira's chocolate shop, which still had all the lights on. And for the moment, Gabriel completely forgot about his worries, forgot about not getting too attached to this place.

"Sir," Ransom said just as she was out of earshot. "If you're trying to flirt with M'am Sari, it's not working."

"I am not flirting," he said, quickly snapping out of his feelings. "And I thought you said you were tired? Maybe you have enough energy to come in early to-morrow to bake?"

"I'm going, I'm going." Ransom held his hands up in the air and beat a hasty retreat. Gabriel watched Sari in the distance for a little longer before he slung his bag over his head and left the Laneways for the evening.

Chapter Seven

December 12

With the number of things currently going on in Sari's life (Sam's move, avoidance of many personal issues including her irrational prank war with her neighbor, the wasps that were coming in and out of her house), she almost forgot she had a meeting with Anton Santillan until he texted her that morning.

Meet you at the lobby lounge at Villa. Wrapping up a meeting here.

Sure, she replied, because whoever Santi got as a supplier for his baked goods was really good at making biscotti, tiramisu and sfogiatelle, and combined with the specialty blend Sari developed for the hotel's café, it was an instant recipe for a good morning. Sari didn't usually personally deliver roasted beans to Tomas Coffee Co.'s clients, but the hotel was midway between her house and the Laneways, and Santi was great at giving business advice over breakfast. Plus, it was nice to get out of the café sometimes, even if it was to walk into someone else's.

Santi ran Hotel Villa, the fanciest hotel in Lipa. He'd taken over the place three years ago, around the same time Sari had opened Café Cecilia, and had insisted on getting all local suppliers for his café and for the hotel itself. Sari had had the chance to stay in the hotel a couple of times, on weekends when Sam wanted the whole house for herself, and she always thought it was extremely comfortable, with the best beds in the world. The fact that the lobby lounge was nice and airy too was a bonus. Santi himself had seemed incredibly stand-offish at first, but had marginally warmed up to Sari in the last three years they'd worked together. He was one of those rare, no-nonsense businessmen who still understood the importance of creating a personal relationship with his suppliers and with the community. Sari always enjoyed their meetings.

Until she walked in, only to find Santi and Gabriel talking in excited, hushed voices, and Sari's mood immediately crashed. Well. No, not crashed, exactly. More like…changed. It didn't *feel* like it was a bad thing, seeing Gabriel without expecting to. It was surprising, sure, but the anger she'd felt over the past few days had boiled over, and now was just a ball of confusion that roiled in her stomach.

She was used to seeing him in the Laneways, used to seeing him frown at her whenever their eyes met. But seeing him somewhere else, in the context of something else, she couldn't quite pin her emotions down.

"…see if I can get a meeting with the Lai Group next week," Santi was saying. "I'm feeling very positive about it. And it's a great opportunity for us. It's exactly what we wanted."

"Oh, that's great," Gabriel said, nodding, although

his agreement was less than enthusiastic. Sari wondered what they were talking about, not that she cared. "Looking forward to it."

"You could sound a little more enthusiastic, you know," Santi berated him. "You were the one who wanted this."

"I know, I know. And you're right. It's an amazing opportunity. Thank you. But I just…oh," Gabriel said suddenly as he turned his head to where Sari was standing. She smiled like she hadn't heard a thing the two of them were talking about and approached the table.

"Sari," Santi said, standing up to shake her hand. In the three years she'd been working with him, Santi never did besos, or anything past what was strictly appropriate. The ever-formal hotelier was handsome in a chaebol heir kind of way, devastatingly handsome, but covered in a veneer of stiff formality that made girls wish they would be the ones to break through it. "Thanks for meeting me here. We were just talking about you, actually."

Whoever managed to break through Anton Santillan's walls would be a fearsome woman to behold. Or man. Or person. She didn't know what his preference was.

"Hmm, good things, I hope?" she asked, sitting in the empty seat between the two boys, and making a concerted effort not to look Gabriel Capras directly in the eye. Which was perfect, because Gabriel was doing a really bad job of hiding the fact that he was looking at *her*.

"Good is subjective," he said beside her. "Santi was haranguing me about our thing."

"Our thing?" she repeated incredulously, wanting to choke and laugh as she ordered a latte and biscotti.

"Well, calling it a rivalry would just make it obvious that you and I have the emotional maturity of five-year-olds," he smirked, taking a bite of focaccia. Just the bread, and nothing else. "Mm, Santi, this is really good."

"Thank you," Santi said primly, sipping his demitasse. "One of the few things I can bake well."

"Are you kidding?" Sari asked, accepting her coffee and immediately dunking her biscotti in it. "I love the baked goods in this place. You made them, Santi?"

"Er," Santi said awkwardly, turning to Gabriel, who suddenly looked like the most smug bastard who ever decided to be smug. The dots connected in Sari's head. Santi and Gabriel were obviously business partners, which was why he was here, and why the lobby lounge was suddenly producing such amazing baked goods. "I actually have a local supplier."

"You?" Sari asked, almost exasperated that she had to put down the langka, pistachio and macadamia biscotti. "Will I ever escape you, Gabriel?"

"I mean," he shrugged, popping another bit of focaccia into his mouth. Sari could almost smell the olive oil, could see it on his lips. "It doesn't sound like you're trying very hard."

Sari made a frustrated sound as she collapsed against her chair, turning away from Gabriel completely to face Santi. No need for him to notice that she'd picked up the biscotti again and started nibbling, because she really did like it, damn it.

"As I was saying," Santi cut in, clearing his throat as he finished his coffee. "Gabriel was worried about the image our bakery was projecting—"

"You're business partners too," Sari sighed, shaking her head. "Great."

"But I was actually telling him that the publicity has been a boost," Santi continued, and Sari could swear she heard Gabriel snickering beside her. That she felt comfortable enough to playfully kick him under the table told her just how much their relationship had changed in a span of twelve days. And that was something she didn't want to dwell on. Not at all. "For both your stores, I imagine."

Sari didn't deny it, but refused to say anything more. Santi excused himself to arrange for someone to pick up the roasted coffee beans from her car. Sari handed him the keys, and Santi gave her a little nod of thanks before he walked out of the hotel, presumably to pick up the beans himself.

"You're business partners with Santi," Sari said, as they both watched him leave. "Is there any aspect of my life that you aren't remotely part of? Maybe I should introduce you to my little sister, you can date her, so the circle is complete."

"Sari," he said with a little sigh, and his curls actually flopped forward a bit at the motion. She'd caught herself staring at his hair quite a few times, she couldn't help it. As if noticing just that, Gabriel raked his fingers through it, and Sari now had the image of his gorgeous, veined hands tugging lightly at his curls. "We both know that your sister isn't the one I want to go out with."

She took another bite of the biscotti and a swallow of coffee. Unfortunately it did nothing to tamp down the inexplicable heat that rose in her belly at Gabriel's ridiculous suggestion.

It's a prank war, remember? she told herself.

"Anyway," he said, brushing focaccia crumbs off his lap, and pocketing his phone, which Sari hadn't noticed was on the table. "I have to go back to the bakery. Things to bake, people to prank, you know."

"Good luck," Sari found herself saying, turning her head to him to say something a little more cutting when very suddenly he pressed his cheek against hers and smacked his lips.

Did he just...give me a beso? Sari blinked, watching Gabriel Capras, infuriating man with the gorgeous curls, walk away from the lobby lounge of Hotel Villa, waving at Santi, who was just coming back inside with Sari's keys.

"You okay?" Santi asked as he returned to their table, and it was a bad sign that Sari didn't even notice Santi handing her keys back until he asked for her attention. She blinked at him.

"Yeah, yeah, fine," she said, shaking her head to clear it. "I'm going to get another biscotti."

Chapter Eight

December 13

Gab had to hand it to Sari. She was an evil mastermind.

An evil mastermind masquerading as a café owner, an evil mastermind with a smile that made his insides feel all mixed up and confused. Because that was all this feeling was, surely? Confusion? It couldn't really be more than that between them. It was just a friendly rivalry. That was all.

The beso at Hotel Villa had been an accident. An instinctual move that he couldn't have predicted would have such a startling effect on both of them. He gave besos to aunties, to uncles when he was younger (their egos were too fragile to handle a beso from a nephew when he didn't look much like a nephew anymore) and friends, all the time. Besos were polite, they were something you did. And he'd given one to Sari, like it was the most natural thing in the world. He'd barely been thinking when he did that, which was a common theme for him. Did that mean he saw her as an auntie? A friend? He really didn't know.

At first, he thought his buoyant mood after leaving Hotel Villa was because of what he and Santi had discussed. How the bakery was doing well on its first two weeks, their plans for the grand opening in January, that a real estate development group had approached Santi the other day about pitching potential businesses to a new mall they were opening up. Malls meant foot traffic and foot traffic meant greater chances of making Sunday Bakery attractive to possible franchisers, or more stores.

But all of that didn't quite match up to the grin that spread on his face whenever he thought of Sari's face after the beso, her face after she realized that he'd made the biscotti she was so clearly enjoying. He was surprised to find that he quite liked seeing her happy and caught off guard, much more than he enjoyed seeing her flabbergasted and annoyed at him.

That giddiness only lasted about a day, until Sari, Café Owner and Evil Mastermind, unleashed a horror of a social media announcement the following morning.

My new favorite bakery, @SundayBakery is having a Cookies for Condoms special! Bring a condom, get a free cookie! Hot tip, the owner loves Tropical Hot Watermelon Wonderland

A stroke of genius, if Gab could say so himself. He would go to the café just to applaud Sari if his store wasn't full of customers carrying contraceptives in their pockets asking for cookies. Because of course, Gabriel was going to do it.

"One condoms for cookies promo!" Faye yelled over the cash register, dropping yet another Tropical Hot condom into the slowly growing bowl of condoms they had to put by the register. Hilariously enough, the customers actually brought more *Watermelon Wonderland* than any of the other flavors. "Ransom, don't think I didn't see you pocketing those!"

"Hey, we're all safe sex advocates here," Gabriel assured Faye, patting her back lightly as he refilled their tray of the promo cookies, simple sugar cookies that he'd managed to whip up quick, each with the Sunday Bakery logo. "I think it's fun. And she totally got it wrong. I much prefer Banana Bliss. It's metaphorical and flavorful."

"You just think it's fun because Miss Sari thinks it's hilarious." Ransom waved a Hawaiian Glee flavored condom as Faye giggled. "Weirdest ligawan ever."

"This isn't a courtship," he told them for what felt like the thousandth time that day, smiling as he handed a customer a cookie in exchange for a Dalandan Delight, the rarest flavor of the bunch. "It's competition. It's about one-upping each other and trying to look the least bit like a fool in the process."

"A little late for that, boss," Faye giggled, shaking the jar of condoms they'd collected so far.

"Hijo," Ate Nessie said, bursting into the shop like there wasn't a line going in, carrying a hand fan that was bigger than the ceiling fan in the shop and waving it around. She looked like she needed to tell him something urgent, and walked right up to the counter where Gabriel was standing and reading the ingredients list in one of the Banana Bliss packs.

"Ate Nessie!" he said in surprise, quickly jamming said condom into his pocket, hoping to God she didn't notice. "What a pleasure to have you in Sunday Bakery. What can I do for you? Or are you finally here to teach me how to make your amazing bonete?"

"Nice try, young man." She rolled her eyes. "But I was told that I could get a cookie in exchange for those balloons you buy in the drugstore."

"Balloons?" Gabriel asked in confusion.

"Yes," she said, waving her closed fan in the direction of the condom bowl. "Balloons."

"You," Gabriel said later that afternoon, opening the door to the fire escape, completely unsurprised to find Sari already there, looking out at the view of the still untouched forest land behind the Laneways. The sun was setting low in the horizon, and when she turned to him with an amused smile on her face, it was like she was glowing and radiating happiness.

Ba-dump, went his heart. *Woosh*, went every thought he'd had before he came here to see her. He didn't know when talking to her at their fire escape had become a thing, but clearly it was now.

"Me," Sari said, lifting her cup to her lips. "Long day?"

"Does Ate Nessie really not know what condoms are, or did you somehow orchestrate this so I would have to defile a whole comb of bananas for an audience that didn't get sex ed?"

Her laughter made the entire afternoon worth it. One thing he'd noticed the day he met Sari, aside from the fact that she didn't like him, was that there was a sadness hiding behind those deep brown eyes of hers. Not that Gabriel had any right to know what it was or why it was there, but it was nice, being the reason for it to go away, even if just for a little while.

So much for not getting attached to this place, an old voice in the back of his head whispered. Gab wasn't even sure who was speaking anymore, his siblings, his father or him. But the Laneways had wriggled its way into his heart, and the person standing across from him was one of the big reasons why.

"Oh," Sari said, getting something from the pocket of her skirt and holding it up between her middle and index finger. Tropical Hot Dalandan Delight. "I would like a cookie."

"We're sold out." He tried to sound apologetic, but he wasn't really. Not at all. "Do you take IOUs?"

"Why not," Sari shrugged, slipping the condom into the left pocket of his jeans. "See you, Gabriel."

Then she bumped her hip against his before she disappeared into her coffee lab. Gab only relaxed when she was out of earshot, and from the way his heart was pounding and his head felt a little bit dizzy, he knew he was in trouble.

"My bananas were very unhappy, Sari!" he called after her, just before he walked back into his kitchen.

Chapter Nine

December 14

Sari got home late the next day. She had been doing that a lot, coming home late, and if pressed, she already had a whole host of reasons why—beans to roast, a specialty client to please, problems with suppliers, matters of concern that only she could handle. But whenever she came home late, she was always disappointed to find that she wasn't the last person in the house to get home.

Sam had been spending almost all her time at the farm. Based on the plans she left laid out in the living room and the calls Sari managed to catch in the mornings of her talking to contractors and electricians, her house project was becoming quite the endeavor. While Sari would never be grown up enough to admit that she was pouting over it, she was grown enough to admit that she already missed her sister, and she technically still lived in the house.

Pulling her re-heated dinner from the microwave (their house help worked days at their house and went home once dinner was made), Sari sat in the dining room set for six and whipped out her phone, propping it up against the wine bottle that they had repurposed into a water pitcher.

Home na me, where na you, she typed, which was very unlike her, but she was bored and lonely, and excuse her for being cutesy.

She was expecting a reply from Sam, but her phone started to ring instead to let her know that Selene was calling. Any time her sister called, it meant it was something important. Sari slid the call to Accept and was treated to her sister's serious face looking at her through the phone screen.

"Hi, Ate," Sari said, scooping a bit of pinakbet and crispy tawilis fish on to her plate. She drizzled fish sauce with calamansi on the tawilis and ate that with a bit of squash from the pinakbet and rice. Always with rice, of course.

"Close your mouth when you eat, Sari," Selene said, and she was in her pajamas and eating dinner too. "Late ka na."

"Hello, ikaw din," Sari chastised her older sister. "Busy at work, teh?"

"Eh, I always eat dinner late." Selene shrugged, and Sari kind of felt bad that she didn't know that about her older sister. Lipa might as well have been a country away from how often they actually saw each other face to face. Once a month, maybe. Twice, if there was an occasion. "Food delivery always takes forever."

A pause. As was the natural trajectory of Sari and Selene's conversations. It was a little weird, she was used to talking to her older sister with Sam there to sort of be the light and happy part of the conversation. But Sam was busy with her life, and now Sari and Selene had to suck it up and talk.

"Something's different about you," Selene commented, peering through the screen as if Sari was holding up a sign listing all of those differences for her.

Well, I'm using a prank war with the new shop next door as a distraction from the fact that I'm scared of being alone in this house where our grandmother was alone, but other than that, I'm good, she wanted to blurt out, but it wasn't the kind of thing that one simply said over the phone. In a family where your parents took up most of the time scratching and clawing at each other, you kind of learned, as a kid, to help yourself. Find out how to do things yourself, because the adults in your life couldn't help you. That was the way her sister had coped, and that was the way Sari had learned to become.

So it affected her own adult life. She was still doing…relatively fine.

"I got a haircut two weeks ago, does that count?" Sari asked, spearing a few green beans with her fork and eating them. "Anyway, you didn't call to ask me how I changed, did you?"

Knowing Selene, there was always a reason for her calls. Sari didn't know what her sister was like with her friends in Manila, but she never called her sisters if she didn't have a reason to.

"It's December 14," Selene pointed out, dipping some sushi in soy sauce and wasabi before she ate it. It looked really good, and had Sari's mouth watering eighty-five kilometers away. "I figured between Sam moving and your holiday rush, there would be some confusion as to when you're attending Simbang Gabi in two days."

"Oh," Sari said, nodding in understanding. Simbang Gabi was just as much a part of Christmas tradition as putting up the parol was. It had mattered to her, being dumped in Lipa at the tender age of fourteen with her sisters, uprooted from the Manila she knew and a little lost in a city that until then, had been a vacation spot. Tradition had helped her find her feet again.

Her grandmother had been only too willing to have Sari come along to the farms, to the factories, explained the qualities of a good bowl of lomi, and Simbang Gabi. Sari drank it all in, and it became a part of her routine, long after her lola had gone.

Sari liked going to the dawn masses at the Cathedral, just because there was always food after, and she liked going before she went to the café to roast beans for the day. Sam preferred to attend the mass the night before, at around 8 pm, so she could still get her wish without having to get out of bed at the literal asscrack of dawn. They compromised, in that Sari put up a fight about it every year, but gave in to Sam's requests to attend the evening mass instead.

That Selene thought it was imperative to call her sisters separately to discuss it meant it was a thing. Had she talked to Sam? Did Sam say she didn't want to talk to Sari about it?

Sari inhaled sharply and rubbed her temple, which was starting to hurt.

"Hey, stop that. Your hands are dirty," Selene argued through the phone, immediately making Sari stop.

"Sorry," Sari muttered. "You talked to Sam?"

"Yes," Selene said, adding more wasabi to her soy sauce. "The house has really kept her busy. I think she's staying there tonight."

"Right." Sari nodded, because she was totally informed of that fact. "I take it she wants to attend the evening mass at St. Therese on Alaminos? That's at eight."

"Yup, that mass exactly." Selene had once commented to her that it was amazing that she knew where all the churches were, and what time their masses were. It was the kind of information Sari didn't even realize she was storing until she had to use it. But she had to admit, it came in handy on Holy Week, where they had to do the Visita Iglesia thing. "And I take it you want to attend the Simbang Gabi at the Cathedral."

"Ate, it's two blocks away! If Sam still actually lives here, and actually gives a real shit about it, it's not *that* much of a hassle." Sari smooshed a squash in half and immediately knew it was the wrong thing to say. But either Selene hadn't noticed Sari's agitation, or she'd decided to let it slide, because she just shrugged.

"I guess you guys are going to have to attend Simbang Gabi separately," she said simply, eating another sushi roll. "You're okay with that, right?"

"I'm always okay," Sari assured her sister, knowing full well that her sister didn't believe her.

"Okay. And that blend for the Carlton Hotel, is that going well?"

Sari frowned at her sister through the screen. "Define going well, Ate. This is my part of the business, I'll let you know if I need your help."

"I'm just saying," she said with all the arrogance of someone who was two years older. "I haven't had an update with you about it."

"Because I'm still trying to perfect the roast, and seriously, lay off, okay?" she said a little testily.

"Fine," Selene finally huffed. They exchanged a goodbye, and she was left alone in the too big, too silent house again.

And still no reply from Sam.

This is getting ridiculous, Sari told herself, standing up to clean up her plate after she finished eating dinner. She was starting to miss Kylo, which was always a bad sign.

She tried to go to sleep. She really did. But for someone who was used to living with her sisters, and before that, her grandmother, the lack of sounds of existence aside from the occasional passing car was maddeningly silent for her.

So, when it was about four in the morning, she drove to the Laneways to open the café a little early. They opened at seven anyway, and it was always good for her to catch up on things like…inventory or something.

Sari had just come up to her coffee lab, leaving her keys and her purse in their usual place on the daybed, ready to get roasting or inventory-ing, when the opening chords of a very familiar song started to play through her walls. And almost like he had been waiting there for her, Gabriel's head popped up on his side of the window, dancing and singing along to "You Make My Dreams" like nobody was watching.

Well, technically, that was true.

Gabriel was really into it too, spinning and head banging along like he had an entire audience eagerly anticipating every move. She was a big fan of his hip thrusts.

Sari decided to walk over to the window and give it a solid knock, shocking him so much that his spatula went flying, sending batter all over his side of the window. Oops.

"Sorry," she said through the window, smiling sheepishly as he sprayed some disinfectant on it and wiped it off.

"It's fine," he said, but she could barely hear his voice over the music. "You okay?"

Sari nodded, and even if it wasn't exactly the truth, having him literally dancing into her day was more than enough to make her feel okay for now. And she didn't know if it was the time of day, or the fact that she really liked this song, but seeing Gabriel was actually a comfort to her.

"Turn it up!" she told him through the window, and Gabriel nodded and turned up the volume a little bit, just in time for Aegis' "Halik" to come on. He pointed to her, because there was no other way to start singing an Aegis song. She pointed at him, and a mutual agreement was made as they both launched headfirst into the song.

And for the first time in a very, very long time, Sari sang and danced her heart out in the middle of her own coffee lab, feeling a little less lonely as she sang the world's cheesiest song to the boy on the other side of the window, who was singing too.

Chapter Ten

The first night of Simbang Gabi ended the way it always did, with the bells of the Cathedral ringing into the dawn. Sari stepped out through the side exit of the Cathedral, right next to the crypt where her grandmother was buried. She smiled and sent a little prayer up to Lola Rosario, as she always did when she passed this way on her walk back to the house. It was still early enough for it to be cold, and because it was the first day, there were more people in the church than ever. Despite the other day's impromptu karaoke session at the coffee lab, Sari had still yawned through the service. Also despite Sam's lack of a reply last night, and not a single, *I'm home, Ate*, or a *where are you*? text, Sari still stopped by the bibingka stand to get them breakfast. Sari liked hers with cheese or sugar grilled on top, Sam preferred red egg on hers, and if Sari remembered right, Selene was the weirdo who enjoyed hers with shredded coconut on top.

No matter the topping, what was important was that the bibingka was there, hot and fresh, not too cloying or heavy, and just right.

She wondered if Gabriel knew how to make bibingka. "Nope, don't go there," she told herself, even if in the twenty-four hours since their clandestine karaoke session, Sari had gone there and back multiple times. Her face now went hot and flushy whenever she thought about the Baker Boy Next Door, the exact opposite reaction she'd wanted when she started this little prank war.

So if she'd dozed off a couple of times during the mass, she blamed Gabriel for it, without question. *How is it possible*, she wondered as she paid for the bibingka and walked in the direction of their house, *to want to wring someone's neck so much and still feel so comfortable around them?*

Because she didn't hate him. No. It was too strong a word to use for someone who was buzzing around her head like a fly. Sometimes she closed her eyes in the middle of planning a new scheme, and she could just picture his face (and that smile) grinning back at her like a puppy with a bone. The more she saw it, the more she wanted to wipe that grin off his face.

Or maybe kiss it. One or the other.

She made it to their house without incident. Sari unlocked the gate and went up the steps to the door. She expected to go in and slide into bed for a few hours of sleep before she had to go to the café. She did not expect to trip on an errant badminton racket on the way in and find the absolute mess that had taken over the living room.

"Susmaryosep," Sari cursed, nearly causing her to drop her bibingka. Her grandmother would have hissed at her for that, seeing as she had *just* come from church and all, but, oh well.

Sunlight was starting to peek through the bay windows behind her, giving her enough light to see the entire living room looked like a typhoon had blown through it. Stuff was draped over chairs, stacked in messy, seemingly random piles. Kylo had abandoned his usual bed in the corner to sleep on top of a small mountain of t-shirts and jeans in front of the kitchen door. He also had a shoe hanging out of his mouth, now half-covered in slobber.

"What? Don't! I have a dog!" Sam's voice was still a bit sleep-rough as she jolted awake from her position on the floor, where she'd slept on her yoga mat and used a sarong as a blanket. She winced and grabbed the side of her neck. "Stiff neck, ow, ow."

"And good morning to you too," Sari said, trying to decide if she was still mad at Sam for yesterday, or if she forgave her for it, because clearly, Sam had other things on her mind. "That's what you get for sleeping on the floor. What are you doing on the floor, by the way?"

Sari tiptoed around the mess of her sister's belongings, forging a path to the kitchen after leaving the bibingka on the dining room table. She might as well make coffee to go with the bibingka while she grabbed utensils.

Kylo lifted his head when Sari approached him. The dog was so massive that he blocked the whole doorway, preventing her access.

"Move," Sari told Kylo, who blinked and went back to sleep. Sari sighed and looked around the topsy turvy living room. "Sam, seriously. What is this mess?"

"I'm wrapping Christmas gifts for the whole barangay," Sam said sarcastically, putting the yoga mat to good use for a quick Downward Dog, Plank then Chaturanga. Sari had never seen anyone do yoga so sarcastically. Sam stood up on the mat and raised her arms over her head before she swan dove into a forward fold. "What do you think I'm doing? I'm panic-packing!"

Sari watched her sister with mild fascination as she went down into a Plank pose, then up to Downward Dog, creating a pattern she repeated a few more times, like she was stretching herself to wakefulness.

"It's a little over a week to Christmas and I have nothing ready. I haven't even made a dent in my Christmas shopping list, and the farm's Christmas party is in three days, and there's a huge debate about if we should have a karaoke machine or not. I missed Simbang Gabi last night, so clearly, I'm not going to get my wish!"

"Oh." Sari nodded, finally giving up and taking a bibingka from the plastic bag, eating it sans utensils. The charred banana leaf at the bottom was more than enough to use as a plate. "You still have time, though."

"I have to comb through everything, take out what doesn't bring me joy!"

"And you decided to find joy at five in the morning?"

"Hey, don't give me your judgey face, Ate. You're the one attending Simbang Gabi even if she doesn't go to church the rest of the year."

"I'm keeping up tradition." Sari shrugged. "Someone has to."

"Tradition! What is this, *Fiddler on the Roof*?" Sam scoffed, attempting to put her books in neater piles before she saw the mess of her old college notes on the side and attempted to fix those.

"When did you see *Fiddler on the Roof*?" Sari managed to open the door long enough to let herself into the kitchen, and used Kylo's backside as a door stopper.

"This isn't about *Fiddler on the Roof*! I was making a point."

"Which is what?" Sari emerged from the kitchen with forks and mugs for the coffee she was already brewing, and went back to her seat on the dining table, the same seat she had occupied since she was fourteen. She picked up another bibingka.

"That you're just as stuck as I am," Sam said, finally putting her hands in prayer position for the last time, nodding her head once before she sat at the chair across from Sari's and took a disk of bibingka. As Sari predicted, her sister went for the red egg. "You don't want to admit this to yourself, but you're stuck too! You're living in Lola's house, doing her job, in her café. And now you're doing Simbang Gabi because she did, not because you have something to pray for. And I know you don't believe that the Simbang Gabi wish thing is real."

Sari frowned, her hand paused mid-pour of freshly ground beans into the French press. That was the last thing she expected her sister to say, but the more the truth sank in, the more it hurt.

Ma. Rosario Tomas was a great grandmother. She loved her granddaughters the way they needed it when their parents couldn't be in a room together for longer than ten minutes. But she lived a very small, particular life, with very little room for new things. After losing her husband in the eighties, she never saw the need to change up her life very much.

She'd made it clear that taking on three granddaughters had been far on the list of things she wanted to do, and Sam had been very vocal about how Lola Rosario made the girls bend to fit her life, instead of the other way around.

But Sari's life wasn't boring, it was…structured. There was a rhythm to it that she knew to follow, routines that she could rely on. Christmases and holidays and planting seasons came and went, and she knew how to move through all of that. She had nothing to complain about.

She certainly wasn't stuck. So why was she so mad at Sam for moving out? Why was it that from the moment she walked into the church that morning, her only thought had been to wish that Sam wouldn't move out of the house?

"You're tired," Sari concluded, standing up to retrieve the coffee from the kitchen. "Go to bed. I'll clean this up."

Sam must have realized that she crossed a line, because she stopped eating her bibingka and took the coffee when Sari handed her a mug anyway. "Sari, I'm sorry, I…"

"It's fine, Sam," Sari cut her sister off, because she didn't want to hear it, or think about it. "Go to sleep."

With a quick hug, her sister went back to her room with the coffee and another bibingka. Kylo looked up at the sound of the bedroom door closing, and seemed to look to Sari for confirmation that everything was fine.

"You go to sleep too," Sari informed him, and Kylo made no further protest, and went to sleep.

Sari looked at the mess of her sister's belongings and felt her shoulders drop. She never liked it when she made her sisters upset, even when she was upset with them. But Sam had made Sari realize that she wanted certain…things outside of what she already had. She wanted a life that wasn't just about being alone in this house.

She looked at the photo of her grandmother that was sitting on top of the piano. In it, Rosario Tomas looked out in the distance, laughing at some invisible thing. Sari glared at her grandmother.

"I don't know what you're trying to say, but whatever it is, it's not funny," Sari said before she started to clean up after Sam, brushing aside thoughts of her own life as she took stock of just how much her sister was taking with her when she left. She wanted to flop down on the couch and sleep, but she knew she couldn't.

All this sudden desire for new things she blamed on one person alone. If he hadn't quite literally danced his way into her life, she wouldn't have started questioning things, or let Sam's words rattle her so much.

Gabriel had unstuck some part of Sari's world, and she didn't like it.

She should like him, really. She liked guys who knew what they wanted out of life, who were go-getters and unapologetic about it. She liked guys who knew how to smile, especially him, with his dimples so deep that whenever her staff gossiped they called him "dimples next door" like Sari wasn't aware of how well that name suited him and—

She spotted a pair of white boots with blue tassel trimmings amidst her sister's belongings. She grinned as a plan began to form in her mind.

Chapter Eleven

Hours later, with apologies left unsaid, Sari and Sam's day continued. The best thing about having sisters, Sari liked to think, was that most of the time, it was all about what wasn't being said, you know? Without talking about it, or sitting down to parse and break it down, Sam and Sari were okay. She liked that about them.

So when Sam walked into Café Cecilia that morning, Sari felt it was only part of her usual routine. She was already behind the counter, showing her new barista how to clean the espresso machine when her sister went behind the counter to give her a huge hug.

"Thanks, Ate." Sam squeezed her tightly.

"I didn't do anything, I just gave you boxes for your stuff," Sari protested, moving out of the hug and to the front of the counter to give her and her sister some room.

"But they were exactly what I needed." Sam launched herself into Sari's back and hugged her even tighter. "You're the best. And I'm sorry I didn't text last night. I thought you were out having fun, and I wasn't really worried about you."

"Is that a compliment to my being responsible, or do you really care so little about me?" Sari turned and pinched her sister's nose lightly so she knew she was joking, before she shrugged out of her grasp and jogged up the stairs to the coffee lab. She needed to retreat a little from Sam's emotions, mostly because she didn't want to feel emotional about this. She was the older sister, it was part of her job to be supportive.

So she was moving away. Sari was going to be fine.

Besides, she had something bigger afoot.

"Ate, why did your busboys just tell me that you're at war with Sunday Bakery next door?" Sam asked, a cookie in one hand and coffee in the other, as the door to the coffee lab opened with a slam. "There was also something about ABBA? And bananas being made sex-safe."

"Don't ask."

"So you *are* at war with Dimples?"

"His name is not Dimples, it's Gabriel, and I have no idea what you're talking about," Sari singsonged, pulling a random book off the shelf from the daybed, and pretending to read. It was one of her favorite historical romance novels, where an older spinster sister tells the viscount off for pursuing her younger sister, but then ends up falling for the viscount himself. Good stuff, but Sari couldn't seem to absorb a word of it, mostly because her sister wasn't supposed to follow her up here.

"You're acting weird." Sam slipped into the space next to Sari on the daybed, making a grab for the book. Sari deftly moved it out of the way and casually glanced out the window. As she expected, she had a perfect view of the street below. More importantly, a perfect view of Sunday Bakery's doorway.

"I'm not. What time is it?" she asked casually, as she very subtly checked her shared window with Gabriel to see if he was there. The kitchen lights were on, but her curly-haired air band mate was nowhere to be found. Maybe he was downstairs at the shop?

"Five minutes to nine," Sam said. "What are you looking at?"

"Just trying to picture this scene I'm reading. The viscount is playing some sort of competitive sport on a huge field, and I don't know enough about white people sports to understand it," Sari said almost immediately, closing the book like she was worried Sam would press for more information.

But Sam was like a fish to food when it came to possible chismis and simply tilted her head at her. Finally, she seemed to realize something and asked, "What did you do while getting boxes for me?"

"Nothing!" Sari lied. Sam narrowed her eyes at her and Sari sighed. "Fine. Something. Just a thing. A quick little stopover."

"A stopover that would have nothing to do with the person who works on the other side of that window?"

Sari laughed, and she knew that her sister was looking at her like she'd just grown a second, third, and fourth head. She was aware that she had never been this excited, or this weird about something, and had never gone this long without telling Sam what she was planning.

"You are freaking me out," Sam said, half amused and half horrified, at least in Sari's ears. "Ate, seriously, what is going on?"

"What's going on is that I am having a little fun." Sari shrugged, so without care or concern that she thought she rivaled Queen Victoria's "we are not amused." "And I'm not boring."

"You are boring," Sam said good-naturedly, squeezing her sister's arm before she paused and studied her. "This is the wildest thing you've ever done in your life, isn't it?"

"I've done wilder."

"Stealing a 1.5 liter of Pepsi from a party when you were super drunk is not that wild." Sam rolled her eyes. "And really? You don't see the un-wisdom of this?"

"Un-wisdom?"

"Avoiding it isn't going to stop me from asking."

"Mhmm." Sari knew she was being a little too chipper as she put the book back in its place on the shelf and walked to the espresso machine.

"Ate," Sam sighed a long-suffering, exasperated sigh. Sari was a little sister to an exasperating older sister herself, so she knew the sound. "But you realize that you're pikon, right?"

"Take that back," Sari almost snapped at her.

"I will not, because you are!" Sam insisted, leaving a bit of dirt on the floor when she stomped her foot. "The littlest things set you off. Just like this morning! You remember when we were kids, and Kiko Villa cut in front of you to get birthday cake, then you tripped him and broke his nose?"

"I was seven, and you are too young to remember that."

"The sight of all the blood scarred me for life. And you also get really, really mad when you're driving."

"Traffic here is just as bad as in Manila! You try sitting in traffic for an hour just to get to something two kilometers away."

"And you cry every time you don't get your way."

"Okay, now we both know that is *not* true." Sari's

voice was low as she glared at her sister. Sari knew that look on her sister's face. When it came to gossip and drama, Sam was like a bloodhound and could smell it a mile away. She also loved sussing out the truth, especially when her sisters were trying not to give it to her. "I cry when I get mad, and that's a very different thing. I can handle this, I can handle myself. It's just Gabriel Capras."

But it wasn't just Gabriel Capras, was it? It was the way he got under her skin, the way he made her roll her eyes at the stupid pranks he pulled. Looking at Sam now in the midst of Sari's planning of this last prank, she saw it exactly for what it was. It was distraction. Distraction from her feelings about Sam leaving her, distraction from her feelings about everything else. It was diversion. But most importantly, it was fun. She liked this, she liked being challenged like this, in ways that she didn't really expect. Who would have thought the boy next door with the impossibly sweet smile would be the one to get her to feel this way?

Sam gasped dramatically like she'd seen Sari's lightbulb moment, and it took all of Sari's willpower not to roll her eyes. She took a sip of her freshly extracted coffee and looked at her sister over the rim of the mug, trying her hardest to keep the smile off her face. She was also trying not to look like she was buzzing in anticipation, because she was.

Sam had always been able to read her like an open book, no matter how much Sari tried to keep it shut.

"You're enjoying this," Sam accused, leaning back against the bookshelf. "I've never seen you smiling like this."

"I am not smiling," Sari snorted, but she could feel it

in the way her cheeks were starting to hurt. She couldn't help it. The anticipation of a successful pranking was just too much.

"You're smiling, and you like being devious." Sam shook her head and laughed. "I love this new side of you, Ate. It's cute. Even if this is the weirdest courtship ever."

"Courtship? What…?"

"I didn't think adults did ligawan like schoolchildren."

"I am *not* making landi, and this isn't ligawan." Sari scowled, and she was pretty sure she looked like a schoolchild when she did so, but whatever. She was not flirting and this certainly was *not* a courtship. She was engaged in a prank war, she was a few minutes away from winning. "I'm facing a challenge. And I never back down from a challenge."

"Sure you do. You back down every time Ate Selene comes into town."

"That's—"

"Different? It's really not," Sam laughed, shaking her head. "I know you, Ate. It's not wrong to admit you're having fun. I like seeing you have fun. This whole secretly devious side of you is wildly fascinating. And I have no doubt you know the limits to this. Just…remember that you're pretty short-tempered, and Gab doesn't know this about you. Don't let this go *too* far?"

"There is no such thing as too far in a prank war," Sari huffed, and almost on cue, a booming sound filled the air, followed by the discordant tinkling of an instrument. A bunch of instruments. Then, a small group of young children in bright yellow and blue uniforms came marching into view, all of them with serious expressions on their faces as they beat their mallets and sticks against drums and lyres to what sounded suspiciously like "Bahay Kubo." Sari hadn't heard "Bahay Kubo" since she was in pre-school.

"What the heck?" Sam sighed, and Sari knew the exasperation of a younger sister more than most, but decided that she was going to ignore her for now. "Where did you even *find* a drum and lyre band at six in the morning?"

"I hired the one from the public school near the house on my way from getting your boxes," Sari half laughed, half shouted, swaying along as the band changed tune to "Hooked on a Feeling," which she didn't even know they could play. Girls in pigtails, blue and yellow tassels and shiny white boots twirled tasseled batons in the air, and a huge crowd began to gather in the perimeter of the performance, taking video as they wondered who this was supposed to be for.

Sari gave in to the urge to sing along, and start dancing. Sam looked a little terrified.

Then *he* came out of the café, and honestly, all of the trouble, the explaining and re-explaining she went through to set this up, it was *so* worth it, seeing the confusion, exasperation and surprise on Gabriel's face. Sari giggled with glee as she curled her fingers closer around her coffee cup, ignoring the way Sam rolled her eyes.

Her sister was right. She *was* having fun. She liked setting this up, she liked sneaking around and getting Gabriel to make that face he was making right now.

Very slowly, his curly head turned and he looked up, almost like she'd told him that she was going to do this, told him where she was going to watch from. There was a crinkle in the corners of his eyes, and his Lipa-famous dimples were on full display. The sight of him made her queasy and giddy at the same time, and she didn't know if it was guilt or excitement. "Hooked on a Feeling" was still playing when he pointed to her, turned his finger around and made a "come here" motion with it.

Sari stuck her tongue out at him in response.

He raised an eyebrow at her. His dimples were at maximum adorability, and had Sari not been the one to do this, she would have immediately floated down to where Gabriel was and bathed in his attention. Because damn, Sam was right. It *looked* like a courtship. It looked like Gabriel had hired the band to serenade her by her window.

"Are you going to go out there?" Sam asked as the band moved to "Can't Take My Eyes Off You," which was just unfair, really, because Gabriel started to dance the way he did whenever he baked, which just automatically brought a smile to Sari's face, until she realized her sister was staring at her.

"Hell no," Sari snorted, shaking her head.

"I thought you never backed down from a challenge?" Sam teased, nudging her sister with her elbow. Gabriel was still watching them with the cockiest expression on his face, like he was fully expecting Sari to go outside. Because she was going to have to, wasn't she?

Oooh, now *that* was the expression she wanted to wipe off his face. His "hello, Sari, I have you cornered" face.

So Sari put down her coffee cup, made a show of brushing imaginary dust from her black and white checkered skirt. Still carrying the air of a queen, she joined Gabriel outside, all breezy and confident and innocent, because really, what could she do?

"Did you do this?" he asked, jerking his thumb at the kids. Was it just her imagination, or did he look amused? The point of this wasn't to *amuse* him. She wanted to…to make him all mad, and infuriated, and, and…

He should stop smiling. Sari could barely finish a thought around a smile like that, and it was dangerous with a capital *D* with matching flashing neon signs.

She merely shrugged in response, because she couldn't be trusted to say anything, and he threw his head back and laughed. His entire face lit up with the absurdity of all of this. Because it was absurd, wasn't it? Sari-sari stores opened next to each other all the time, selling the exact same wares, and petty rivalries like this had never emerged.

He ran his hand through his hair and looked at Sari, and she just…she knew that his smile was all for her, warm and happy. It made her think of hot caramel on cool vanilla ice cream. But he was laughing, which meant that he didn't hate this. The crowd seemed to sense it too, because they started to cheer at the sight of them standing together at the stoop of each of their shops, as if daring the other to come close.

"Kiss! Kiss!" someone chanted, and everyone started to join in.

"Excuse me?" She scrambled for an excuse without actually saying that this was her fault. "There's no mistletoe!"

"There's no what?" People in the crowd seemed totally confused.

"Is that drugs?" one particularly ornery person asked.

"It's not drugs, that's probably a contraceptive."

"Not the outcome you predicted, is it?" Gabriel asked, and he was laughing really, really loudly now. So loud that he could have topped the big bass drum when it came to decibels. "Maybe we should just give the crowd what they want."

"Hmph. You first."

"Is that a challenge?"

"I don't know, Gabriel. Is it?"

But instead of saying something in response, Gabriel stopped laughing. He never did stop smiling though, and held out a hand for her to take. Sugar particles always seemed to be stuck on his hands, and Sari could see them sparkle in the sunlight. Had she been a more naive person, she would think this a sign. Or a Christmas miracle.

"Don't you wash your hands?" she asked him.

"Yes, of course I do. Take my hand, Sari," he said with no force whatsoever. How did he make his voice that deep, and still so warm? It shot through her body, like the caramel in coffee, making her fingers tingle.

God help her, she took it. She didn't know what possessed her to take his hand, but she wasn't going to be the one to disappoint their little audience. Very suddenly, she remembered that morning where they were both on their own sides of the window, dancing together, but still apart. This felt very much the same, but this time, Gabriel was in solid, touchable distance, and she was about to kiss him.

"I brushed my teeth this morning, if that helps," he said.

"It doesn't," she clarified. "So are you admitting defeat? I win?"

"Defeat? Never." He grinned, and it made Sari's entire body tingle. "This is me going first."

"I-is that a challenge?" She hated that she was stuttering.

"Is that consent?"

Sari squeezed his hand, warm and big and much, much bigger than hers. She put on the most unaffected face she could muster, hoping that her cheeks weren't as red as she thought, hoping that she wasn't smiling. She probably was, though, because her face always betrayed her, and her cheeks were burning. Honestly. If only she could actually project the level of cool she imagined she had, she wouldn't end up in situations like this.

Not that this situation was bad, per se, it was just… exactly what she wanted. She never thought she would get exactly what she wanted more than once in this life.

She tugged his hand to pull him close. She was now close enough that she saw him swallow thickly, the only sign that he was nervous.

"This is consent," she told him. "Make it good."

With a deftness that she didn't think possible for a man as tall as him, he lifted her hand and twirled her around, and her skirt flew around her. Sari's entire world spun and her feet were a little unstable before she felt her back press against his warm chest. In the warm December sun, Gabriel's chest radiated heat, felt comfortable, and Sari wanted to curl up into it and nap like a cat. She didn't think bakers had such firm muscles, but hey, she wasn't about to complain when Gabriel was so in control of the situation.

She could feel his breath against her neck, smelled freshly washed sheets, sugar and cinnamon on his skin.

Was she just imagining it, or did he take a little sniff of her too?

With their arms tangled up in each other, he twirled her again. Now she was looking up at his face. His eyes were sparkling with mischief, and she tilted her head slightly just because she wanted to see more. He slid a hand down her back, pressing lightly on the base before he eased her backward, and Sari was about to fall, she was sure, but his hand supported. Gabriel gently dipped her, her entire weight supported by his arms. Their eyes locked, and Sari didn't want Gabriel to be the only one doing anything—she pressed a hand on his cheek and kissed him.

It was a quick kiss, barely even scandalous had this been anywhere else. But this was the Laneways, a small community that loved drama just as much as they loved free food. The whole thing occurred in seconds, but those precious seconds were enough, making the entire crowd cheer in delight as Sari and Gabriel looked right into each other's eyes.

Sari would like to personally note that Gabriel Capras had really gorgeous eyes.

They were smaller, but they were full of warmth and happiness, with the kind of full lashes that she could only achieve with copious amounts of mascara, which wasn't fair at all. Those eyes were dancing with mirth and amusement, like he couldn't believe this was actually happening. His lips were curved in the slightest of smiles, his hair curling around his face. Every line on his face deepened when he smiled, but it only made him look sweeter and much happier. Sari felt her face burn and her heart pound.

"I like that look on your face," he said softly. "Your 'I hate you so much I want to kiss you' face."

"We need to talk," she told him, looking up at his eyebrows, which were a lot less distracting than his eyes.

"There are more subtle ways of getting my attention, sweetheart."

"I didn't think you would get the hint, dimples." She rolled her eyes, but pressed her lips together to keep herself from smiling. She gently pushed him off her, and Gabriel relented easily, before he turned to their little audience and waved. To the drum and lyre band he started to applaud, and let them take a little bow.

"Iced tea and snacks in my café, as promised." Sari nodded to the group, and twenty-something kids and their supervisor all headed into Café Cecilia, leaving Gabriel and Sari standing in the spot between their two shops, looking at each other under the warm glow of the recently lit Christmas lights. She turned to him and started to laugh.

"What's so funny?" he asked her, placing his hands on his hips, and his dimples were out and on full display.

"Nothing," she said, but immediately took it back. "Everything. This whole prank thing. I can't believe you didn't save any brazo de mercedes for me."

"I can't believe you made me demonstrate the proper use of a condom to Ate Nessie." He shrugged casually as he stuffed his hands into his pockets. "And now this whole thing. You must really like me, Sari Tomas."

"I…don't," she said, but the words sounded weak even to her. Gabriel took one step closer to her, a little grin playing on his lips. Sari's cheeks suddenly felt very hot. This was the Philippines, it was hot all the time, but then again this was Lipa in December, and she was very, very flustered about it. "I don't like you."

"What did I ever do to annoy you?"

You made me want you, when I've never wanted anything else for myself, she thought.

"Oh, I don't know, blaring 'When I Kissed the Teacher' during my barista training class the day we met wasn't pleasant." She scowled at him, but really, she'd lost all fight the moment he'd dipped her in front of a crowd. Sari still felt the touch of his lips against hers, still thought of the way he'd looked at her through the window and asked if she was okay.

"That was an accident, I swear," Gab chuckled, holding his hands up in surrender. "I just really like listening to ABBA sometimes."

"And your big neon sign casts a glare into my store."

"Well, one of us *had* to make the warehouse look attractive from the street."

Well, *that* stung. Sari was proud of her store and what it looked like, and she didn't like that Gabriel felt it was fine to comment on it the way he did. Immediately she backed off, pushing aside everything that had just happened for this little slight. *Pikon,* she heard Sam's voice in her head, but ignored it.

"I don't want to talk about this anymore." Sari shook her head, and turned back to her place, noticing the way Gabriel's face had dropped a little. "I have half a classroom of children in my café, a private cupping to arrange—"

"A what?"

"My job. I'm here to do my job, making coffee. That's all."

"Well, I bake things, and that's *my* job too," he said

defensively, and Sari wondered what she'd said to make him suddenly put all of his guards up. And for Gabriel, who seemed completely unaware if he even had guards up, it was odd to see him do that.

But she hadn't known him for very long, and she shouldn't be thinking these kinds of things. If she was a different person, a better person, she would ask him what was wrong. But she wasn't. So she didn't.

"Are you sure you don't want to go out on a date with me?" he asked suddenly, and Sari knew a defense mechanism when she saw it, mostly because she'd just played an elaborate prank on him to avoid thinking about her sister's impending move. There was no way that Gab was serious. He couldn't be.

"Sure. November 31 work out for you?"

"I…oh. You almost had me there," Gab said, shaking his head as Sari shrugged casually. They were both grinning at this point. "I believe the next prank is mine, sweetheart."

"I'm looking forward to it." Sari nodded at him before she turned her heel and walked back to the café, taking a to-go cup of coffee and ignoring the knowing looks Sam was giving her.

"Rosario, you cannot be serious," she said, adopting a British accent she probably picked up from watching *Pride and Prejudice* too many times. "You're really dating the Baker Next Door?"

"It was just for show! I was trying to prove a point."

"In his mouth?"

"I'm going back to work. Go inter-crop a plant or something."

"Oh, scary." Sam rolled her eyes before she followed her sister back up to the coffee lab. From that point of the morning, all through lunch, she and Sam talked business—how her new cacao trees were looking, a new batch of Liberica that Sari needed to roast, if there were any issues at the roasting and packing facility that they needed to sort out. It was work, and it was the kind of work that usually would have soothed Sari. But not today, apparently. Today she felt a little jumpy and out of her skin, like the kiss from this morning (it was *barely* a kiss, to be honest) still lingered on her skin.

The rest of the day was relatively quiet, thank God. Sari was standing behind the counter again, humming along to the Christmas song playing on the speakers as she made candy cane coffees for the group of teenagers who had asked to shoot a music video for class in the café. From what Sari could tell, it was an adaptation of *Ang Mag-anak na Cruz*, which she distinctly remembered not reading in high school.

"Rosario!" One of her regulars, Mrs. Vargas, came into the café looking a little flushed and terribly excited. "Yoo-hoo, dear!"

"Yes, Tita V." Sari smiled. "Spiced hot chocolate or barako?"

"Spiced hot chocolate with ice, please, I'm melting," Mrs. V laughed, sitting in her usual seat by the window. "Come and sit with me for a moment, and tell me all about that delicious bedimpled boy next door."

Sari wrinkled her nose. "There's nothing to tell though."

"That's not what I heard through the grapevine, though! I heard you were serenading him with a marching band this morning. I love it! You don't see a classic ligawan nowadays, you know? It's all texting and chat-

ting and Twittering, but that? *That* is romance. Good
for you, hija, taking charge like that."

"I wasn't—"

The door to the shop rang just in time to interrupt
her. Sari looked up at the door to see one of the shop-
girls from Meile's Garden a few doors away holding a
bunch of flowers in one arm. The stem had spiny little leaves, and branched off into flower heads with the
most adorable blossoms, huddled together and shiver-
ing in the wind. Sari could almost hear laughter coming from the blooms.

There was a brief moment where she was reminded
of the way sugar had seemed to dot Gabriel's hands that
morning. *Baby's breath*, Sari's brain supplied just before cutting off thoughts of Gab.

"Flower delivery for Sari Tomas," the shopgirl said,
holding up the bouquet.

Beside Sari, Tita V gasped. "Oh, hija," she cooed.
"That is *so romantic*."

"What?" Sari nearly dropped the coffee cup she was
holding. "I didn't order flowers."

"Of course you didn't," Tita V happily supplied.
"Your boy next door did."

"It's a special delivery," the shopkeeper explained,
before Sari could correct her. They turned to the door,
where Sari could see two more shopkeepers and the
shop owner herself crossing the street to Café Cecilia, each one of them carrying huge bouquets of the
same flowers in both arms, two to a person. Half baby's breath, half carnations. From what she could see
of the flower shop's storefront, there was still a whole
multi-cab full of buckets and buckets of baby's breath

and soft pink carnations that supposedly belonged to her. "There's a card. Should we unload them here?"

Sari frowned and let them. As her entire floorspace became slowly invaded by the prettiest sea of pink and white, her staff and customers very unhelpfully pointed out the obvious.

"Ay, M'am Sari has a secret admirer!"

"Well, after this morning, it's not so secret any-more…"

She pointedly ignored them, taking the card and greedily opening instead for clues. *This has to be a prank*, she thought. His handwriting was messy and haphazard, like he'd scratched off the note without much care or thought. Even his baking was like this. But even with Gabriel's seeming lack of care, Sari knew that each and every bake in that shop of his was perfect and made with love, and clearly this prank was the same way.

Just to let you know that I was thinking of you. Date?

Sari looked up to the wall she shared with Sunday Bakery, and suddenly felt her heart thumping in her chest, her hands get cold. Because this wasn't a prank anymore. This was…this was ligawan. Real, honest to goodness ligawan, something he did because he was thinking of her. A lot, apparently.

"I…" was all she managed to say before she slipped the card into her apron, grabbed a handful of the flowers and headed up to the coffee lab, telling her manager that they could handle this. Because she certainly couldn't.

Still holding the flowers, she looked frantically around the shop. The daybed was too close to the window, her office desk was too small. She headed out to the fire escape, which was thankfully, empty. The door on his side was closed, and she exhaled a slow breath as she sat down, letting the slats of the metal flooring dig into her butt as she considered the lovely blossoms.

Falling in love wasn't exactly on Sari's radar. She legitimately thought she was past the age where she still fell in love. She was twenty-nine, after all, and kids her age were getting married and having babies and moving into mid-size condominiums in Manila. But this gesture of Gabriel's, which would have certainly irritated her two weeks ago, now touched her heart in ways she'd never experienced before.

I was thinking of you. It was such a simple sentiment, a sweet one, but it meant more to Sari than all of the little interactions they'd had over the last two weeks, meant more to her than anything else. He was thinking of her, and she didn't feel alone.

She looked up at the closed fire exit door to Sunday Bakery and smiled. She slipped the bouquet through the latch of the door without really thinking about what that was supposed to mean, and went back into the shop to handle the thousand other flowers that were waiting.

"What in carnation," Sam said a few hours later, plucking one of the scentless pink blossoms from one of the little milk jugs they used as vases on the customer tables. "I go back to the farm for a few hours and suddenly this happens?"

Sari raised an eyebrow at her. She hoped her sister didn't notice that her cheeks had been pink the whole day, just like the carnations. "You think you're the first to make that joke? Kira beat you to it. As did Mrs. Recto. And the mayor. And his wife."

"You know what, I take it back, you and Gab are perfect for each other." Sam rolled her eyes, tapping the flower against her sister's nose. "It's a Christmas miracle. Sari finally finds The One."

Sari snorted and hid a smile behind a bunch of flowers placed in a repurposed iced tea bottle. She was so happy it was getting a little bit embarrassing. But because her sister knew her all too well, Sari heard her snicker with laughter anyway.

"Two lonely, petty masters of their craft that refuse to see how perfect they are for each other."

"What was that?" Sari pretended not to hear, attempting to school her face into impassivity while she rearranged the cups on top of the espresso machine. Not that the cups needed rearranging, but Sam didn't know that.

"Nothing, nothing, not a thing, Ate! Clearly, I'm just a fly on the wall here." Sampaguita Tomas rolled her eyes before she twirled the carnation in her fingers. "And Ate Nessie and the titas aren't already planning your wedding outside. I hope you like pink and white for a color scheme."

Chapter Twelve

December 18

"Good morning, sir!" Gabriel's staff greeted him chirpily two days later, and he greeted them back with equal enthusiasm. He'd seen the flowers Sari left at his door, and he took it as a little gesture of thanks.

The flowers had been a bold move on his part, and a brilliant one, because it served the dual purpose of being sincere and possibly being interpreted as a prank if she didn't feel the same way.

Somehow, he'd known she would like it.

Ever since he'd accidentally given her a beso on the cheek, possibly even before that, Sari Tomas had occupied his thoughts. He hadn't come back to the Philippines, come to Lipa, to fall in love, but he was a big believer in the grace of the universe, and he wanted to roll with it for as long as he could.

Well, Santi did say this was good for business, he told himself, trying not to think of what his father could possibly make of all of this. Hunter Capras was way too serious to appreciate a prank like this, even with nine kids and a particularly nefarious kitty. His mom, maybe, would think this was cute.

"Where did you get all these flowers?" he asked innocently as he walked through his bakery, which was doing a good job of currently looking like it was a flower shop that sold only pink carnations and baby's breath. "And Ransom, don't think I didn't see Sab posting on Facebook with a bouquet you gave her!" It was as if his little prank war with that café next door had sparked a revolution in the Laneways. He'd heard rumors of grand gestures happening left and right, Christmas gifts coming into the Laneways by the truckload, so much that their local delivery service had complained. Love and Christmas magic were in the air, and Gabriel pretended he couldn't see it.

His phone buzzed with a message. It was from the family's group chat, where they talked about everything from global warming to the time Bubbles the cat ran straight into a glass door. It was supposed to be a group chat for schedule coordination (nobody ever talked about how much of a logistical nightmare nine kids was), but had now evolved into being part of the family's daily life, a way to connect while everyone was living their own lives.

Mom: Good morning, children. Send a siomai emoji so I know you're all alive.

Although most of the family still lived in their house in Alabang, the Capras family was always in at least three or four different places at once during the week. Gabriel in whatever country he was working in, Lily and Daisy sharing a condo in Ortigas because of work and Rose and Ivy in a dorm in Katipunan for university.

Check-ins became mandatory, and weekends in Alabang necessary for those still in the Metro Manila area.

Gabriel, the idiot, was in such a sentimental mood that he actually replied, dumpling emoji and all, when he hadn't replied before.

Mommers: Gabriel! Good morning! I haven't heard from you in so long! How is Melbourne? Did you eat breakfast?

Papa: Yes. Report.

Kuya Gab: Oh it's fine. Nice and cold. The usual.

Lily: How strange…when it's summertime in Australia.

"Shit," Gabriel muttered, wishing he could take back his emoji. The thing about lying to your whole family was that it was hard to sustain that lie. Four years ago, when his father told him he basically wasn't good enough to sustain his own family, Gabriel had made the rash decision that he couldn't stay in Manila. He'd packed his things and took a job working in bakeries and patisseries in Hong Kong, Osaka and Singapore before he finally ended up in Melbourne. As far as his parents knew, he was there, living in a studio outside the CBD and baking bread for a bakery on Little Bourke Street.

Lily and Daisy knew otherwise, though. He quickly switched chat groups and sent a private message to Lily. He loved his little sister more than a lot of things in this world, but most of the time he thought she was way too smart to be the younger one. That someone up there had messed up on the birth order of the Capras kids, and now the family was stuck with the disappointment as the oldest kid.

Gabriel: Hi can you not laglag me in front of mom and dad tnx??

Lily: Hi, can you text like a normal person? It's not my fault you said it's cold!! Dad still remembers that we don't like Australia for Christmas because it's hot! Also, can you please tell them you're in Lipa already? The other day Mom was texting me to ask if you could buy her eucalyptus oil, and you can't.

Gabriel: Baka someone's selling on Shopee or Lazada pretend I sent it to you. I can GCash it or something.

Lily: I can't believe I'm not the oldest in this family.

Gabriel: U n me both.

He felt bad for leaving his sisters stuck with having to lie like this, he really did. But Gabriel was old enough to know that he had to make *something* of himself, and he needed to do that not in Manila. His father would try to be way too involved, and Gabriel would always be on the defense, which only made things uncomfortable for the entire family. And while Lily and Daisy couldn't understand why he needed to do this, they loved him enough to keep his secrets without question.

It's better this way, he thought whenever he found himself missing them. When he finally got the mall deal and left the Laneways, there would be nothing his father could say about it except, "good job."

Gabriel sighed and switched back to the family chat group to rectify his mistake, posting a photo of the lemon loaf he'd made this morning, making sure that there was nothing in the background to indicate specifics of his current location.

Gabriel: Oh you know. Once you leave the PH everything else seems cold in comparison

Lily: You can't see, but I'm rolling my eyes.

Gabriel: You cant see but I love yew baby sister

Mommers: Hay naku. Those people are really making you work hard, @Gabriel. When are you coming home for Christmas?

Gabriel swallowed thickly. In his brilliant plans to be home and not be home, he hadn't even considered Christmas or any big holidays. He supposed he would have to go home at some point, but how?

He didn't have the answers yet. But with his father seen-zoning every message that came through, he knew he was going to have to come up with something. Something to talk about in the This Should Be The Gang group chat shared between him, Daisy and Lily. Yes, there were factions in the Capras family. Don't tell the little kids.

Gabriel: Wish u guys cld smell this lemon loaf!!!

Mother: Looks goody! Miss you, anak!

Gabriel: Miss you too, Mom! Kiiissss.

Lily: Hay nako.

Gabriel: You too, Lily. Kissssss.

Mindy: I'm here too, hellooo???

Gabriel: Didn't see u there Minders. I don't miss you.

Mindy: Liar, you love meeee!

Gabriel: Sige na, sige na. BYE NA.

Then he put the group on Mute for the next twenty-four hours. When Gab had told his younger sister of his madcap plans, Daisy had put on her one-semester-of-Psych-101 hat and told him in no uncertain terms that running away to open a bakery to spite their father wasn't going to fix his problems. That lying to his family about still being in Melbourne when he actually was back in the Philippines was a bad plan.

He knew that. He wasn't a total idiot, but he took things a little too far when his emotions ran high. His siblings always told him that he went too far when it came to these things, like the time he'd told the twins that they were adopted after they used his favorite shirts to paint in, and they believed him so well that they actually tried to run away to find their real family. Or that time he convinced Ivy that diarrhea was contagious and she'd refused to sit with the family for meals for three days straight until his parents figured it out.

His finest moment had been when he swore to Daisy

that he put sriracha in the red velvet Carmen's Best ice cream, and she looked so utterly torn between believing him and not believing him that she actually started crying as she ate the ice cream and discovered that he hadn't put sriracha into it at all.

Just like you went a little too far with Sari and the flowers, his traitorous brain reminded him. He hadn't seen head, tail or fin of his favorite barista in the last couple of days, despite her leaving some of the flowers in his doorway. What if what he thought was a gesture of thanks was actually a gesture of "no thanks"? And how was he supposed to clarify that when he never seemed to be able to catch her?

In short, once again, Gabriel had gone too far, and now Sari was never going to talk to him. He was an idiot. An idiot who'd given an entire city's worth of carnations and baby's breath to a girl he liked. This was a prank war Gabriel was sure that he had just lost.

It was the Christmas party tonight. There was no way they were going to miss that, and Gabriel could talk to her then.

"What is that?" Gabriel asked Ransom, who was carrying a wet rag and a box of chalk in his hands. "Where are you going?"

"Out to the chalkboard. Miss Sari left a little message for you this morning." Ransom gave Gab an odd look, like he wasn't sure how on earth he ended up employed by a guy like him.

Hey, Gab wasn't sure how either, but that didn't matter so much right now, his heart was thumping in his chest as he made a mad dash to the chalkboard outside. The last time he'd looked at the thing was last week, when she wrote He's Got Big Buns.

Some part of him blamed that damn kiss in front of the marching band. That sudden, spontaneous, sweet, extra special first kiss that should've happened at the end of a first date, not in front of young, impressionable children and their guardians. If he were a good guy, he would've pulled her aside before doing anything like that. But he wasn't a good guy. He was the guy who went a little too far.

He ran so fast that he actually skidded on the brick floor outside, and caught himself before he face-planted the floor. He ended up face to face with the sign, written in Sari's pretty script hand.

If you were looking for a sign, this is it.

Oh. Gabriel's face felt a little hot. This is it. He didn't screw it up. He felt like shouting and dancing. He felt like walking into that café next door and kissing Sari much better than a super random kiss in front of strangers.

"I don't get it," Ransom said behind him, still holding the rag. "Is it a private joke? You're in a good mood suddenly."

"Of course I am," Gabriel said, still smiling, bringing out his phone to snap a picture. He needed to remember this. Needed to reciprocate somehow. Was skywriting too much, or just right?

"Does it have something to do with your girl next door? Not that I think she belongs to you, or anything. Or that I know anything. Or that everyone thinks you're together. Unless you are. Together, I mean."

Gabriel turned his head slowly to narrow his eyes at Ransom, who usually did not have a chismoso bone in his body. He was, however, Ate Nessie's son, and very much a Mama's Boy, and that instantly made him suspect.

"I'm in a good mood because today is the Christmas party," Gab said, slipping his phone back into the pocket of his apron and standing up to his full height. "Our first Christmas party."

"A little help here, please?" a voice behind them said, and both Ransom and Gab turned to see Santi coming up to the store with his arms full of what looked like a mini-refrigerator, still in its box. Ransom and Gab immediately ran up to help him, and once they had the thing well in hand, Santi let go.

"Seriously, dude?" Gabriel grunted as he and Ransom brought the mini-ref inside the store to put to one side until the Christmas party.

"What?" Santi asked, walking to the sink to wash his hands. "It's for the raffle tonight."

His staff had been talking about the Christmas party since the day they had their soft opening, and Gabriel had to admit he was equally excited. Like most events surrounding the holidays, the Pinoys just did it better. And a company Christmas party always meant tons of food, games, huge raffles and group presentations that were sure to be mind-blowing. On the Laneways, the Christmas party was when all the stores, their staff and their owners came together to eat, drink, be merry and conquer the annual karaoke contest. Both Ransom and Faye made sure to talk Gabriel's ear off about it, hyping up their boss, who had never attended before, for the Best Christmas Party of All Time.

"Ready to win the karaoke contest, boss?" Ransom asked.

"A performer doesn't get ready, he stays ready." Gab grinned.

"Well, if you're going to win, it's going to have to be this year, because we don't know where we're going to be next year," Santi said, giving Gab an odd sideways glance.

"What?" Gab asked, a little confused.

"If the mall deal comes through, I mean," Santi explained, crossing his arms over his chest to face his business partner. "You know. The one we decided we would pursue for Sunday Bakery?"

"Of course." Gab nodded, because Santi was right. The mall deal was what they both wanted, the logical next step for the business, and the logical next step in Gab's Plan Let's Impress Dad For Once In Our Life. And it was a fantastic opportunity. Who didn't love the extremely high foot traffic of a mall?

Gab couldn't seem to hold on to that thought for as long as he used to. Why was he more excited about the upcoming Christmas party than he was about potentially getting a mall deal?

Because you went too far, and now you're way too attached to this place, was the answer, and this time, he heard it in Lily's voice. Lily, the voice of reason in his head, and always one who was ready to deliver the harsh truths.

"Gab, you could just say if you don't want the mall deal," Santi said to Gabriel as they went upstairs to the kitchen, where Faye was already waiting for him. "It's something we both have to be all in for, if we're doing this."

"Yeah, no." Gab shook his head.

"Could you be more specific?" Santi asked, crossing his arms over his chest and tilting his head to the side.

"Yes, I still want the mall deal, and no, I know we have to be all in for it." Gab sighed deeply, placing a hand on Santi's shoulder. "Sorry I keep flip-flopping about this. It's an air sign thing."

"Gabriel, I like a lot of things about you," Santi said, which was probably the biggest compliment he'd ever paid Gab in the time they'd been working together. "Your belief in astrology is not one of them. But tell me the moment you change your mind, okay? I don't want to do this if you're not ready."

How could Gabriel not be ready for a mall deal? He'd spent years being told that this was the only way his profession was going to be good enough, and he was going to have to be good enough.

"I'm ready," he said, more to convince himself than Santi, throwing on his bandana as if to prove it further. "I'm ready. I'll see you at the Christmas party tonight?"

"I'll be the one spreading Christmas cheer," Santi deadpanned, which made Gabriel laugh. He wanted to bet that he was one of the few people in the world who knew that Anton Santillan had a penchant for dry humor. "See you later."

"Bye, Santi!" called Faye, who before that point was reading from her phone in the corner and wearing a pair of earphones while waiting for a batch of cookies to finish cooking. He didn't miss the blush on her cheeks when Santi gave her a tiny smile and a wave.

"Crush mo?" Gab teased as soon as Santi disappeared downstairs. And Faye, his twenty-year-old part-time worker and baking apprentice, the same age as his little sister Rose, blushed furiously and frowned.

"No," she said a little too loudly. "Stop it, boss. Seriously. STOP."

"O ano, should I ask if he's interested?" he teased, picking one of the just-cooled cookies and taking a bite. He loved this particular recipe. His sister Daisy had gone through a domestic goddess streak when she was fourteen, and made enough cookies to fill five ice cream tubs for Ivy's seventh birthday. She'd accidentally added crushed pretzels in one of the batches with the gooey, grated chocolate and walnuts, and created a winner. The Capras kids had scrambled for those cookies and played tong-its to establish ownership of said cookies.

Just like Daisy's, these were snappy and crunchy, the kind of cookie that left crumbles on your lap that you wanted to eat. Faye was getting really good at this.

He looked over at their neon sign, bright red and loud, reminding his customers that "it only takes a bite," and grinned at the thought of the glare it cast in Sari's shop. Then a thought struck him.

"If you weren't paying me, I would hate you," she grumbled.

"What was that?"

"I was saying, Manang Nessie said you should bring sansrival for the party tonight," Faye said a little too loud, and with a smile that was a little too wide. Gab was always thinking of what to bake next and it was sometimes hard to keep track of the things he'd already promised.

Gab gave a low whistle. That was a huge promise that he maybe should have remembered giving, because a sansrival was no joke. Everyone had a favorite kind—some liked it when the nutty meringue layers in between the buttercream were crisp and crunchy, others preferred it soft, mallowy and chewy. Some purists didn't think that a sansrival should be flavored with anything else but cashew, others liked to experiment with pistachio, almond or macadamia nuts.

And then there was the buttercream, the thing that bound the entire cake together, generously sandwiched between the layers of the meringue. Too cold and buttercream was flavorless, too warm and it melted. Some liked it sweet, others liked it closer to butter. Some wanted it flavored with coffee or rum.

Damn. It was like a challenge. Bake the perfect sansrival and win the hearts of the people he was going to leave anyway.

"Well, no time like the present to start," he said, stretching his arms over his head as he pushed the thought aside. "I don't really like making sansrival."

"Why not?"

"It's hard to please everyone."

It was also the birthday cake he'd baked for his younger sister Rose on her sixteenth birthday. He'd already been midway through culinary school then, on the brink of quitting yet another college course, ready to accept that he was just going to fall even farther behind, when his mother had asked him to make something for Rose's school party. So he made a sansrival, and it was like the entire world made perfect sense. When he baked, he was in perfect control of the ingredients, making magic he couldn't quite explain. And everything fell into place for him, in a way that the three other courses he'd shifted out from hadn't. He loved baking. He loved making his family happy with the things he made.

So he ran with that, and never looked back.

He liked to think this was the cake that had started and ended it all. Baking the cake made him think about baking, baking eventually made his father tell his son to "be serious." Because Gab was a man, and a man didn't dally around with random courses and hope something stuck. Because a man who wanted to support a family didn't bake his way to it.

"It's a waste of your time," his father had told him. "You're never going to earn enough to make her comfortable the way I did for the family. Just get a regular job, anak."

"You never told the girls that they were wasting their time," he pointed out.

"That's different. They're girls, who will become wives. You're a *man*, Gabriel, and people will expect you to be able to support a family of your own, and I don't see how you're going to be able to do that by baking for other people. For once in your life. Take yourself seriously."

The memory stung him, four years later. He'd spent the four years trying to outrun all of those memories, only to have it come running back and smacking him across the face here in Lipa.

There was a reason why he didn't particularly like making sansrival.

"I should get started," he said, grabbing an apron and putting it on. "Faye, care to help? Mastering your meringues is a key skill in baking."

"Yes, boss!" she said enthusiastically, following him up to the bakery. He hated to admit this, but his mood had dimmed spectacularly, and he wasn't sure that even a Christmas party was going to make things any better.

Chapter Thirteen

December 18, Laneways Christmas Party

Several hours and one carefully made sansrival later, Gab took back his earlier statement.

A Christmas party made *everything* better.

They had sectioned off the back end of the Laneways, creating a huge party space under the strings of twinkle lights. A makeshift marquee was set up to protect from the rain, but it only made the entire scene look like the inside of a circus tent. Mismatched tables and chairs were set up, the buffet table groaning with the amount of food it carried. There was apparently going to be a pretty big raffle—Gabriel could spy a washing machine, stand fans and…was that a TV?—up for grabs along with the two mini-refs courtesy of Hotel Villa and Sunday Bakery.

Someone brought in giant white parols on bamboo sticks and set them up around the front, so it looked like a stage fit for a show. Sari clearly had flowers to spare, and now the stage and the tables were full to the brim with baby's breath and carnations and other flowers from Hope's Garden. With the cool nip in the air and Jose Mari Chan's "Christmas in Our Hearts"

on repeat, it was a scene that could make the biggest
Grinch's heart grow several sizes too big.

"This party is fancier than my debut, and my dress
had a train," Kira Luz said, sliding up to him, holding a plate of lechon in one hand and one of his caramel banana cupcakes in the other. Gab had sprinkled
crushed banana chips on top of the cupcakes, making
them extra fantastic to eat, but not quite a taste match
to the lechon. "You remember? I think I made you one
of my eighteen roses."

One would think that someone who made chocolate
and tasted it for a living would be a little more discern-
ing with her tastes, but Gab didn't judge. He'd known
Kira since college, and he'd always thought she was
a bit of an odd duck, but she gave too little shits for
anyone else to care. She was the one who had called
him seemingly out of the blue one day while he was in
Melbourne, after months of not talking, with a simple
question.

"The shop across from mine at the Laneways is open.
You should get started on that bakery."

So Gabriel owed Kira a lot. That they met through
one of his exes was something they very rarely talked
about anymore, and he really appreciated that.

"I remember," Gab chortled, shaking his head. "We
were freshmen. We danced to a *High School Musical*
song because we thought it would be ironic."

"'Bop to the Top'! Oh God, so dorky," Kira laughed,
shaking her head as she made a face. Gabriel glanced
at her and noticed that Kira had exchanged her usual
chocolate-splattered apron for a pair of loose black pants
and a bright pink tank top.

"You look nice," Gabriel commented, unused to seeing her outside of her daily uniform of denim shorts and tee shirts.

"Thanks!" Kira said, giving him a little twirl with her loose pants. "I managed to clean up a little. I had a minor chocolate explosion in the lab this afternoon."

"Are you all right?" Gab didn't even know that chocolate could explode, much less in a minor way.

"Of course! I didn't even have to go to the hospital this time," Kira said proudly, after she'd dunked the piece of lechon in sauce and eaten it. "How goes your sad seduction of Sari Tomas? I can't go anywhere in the Laneways without someone talking about that lyre band flashmob. And all of the baby's breath and carnations. I had people asking me if they could have weddings in the Laneways, which is probably a good idea, don't you think?"

"Sari hired them," he said defensively. "And the flowers are just flowers."

"I heard you dipped her, then *kissed* her."

"You make that sound dirty," Gab scoffed. "It was barely a kiss. I've seen spicier kisses on Korean dramas, and those with the slow burn romances are always so tame."

"You haven't had sex with Sari, have you?"

"Wow," he choked on his Royal Tru-Orange soda. "You are *not* subtle."

"Neither are you, if you heard the rest of the Laneways tell the story. And I'm a Gemini, being unsubtle is part of who we are." Kira chomped on the cupcake. Gabriel's entire face scrunched up when he imagined what those two things tasted like together.

"Hungry?" he teased.

"Starving. I had to make three hundred wedding favors today, a chocolate sculpture for a congressman's daughter and then, the great explosion happened. I've been eating since the food came."

"Do chocolate explosions happen often?"

"More often than you think. The pizza is amazing, you should get one."

"It should be. It's from La Spezia."

"Ugh, that place in Hotel Villa that charges way too much for pesto because they serve it with twirly pasta?"

"Yes. Santi's place," he said, wondering how often Kira ate in Hotel Villa to know.

Kira scoffed, frowning in the direction of the pizza. "No thanks. But tell me more about Sari! You were telling me about your pathetic seduction of the most ice cold girl in all of the Laneways."

He opened his mouth to tell her off for that, but Kira held a hand up to stop him before he did.

"Please don't patronize me by denying it. I know her, I know you, and I know your signs pretty much line up. Capricorns are known for two things—accepting undue responsibility and being lone wolves. Sari has always been a lone wolf that's particularly resistant to new things. So how are you and your neighbor 'getting along'?"

"Fine."

"Ah, so it's going badly."

"Not bad per se," he said, trying to find the words to describe his relationship with Sari Tomas. Clearly they had stepped past the hating each other stage and were… somewhere he couldn't quite identify. *If you were waiting for a sign, this is it.* "But we're not exactly where I want us to be yet."

"And where is that somewhere?" Kira asked, taking a bite of her cupcake.

"Harmlessly flirting with each other?" he said hesitantly, and the image of Sari's lips against a coffee cup, her eyes fixed on him with murderous intent, filled his mind.

What was it about a girl taking a drink that was so attractive? She'd worn lipstick that day on the fire escape, he remembered. The day when he'd gone out and just knew she would be there. He remembered how her body felt in his hands when he'd dipped her in front of the store, how her breath escaped her lips in quick gasps.

"There is no such thing as 'harmless flirting'!" Kira protested, her cheeks burning, but Gabriel didn't know why. "It's like saying 'carb free cookie', 'traffic free roads' or 'white chocolate with cacao'. It sounds perfectly logical, it should be true, but it's not real. You know what *is* real, though?"

"No. But I'm sure you're about to tell me," Gabriel grumbled.

"What's real is this cupcake! It's ah-*mah*-zing, and I mean that from the bottom of my heart." Kira held up the cupcake, which was already halfway gone. "Why does it have, like, a milky, cereal-ly flavor?"

"The cupcake was soaked in cereal milk."

"Shut up, that is *amazing*! Your family must love having cake in the house all the time. I can imagine your fridge, diabetics must cower in fear."

"Actually," he said in a small voice. "My family doesn't know I'm here."

"In Lipa?"

"In the Philippines. They ah—still think I'm in Melbourne," he said, because there was no way that he could lie to Kira, because if anyone knew anything about his life outside of the Laneways, it was her. She'd been to his house in Manila, had met some of his siblings. He was pretty sure she even helped Mindy get in to one of the many orgs she'd signed up for.

"Ohhh classic Libra. Indecisive, avoids confrontation, preferring a harmony that one can only get from the lands of Batangas." Kira raised an eyebrow at him. "I've known you for ten years, and I've never known you to avoid the onslaught of Capras kids when they run toward you. You're close to your family, right?"

"Well. I'm the oldest," Gabriel said, and that was all he was going to say on the matter. Really, Kira knew how to be scarily accurate sometimes, but he'd learned to remind himself that she was shooting in the wind and that horoscopes could mean absolutely nothing. *Typical Libra*, she would tell him.

"Sari!" Kira exclaimed suddenly as Sari walked into the park, wearing a blue dress with white polka dots, fresh as a morning breeze. Gabriel's heart flipped as he remembered the words she'd left on the chalkboard. *This is it.* She looked beautiful, and had a smile on her face that was so bright, it rivaled the brightest parol in the party. And she always seemed to smell like coffee. He liked coffee. "My favorite Capricorn! Have you had some of this amazing cereal banana cupcake? It's deliciousness wrapped in a hug."

"The hug is called Swiss Meringue Buttercream, and Sari doesn't want any of it," Gabriel said, and yes, he was completely aware that he was being petty. "Right, Sari?"

"If you're trying to bait me, it's not going to work," she said wryly, looking at Gab.

"Lies," Gabriel and Kira both said at the same time, in completely different tones.

"Oh, by the way, I signed you up for the karaoke contest." Kira grinned at Gab, nudging him with her elbow.

"What?" he asked her, aghast.

"Yeah, it's required for every new shop owner on the Laneways," Sari chimed in. "It's in the lease."

"It is not," Gab argued, mostly because he wasn't sure, making Sari and Kira laugh this time.

"It's still required, though! Duets are allowed, I'm just saying," Kira said breezily. "Oh, is that Anton Santillan? Ugh, he's got a frowny face on. I feel the need to keep him away from the merriment."

She turned from them, put the now empty lechon plate aside and picked up another cupcake, although it wasn't clear if she was getting it for Santi or for herself. Gabriel could see Santi in the distance, peering nervously at the party like he was unhappy with what was going on inside. Kira was already halfway across the venue when she stopped and turned her heel to face him and Sari.

"Oh, Gabbers!" Kira yelled. "I heard your one-year lease was just finalized! Congrats!"

A feeling bloomed in his chest when Kira said that, and Gabriel couldn't process it. Was it pride? Happiness? Both? He wasn't sure. But whatever it was, it felt right. Just like when he made that sansrival. But then, Santi's words from earlier that day followed him, reminding him that the reason why they only got a year's lease was because they were fully expecting to be in the malls, and not the Laneways, next year.

"Congratulations," Sari said, the soft smile on her face more beautiful than any fierce, angry look she could give him. "It's nice, isn't it? Like you found your place in the sun."

Then she directed that smile in his direction, and his heart bloomed. There was no anger or derision or "I can't believe you actually exist, you annoying creature," just…recognition. Maybe even mutual understanding.

"How long will it last?" he asked her, even as he wondered how he could leave this place after only a few weeks here.

"Not long," she giggled before she picked up a marshmallow-less hot dog on a stick. "Now if you excuse me, my baristas are about to do their dance number. I've been banned from rehearsal, and I have to sit in the front row and take videos."

She moved away from him, about to squeeze through the crowd and disappear, when Gabriel yelled the first thing that popped into his head. He wanted to admit defeat. She had him. He wanted to ask if they were okay, if it was safe to call off the troops and the dirty baking puns. He thought it was time, especially if she was going to look at him like that, and say things that he couldn't form with words.

"Sari! Date?"

She looked over her shoulder, her long locks swooshing around her face like she was in a shampoo commercial. Jesus Christ. She shouldn't do that. If Gabriel hadn't eaten quezo de bola and fiesta ham earlier he would have been light-headed. The dots on her dress seemed to dance, and he caught a flash of the gold sparkles she put on her eyes. Gorgeous.

"Only if you score a hundred on the karaoke contest!"

"Sing a duet with me, then," he called back. "Your song choice!"

That made her stop in her tracks, and Gab was so ready to argue with her, tell her all the reasons why she had to sing with him (he didn't have a lot), but reason was lost on his tongue when he realized she was smiling. She walked back to him and took his hand, dragging him to the stage.

"I know the perfect song," she said, going up to the machine. The entire audience roared with cheers as the opening bars of the song came on. And Gab couldn't blame them—this was an iconic karaoke staple, a great choice, really.

He just wished he didn't have to be the one singing "Sinta" by Aegis.

Sari had a beautiful voice, by the way. It didn't have the raspy, rocker quality the song needed, but she got the pitch and the tone. The extent of Gab's musical experience came with living in a house prone to spontaneous bursts of singing, so he managed well enough. But the crowd was just eating them up, screaming, recording on their phones like they were the hottest thing to hit the stage since…well, since Aegis.

They jumped into the chorus and naturally turned to each other. Their voices did not blend at all, but he didn't care, he didn't care when she was looking at him like that. Oh, and her hand was moving, where was her hand going?

OH Sari was about to—

"AYYYY!" The entire front row of their audience seemed to collapse in kilig and delight as Sari and Gab clasped hands, looking at each other as they sang.

And no, his voice wasn't shaking. But the Christmas lights were glowing in Sari's eyes and she looked so happy that he couldn't help but smile too.

And just like that, the song was over, and the moment was over. Sari was bowing to their audience, and Gab was still looking at her. He couldn't believe he'd just sang *that* song with her. You just couldn't sing "Sinta" without really believing deep in your heart that you were crazy in love with the other person. Had this been a music video, there would have been images of them running through a sunflower field, holding hands and laughing.

The karaoke machine began to play triumphant music, and lo and behold, they got a perfect score.

"So," Gab said, leaning a little closer so she could hear, and away from the mic so nobody else could. "About that date?"

Sari pressed a hand to his chest, not pushing him away, more like to steady herself than anything.

"I'm all yours," she grinned. The entire population of the party burst into another round of screams and laughter.

Chapter Fourteen

December 19

Sari was still absentmindedly humming "Sinta" when she drove up to the café after Simbang Gabi. This time, she was carrying a bandehado of biko that the seller proudly pronounced was the favorite of the high society set in Manila. Sari didn't know how she was supposed to finish a whole bandehado by herself, so she brought it to the café to share with her baristas.

It was a Thursday, which meant that today was a roasting day for Sari. The café had the most customers from Friday to Sunday, and so she always did a big batch roast on Thursday to make sure the coffee was fresh. She used the Tomas Coffee Co. robusta blend on a medium roast. Sure she could teach one of her baristas to do it, and she had, but Sari liked to be more hands on in the business than she had to, and this was just one of the things she loved about having the café.

She'd just finished pre-heating the roaster when she heard a growl of frustration from the other side of the window. She looked up and saw that the kitchen lights at Sunday Bakery were on, and there was Gabriel, actually angry and frowning. She'd never seen him like that. Then again, she hadn't known him for very long.

She knocked tentatively on the window, and his head jerked up, his curls flying. Shock gave way to a little smile that didn't quite meet his face.

"What's wrong?" she asked him, and it showed her how agitated he was when he frowned and mouthed something that looked to Sari like, "nothing."

"Something," she said back, and Gabriel must not have been able to hear her either, because he headed in the direction of the fire escape, and she did the same. Their doors swung open at the same time, and they stepped out together. He was already wearing his apron and his bandana, and he was holding a pretty sizable jar with what looked like dough inside.

"My starter didn't...start," he said, his nose wrinkling because it didn't sound like the right word to use. "I've been baking for at least ten years, and I can't get my damn sourdough starter to start. Of course I already *have* a starter, Belinda is five months old and living happily in Fairview, but I can't get her."

"Why not?" Sari asked, and the look of surprise on Gabriel's face told her that he hadn't been planning on telling her why, except now he'd talked himself into a corner about it. "Gabriel, it's all right. You can tell me. Or not, if you don't want to."

"I think I should," he said, sighing like he still really didn't want to, and put the jar of non-starter against the corner of the fire escape nearest to the wall. "My family has no idea that I'm here in Lipa. They think I'm still in Melbourne. Some of them probably think I'm in Singapore or Bali."

"Okay, but why?" Sari asked, immediately confused.

Although she didn't always get along with her sisters, she couldn't imagine them not knowing where Sari was, couldn't imagine lying to them the way Gabriel was, which only reminded her that they really didn't know each other all that well outside of the Laneways. "Do you guys not get along?"

"I think we do." Gabriel was still frowning, and she didn't like it. Sari understood only too well how hard it was to articulate how you felt sometimes, whether it was because you felt guilty for feeling it, or knew your feelings would hurt someone else. "I love them. But they just got used to the idea that I liked wandering from place to place. Hell, I thought I would always wander from place to place. Did you know I switched courses three times in the span of five years in college?"

"I didn't."

"Yeah, it took me a while before I realized that I liked baking, and even then…" He trailed off, and Sari wished that he wouldn't. She was just discovering the other sides to Gabriel, and she wanted to know more. "Anyway. It's easier to let them think that I can't stay in one place until I'm sure I can do it here."

"You think you can?" Sari asked. "Stay here, I mean."

"Maybe," he said, and she didn't love that his smile was a little wistful, still unsure. For someone like Sari, who had found Lipa and stayed here for as long as she had, seeing someone who still felt so rootless reminded her of the times she used to feel just as lost. "I like it a lot so far. The people could be nicer."

"The people are trying, really hard," she said, and ala eh, she'd actually made him laugh! "Does your family want you to stay in Manila?"

"My father certainly does," he said, and his face grew dark at the mere mention of his father. "He thinks that as a man, and as the oldest of my family, I have a duty to take a regular, steady income job and support my family. Because that's what a *man* does."

"I think getting a job and supporting the people we love isn't exclusive to guys," Sari added, and Gabriel nodded in agreement.

"Yeah, and what does that even mean, anyway, being a man? I have one sister who manages a hedge fund, and she kicks ass and takes names in the name of money, or whatever it is she does. The other is so good at what she does her company wanted to send her to Switzerland for a year. I have another sister who saved for five years then took herself on a trip to Paris, because she thought she deserved to fulfil that dream. Then the younger ones are just figuring out what they want to do, and it's great."

There was a glow of pride that came to his face when he started talking about his family, and he tugged at Sari's heart. It was easy to see that he really did love them, and she wondered how much he missed them, when he was much closer than they all thought.

How bad did things have to be that Gabriel felt the need to lie to all of them about Sunday Bakery? Why did he seem almost ashamed of what he'd been able to achieve?

"I just don't understand why my parents raised me to think that I can be anything, I can do anything that I wanted, only to tell me later on that who I am isn't enough for them," he muttered, stuffing his hands in his pockets and kicking a bit of dirt from the metal flooring. "You know what I want?"

"What you really, really want?" she asked, and score two points for Sari, because she'd made Gabriel laugh again.

"I want to go to Paris," he said with a little smile. "Just like Mindy did. I want to do that, but I want to spend an entire day sitting in a boulangerie eating all of the bread, with the fancy butter. Maybe even have a coffee or two, so I can think of you."

"Bold of you to assume that I don't want to go with you." Sari smiled. "I've never had to drink coffee from a bowl, and I want that experience. Everyone tells me the café culture in Paris is completely different from Seoul, or Japan."

"I hope so." Gabriel was smiling a little now, looking at her. "I love Seoul, though. Every café has a different vibe, and for some reason *all* the coffee is excellent. Australia I feel like is all about the brunch experience— avo on toast, all the ways you can eat eggs in a croissant, things like that. Hong Kong and Japan are about the teeniest tiniest cafés, with the most minimalist aesthetic. Good luck finding a filling meal there. Seoul is a little more varied, I think. You're literally spoiled for choice when it comes to the cafés there."

"Have you ever been to Café Revolver in Bali? Or Café Mexicola?"

"Cool for the gram, but I didn't stick around long enough to decide if I really liked their stuff." Gabriel shrugged.

"Whenever you have to eat someone else's bread," Sari said, because she might as well, if they were doing this. "Do you always feel like you're trying to compare it against yours?"

"All the time!" he exclaimed. "I'm the worst kind of

customer. Especially if their bread is better than mine?
It makes me feel so competitive."

"I want to change the entire coffee menu at Mary
Grace," she said in a soft voice, because speaking any
louder than that would anger the aunties who loved
that place.

"Sari, that's blasphemy!" Gabriel gasped, even if he
was still smiling.

"I love their food, I love their pasta and their desserts, but if I'm paying five hundred pesos for a meal
and dessert, my coffee should at least taste better than
what I would get at home!"

It felt good to talk to him about these things. It felt
good to talk about cafés in general, because Sari realized, she didn't really have anyone in her life to talk to
about these things. Sam had always preferred travelling
locally, it was more exciting that way, she said. And Sari
didn't think Selene had traveled for leisure since they
started the business. Kira liked cafés too, but tended to
stick to the ones she knew.

So this was nice.

"I should let you go back inside," Gabriel said. "I'm
sure you're busy."

"I am." Sari nodded. "I hope you finally get your
starter on."

"I'll figure it out," he said, picking up his jar. And
the way he smiled at her, the way her heart was quick-
ening its pace in her chest, Sari legitimately thought
that he was going to kiss her. Maybe it was just the
morning light, the way it hit his face, because he just
looked so happy to be there with her, that she wanted
to kiss him too.

She placed a hand on his chest, possibly the most

bold thing she'd ever done. His eyes widened for a second before they softened. And Sari knew she liked the right guy when he bent his head down a little, his nose already brushing against hers, his eyelashes fluttering against her skin. She reached her other hand up to his cheek, just so she could brush her fingers against his dimples.

"I feel like I've waited forever for this," he said.

"It's been two weeks. More or less."

"I've always been impatient."

Then he pressed his lips against hers, and Sari's heart completely opened up, in a way it never had before. She never realized how lonely she felt until Gabriel kissed her, like she was safe, like she was wanted, like he was thinking about her. She pulled him in closer, and he wrapped his free hand around her waist, the other still carrying the damn jar of starter.

In the distance, she heard the sounds of familiar beeping, and she remembered. She was supposed to be roasting beans.

"Was that my timer or yours?" Gabriel asked hazily as they separated. Sari turned her head to the direction of her coffee lab, and he stole a kiss on her collarbone, making her insides feel all warm and melty like hot caramel.

"Mine, I think," she said, and he sighed, like he knew she was about to leave. Sari squeezed his cheeks together and pulled his head up gently so he could look at her. His smooshed up face was hilarious, and she giggled.

"I'll talk to you later," she told him, and it wasn't a question, but a promise.

"Hopefully I'm actually productive by then," he

sighed, and she smacked him on the forehead with a kiss before she left the fire escape. For some reason, she was very aware that he was watching her and looked over her shoulder.

"I love it when you walk away," he said dramatically, and she laughed and closed the door behind her.

Chapter Fifteen

December 19

He had kissed Sari Tomas.

Gabriel had *kissed* Sari Tomas.

Fuck, it was wonderful.

Gabriel decided to celebrate the occasion with a mango-and-cream cake (because what was the point of being a baker if you couldn't bake when you kissed a girl that you really liked). Mango and cream had been a combination on a famous cake from Red Ribbon Bakeshop when he was a kid. The current iteration of Red Ribbon still had it, but it wasn't quite the same. The mango cake that Gab remembered was a delectable tower of chiffon with pieces of fresh mango in the Swiss buttercream. The cake was a study in pillowy lightness and sweet cream, all flavors just there to highlight the amazing mangoes from a legendary mango farm in San Antonio, which happened to have a few out-of-season mangoes.

Would Sari be able to resist that?

"Are the mangoes here already?" he asked Ransom, who was still blinking away post-lunch sleepiness with a cup of barako from next door. Gabriel had to stop for

a second, because the strong, punch-you-in-the-face
barako was starting to smell like home.

"In the kitchen. Blossom Farms also sent over some
of their Red Lady papayas. They thought you might
want to experiment with them."

"Hmmm." He ran his hand through his hair as he
thought. In his experience, papaya was sliced up and
served with generous heaps of condensed milk. What
could he do with that? "What do you guys think, pa-
pie-ya?"

Both Ransom and Faye, who was sitting in the corner and reading one of Gab's baking books, cringed.

"Tough crowd," he chuckled. "I'll think of something. Faye, come up and help me with the mango cake
in ten minutes?"

"Fifteen?"

"Sure." Gabriel shrugged. His fragile ego could handle a bit of insubordination.

With a little spring in his step, he headed upstairs
to the bakery, pulling his hair back in a bandana so he
could get to work on that cake. Perfection didn't make
itself, after all. He put on his Christmas playlist and
started to sing along to "Kumukutikutitap" to get into
the mood.

He threw on his apron, thoroughly washed his
hands and mentally ran through the list of ingredients
he needed for the cake. He could make chiffon in his
sleep, his training and culinary school had seen to that,
but the perfect ratio of the mango to the Swiss meringue
buttercream was all Gabriel. It had to be sweet, but more
mango sweet than sugary sweet. There had to be little
resistance when you cut into the cake, and it had to fill
the tongue with cream, just enough to taste the fresh-

ness of the mango. And with mangoes like the ones he had, it had to be the star of the show.

He was distracted by the basket of mangoes waiting for him, yellow jewels in a banana-leaf-lined kaing. He picked one up and took a sniff, loving the familiarity of the promising, slightly floral scent on the soft mango skin. Philippine mangoes didn't have that syrupy quality he seemed to get in Taiwan or in Japan, and he much preferred it without. Mangoes here were a bit more subtle in their sweetness, and had a warmth to their flavor that he couldn't find with any other fruit. With a practiced hand, he picked up a clean knife and cut the mango into three parts, expertly separating the cheek-sides from the seed that ran through the middle.

When he was younger, his mother would cut the inside of the mango cheeks into diamond shapes, making them easy to pop up and eat without a spoon, handing them to Gabriel just before she reminded him to share. The concept of sharing had eluded him for a good long while—how could he share something that was already *his* to begin with? But slicing up mangoes always reminded him that the best things in life became even better when shared with someone else.

Today, he didn't have anyone to share with. It seemed silly to call one of his siblings to drive two hours to Lipa just for half a mango, not that he was about to do that anytime soon.

He looked up at the window he shared with the coffee shop and saw that Miss Sari was in residence, wrestling with the most intimidating-looking coffee machine he had ever seen in his life. It had a computer and everything, and was it actually making a graph?

He would never understand coffee-making. Gabriel

knocked on the glass, loud enough for her to look up and turn to him, her momentary confusion quickly morphing into a brilliant smile.

You kissed her, he thought, smiling back. *And she liked it.*

He held up the mango, hoping she would get the message. He'd even cut it into diamond shapes, just like his mother showed him. Sari's face immediately brightened at the sight of the mango, and Gab felt his heart stop in his chest. He'd been aware, the first time he saw her, that she was beautiful. She had delicate features, a heart shaped face, and dimples that came out every time she tried to hide a smile.

He didn't know why he liked provoking her so much, but he did, falling deeper and deeper into the pit of her light brown eyes until just the thought of him made her frown the way she did. But there were moments when her gaze softened, just like this, that made him feel like it was worth it.

But with that soft gaze, she revealed a sadness behind her eyes, the pressing weight of the world that Gabriel wished he could carry for her.

They met in the fire escape, quietly eating their mangoes like it wasn't a rare treat to have them so sweet in December.

"Something on your mind?" Gabriel asked gently.

"Oh, lots of things," she said quickly. "Lots and lots of things, constantly looping in my head. I have an intro to running a café class at the end of the week that I haven't prepared for, inventory, purchase orders, Christmas gifts to think about. And then we kissed."

"Yes, we did." He wriggled his eyebrows suggestively at her, which only made her laugh and elbow him lightly in the ribs. But her smile faded as she seemed to remember something she would rather not think about.

"My sister Sam is moving out in two days and she doesn't have a rice cooker," she said, using her thumb to clean up a bit of stray mango on her lip. "Not that the rice cooker is the most important thing, but she doesn't have one."

"I've heard amazing things about the Xiaomi one," he told her, because it was just one of those random things he'd picked up from his family chat group. "I can ask around…"

"It's not that," Sari giggled, and she squeezed his arm as if to let him know that she was grateful for the gesture. But even then, that sadness was still on her face, and Gab didn't know what he could do to take it away.

"I feel like parts of my life are falling away," she said, pressing the heels of her hands against her closed eyes. "I've lived with my sisters all my life. We were together when our parents were fighting, we were together when our parents split and we moved to Lipa. We were even together when we studied in Manila, one after the other.

"When Lola died, the three of us rallied to go against our father when he suddenly showed up and lost the company their biggest client. But after that, we kind of…went our separate ways. Together in the business, but separate in everything else. And now Sam's moving out, and I'll be…" She paused, like she didn't know the right word to use. And because Gabriel understood what she was feeling, he knew perfectly well that it wasn't that she didn't know the right word to use, it was that she didn't want to say it out loud.

"Alone," he said, and the word hung heavy in the air, and he knew she could feel it too.

"Yeah," she said, the confession so soft that his heart wrenched. Then and there, he realized that he was the last person in the world to give her advice.

He didn't know anything about her family business, in fact she was the business veteran between the two of them. He understood sibling relationships, but what right did he have to comment on hers when he had put a deliberate wedge in his relationship with his family? But while he couldn't advise her, he understood her. He could listen to her.

He hoped that it was enough.

"And now I'm supposed to think of Christmas gifts for my friends' kids? I mean, are you still friends with people you only interact with through comments on social media?" She chuckled in that way people did when they were trying their hardest not to sound pathetic, fully knowing they did.

"I didn't know you were supposed to give gifts to your friends' kids."

"Well, you are if they made you swear in front of God to be called ninang, and provide Christmas gifts," Sari sighed. "And I don't think four-year-olds want coffee beans."

"Yeah, a downpayment on a condo would be more appropriate," Gabriel commented dryly, because he was good at that sort of comeback, too. It actually made Sari *laugh*. He felt a little sense of victory at the thought that he'd done that.

"How unfair. I recall being extremely happy getting a crispy new twenty peso bill for Christmas at that age," she said, inspecting her mango for any remaining bits of flesh that she hadn't eaten yet. "God, this mango is amazing. Where did you get it?"

"A magician never reveals his sources." He waved his hand around like he could conjure a fresh mango in seconds. If only. "But it's from a farm in Zambales. People say their mangoes are magical. There's a whole legend behind it where the women who run the farm have to be married with kids for the mangoes to be good."

"They marry…kids?"

"What? No, they get married and then have kids. Basta, it's magical."

"Sure, magical." Sari laughed, for the second time in one sitting, and honestly, it felt like progress to him. "I feel like people always underestimate just how amazing running a farm is. Not to mention how difficult it is to run a business with your family."

"Is that how you guys feel about your coffee?" Gabriel said, and ignored the little twinge of guilt that bit at his heels whenever someone mentioned the f-word. This was the Philippines, where families were ingrained in your blood and were as important as the place you lived. You were made up of the family you were born into and the last thing you ate. He'd chosen to put his family aside for now, trying not to need them, and he didn't. But that didn't mean that he didn't miss them all.

"It is." He wondered what had happened in Sari's life that she sighed that deeply at the thought of her legacy. "It's complicated. Someone works hard to build it up, someone wants to just sit around and benefit because they weren't asked to do the work, and eventually things break down. Thank God my sister Selene was smart enough to take over when she did, give it to us the way she did, or else I wouldn't… I wouldn't have anything."

"I'm sorry. I don't know what happened exactly, but I sort of understand. That moment when you realize that they love you, but they don't *understand* you," he said, because he understood that too. How odd that he hadn't known Sari for very long, but then found someone who understood him. Their situations weren't exactly the same, but recognizing yourself in another person, that was special. That was important.

"The glass shatters, and you realize that everything's a lie." Sari nodded, her gaze far away. "You're holding on to what you have so tightly, and you don't realize you're choking them."

"What about you, Sari?"

"What *about* me?"

"Even if it was your sister who, I guess, organized things for you and Sam," he said, because someone who remembered the names of his eight siblings remembered the names of other people's. "You took on the challenge just as much as they did. And I see you in your coffee lab, you're constantly working, and when you work, you have this little smile on your face when you know it's going well. You love your work, and I don't think you should discount that."

"I do." She nodded. "I love it. But what else do I have beyond it?"

Me, he wanted to say. *You have me.* Even if he was leaving the Laneways, was fully expecting to leave the Laneways really soon.

"What do you want for Christmas?"

Sari tossed her now flesh-less mango cheek into the bin in the fire escape. Then she looked at him, a tiny smile playing on her lips like she was trying to see if he was really asking her. Gab didn't think he had the answer to that.

"You."

He choked on a mango.

"You giving me the address to the magical mango farm," Sari added. "It's in Zambales? I want specifics."

"I'm not that generous." Gab managed to regain his composure long enough to come right back. "But I will think of something nice. Something I can give to you. Something I can wrap in a bow. As a neighborly—no, a friendly gesture."

"Ah, so our relationship is progressing, is it?"

"Don't you think it is?"

"Oh, I do," Sari agreed, nodding, and oh, was that a blush he could see on her cheeks?

They lapsed into comfortable silence, and Gabriel couldn't help but steal a glance at Sari. She had her arms crossed over her chest, the scent of coffee wafting over to him from where the breeze passed her. Christmas was knocking on their door, so close he could taste it, and there was a nip in the air that you could only get from the highlands. Not cold enough to put on a jacket, but noticeable enough that he didn't feel the desire to jump into a swimming pool anytime soon.

Sari's lips were lightly pursed, as if caught in between filtering her own thoughts and saying something to him. Her creamy skin looked like it needed a good kiss, and he wondered what it would feel like to place his lips on that little pulse point on her neck. Would she taste like coffee? Sugar?

He wanted to kiss her again. It had been six hours already.

"Go on a date with me?" he asked, because he really wanted to spend time with her outside of the fire escape, outside of the Laneways. He wanted to keep making her smile.

"Why do you keep asking me out?" she said instead, chuckling like the question was ridiculous. Gabriel frowned, immediately hurt by the question. It wasn't a rejection per se, but he would have thought that she would want to go out on dates with someone she was sharing kisses on the fire escape with. Or maybe he was missing something? His sisters did always say that men could be dense about a lot of things.

"Is it making you uncomfortable? I'm sorry," he said quickly, because that was the last thing he wanted to do. He wanted to make her blush, and smile, he wanted to see her kilig, not scared or uncomfortable. "I'll stop if it is."

"No, it's not, it's…it's actually very flattering," she admitted, and he could have sworn he saw her cheeks warm as she looked away from him. "Even if it's not real."

"Why would you think that it wasn't real?" he asked suddenly and sharply, and he didn't mean to change the tone of the conversation so quickly, but Sari had touched a very sensitive nerve. "Did you think I wasn't serious?"

Her eyes widened, although he wasn't sure if it was surprise. *Great job, Gab, you've officially freaked her out because of your insecurities. Sari is not your father.* He didn't know why, but the voice of conscience in his head sounded like his sisters. All six of them.

"I don't know," she said, her eyes still a little wide, wary and cautious. "It's just that everyone here keeps asking if we're together, they think we're courting each other, and we've kissed, but last week I was planning your murder, I... It's getting confusing, to say the least."

"How?" he asked.

"How is it confusing?"

"No, how were you planning on murdering me?" He was genuinely curious. "I've planned many a murder on our cat whenever he thinks my pant legs would make good scratching posts."

"Oh, you know. Just the standard baking accident, surely that super sharp knife wasn't meant to go into his chest, that kind of thing." She shrugged, and he liked that she just went with it. "I don't exactly have a frame of reference for being asked out on a date that...frequently. You seem very sure of what you want."

Relief whooshed through Gabriel so quickly that he had to laugh.

"When you know, you know," he told her with a shrug, as if life was that simple. "You know?"

"Not really. I could be a snorer," she said. "Or really bad in bed. I could be a cat person, when you are clearly a dog person."

"Are you?"

"Bad in bed?"

"A cat person?"

He didn't miss her cheeks burning pink before she looked away from him. "No, but that's not the point, is it? How do you know?"

"Know what, Sari?"

"Know that you like me?"

She asked him like he held all the answers to a secret she'd been trying to know for so long. Gabriel shrugged like he did this all the time, which he never did. He always had to be the smooth guy, the cool guy, the big brother who knew everything, because he had to be. He was older. People expected him to know everything. Little did his younger siblings know, he was struggling just as much as they all were.

"You make my cells rise," he started.

"What?"

"I read it in a book. When you find something that makes you incandescently happy, it feels like all of your cells are rising."

Sari's brows met in between her eyes, and Gabriel was sure she'd heard that before. "You got that from *The Life-Changing Magic of Tidying Up.*"

"I did. But doesn't mean it's not true. When I see you smile, I want to figure out what made you happy. When you get that little annoyed but amused crease between your eyebrows, I hope I'm the reason for it, because you think I'm funny."

"I do."

"I want to take away whatever it is that's making you sad, and I'm not going to lie, I want to kiss you again. It's been six hours, Sari, I need you to kiss me again."

Her cheeks immediately flamed even redder, and Gabriel couldn't help the little frisson of kilig that ran up and down his system. This Charm Offensive thing was working really well for him so far.

"Why don't you come over here and kiss me, then?"

"Oh, sweetheart. Is that a challenge?" he asked, raising an eyebrow at her like he was asking her to make it real. And that actually made her smile. It warmed his heart to know that he was the one to put that smile on her face. "Because you have a bit of mango on your lip."

"Oh, I do?" she asked, nibbling at her bottom lip. "There?"

"Just missed it. May I?" he asked, and Sari nodded. Reaching out, brushing his thumb against the soft skin on the bottom of her lip where a bit of mango still was. Then, he didn't even know why he did it, he put his thumb against his lips and sucked.

The effect on her was instantaneous. She sucked in a breath, her eyes wide and dark, before she swallowed. He could almost hear her heart thundering in her chest as she looked at his lips. No. Wait. That was *his* heart he was hearing.

His hands were on the sides of her face now, his thumbs brushing against her cheeks.

"May I?" he asked again, not knowing why his voice was so shaky.

"Yes." Sari's voice was breathless, but Gabriel still went in slow. He touched his lips to where the bit of mango was, as if expecting it to be sweet. Her lips were still wet from its juice as he tasted her. Sari sighed, her body relaxing against his hands, and then they were kissing, a mix of mangoes and sugar, mangoes and dark roast coffee.

"Gab." Sari pulled away suddenly. "Gabriel?"

"Hmm?" He liked the way she said his name, the way she emphasized the last syllable the way they would in old-timey dramas.

"Go out on a date with me," she said, and he noticed that her hand was clutched at the front of his shirt, and he liked it. She tugged at him a little, and they kissed again. "I'm going to Simbang Gabi in the morning at the Cathedral. Come with me."

"Um," Gabriel hesitated. His family was still very much on the religious side of the spectrum, but he hadn't gone to church in forever, even on the important days.

A hazard of travelling, he'd said, but really, it was just that going to church reminded him of his family, and he'd needed a bit of space from them. And, he wasn't ashamed to admit that going to a Catholic mass elsewhere around the world was just not the same as in the Philippines. The songs hit different in Tagalog.

"I know you can't make a wish, since you missed at least four days," Sari said. "But if you've never been to the Cathedral, you can check it out. And I heard you can also make a wish if it's your first time at a new church."

"So many wishes, who needs prayer?" He raised his eyebrow. She shrugged. "I suppose I could get Ransom to come in and put the bakes in the oven tomorrow. He'll hate me the whole day, but he'll get overtime."

"Ransom can have all the coffee he wants again if he comes in tomorrow morning," Sari told him, and her face lit up with happiness. It was finally happening. He was going on a date with Sari Tomas. Sure, he never thought he would ever go on a date that included Catholic tradition, but then again, nothing about his experience in Lipa so far had been predictable.

"So you'll go with me?"

"Yes." He nodded. "Consider it a date. Seal it with a kiss?"

"Okay." She kissed his lips, a quick little smack that made him laugh. "Done."

"Ala eh." He frowned, which made Sari laugh.

"You're using it wrong."

"You're incredible, you know that?" he asked her, and he meant it in every sense of the word. He admired her dedication, he was awed at her strength. He loved that she knew when to laugh at the joke, and knew when to challenge it. And she pulled really good pranks. "Even if you never taste my baked goods."

"How do you always manage to make that sound dirty?" She laughed, pressing her hands to her cheeks.

"It only sounds dirty because you think it's dirty," he pointed out to her, because he was good at that kind of thing. She raised a brow like she didn't believe him, and he couldn't deny that it stung a little. "But really. I'm great at making cake. Children have cried, women have tossed underwear at me in offering."

She stuck a tongue out and frowned. "That doesn't sound appealing. Or sanitary!"

"I'm trying to give myself a rockstar vibe. Is it working?"

"No." She shook her head.

"The point is, you really should try my cake sometime."

"Only if you try my coffee," she said before she turned to him and ran a finger across his collarbones, and down the middle of his chest. "I make it really hot."

Her voice dipped at that last sentence, and Gabriel could almost see her smiling wryly at him from the rim of a coffee cup, just before her lips touched the dark liquid.

Her eyes were focused on nothing else but him, kindling a flame of attraction that he harboured for her. Gabriel cleared his throat to get the image out of his head. He'd barely calmed down from the kiss. Kisses.

"See, it's dirty when someone else does it to you." Sari's tone was light as her laughter before she made her quick escape, heading for her side of the old warehouse.

"So, date?"

"Yes! Date!" She waved her hand behind her like

this wasn't momentous. Like it was no big deal, and like she hadn't told him how much she liked it just a few minutes ago.

It made him grin like an idiot. The entire place could be in total chaos and he would be absolutely fine. Good, great, happy, utterly fantastic. Nothing could kill his mood, absolutely nothing.

Not when he'd just kissed Sari Tomas.

Chapter Sixteen

December 19

You know when you have a major deadline coming up, and you know you have to do something about it, but instead you end up completely dithering and doing something else?

That was what Sari felt like when she went back into her coffee lab after sharing that mango with Gabriel. But the thing they never tell you about dithering, it was fun. It was wonderfully distracting. And God help her, she liked it.

When did Gabriel become so cute, by the way? He'd popped up on her fire escape like an oasis in the desert, all sexy features and a warm gaze, listening to the things she had to say. It felt so wonderful to have someone be there for her, just…listening. Without telling her what she could have done to make things right, without judging her, and without any agenda. It made her feel important, and *seen*, and Sari would never forget that small act of kindness from him.

Her phone lit up to let her know she got a text message, and she felt like she was being reprimanded for daydreaming. She was in the café, picking up a bag of

Benguet coffee beans from a local supplier that was looking to partner with them on a blend.

Selene: Just got to Star Tollway exit. Will be there in a bit.

Sari inhaled and exhaled sharply. Selene Tomas texted the same way she lived her entire life—efficiently, straight to the point, and with very little emotion. When their entire family was falling apart, the business all but vanishing in an all-powerful snap, Selene had glared the problem straight in the eye and told her sisters exactly what to do, pushing on like she'd been expecting it to happen the whole time. Her sister was a rock, and next to Selene Tomas, Sari felt like singleply tissue paper slowly dissolving in water.

Sari's phone began to ring, and she picked up on the first ring without checking to see who it was.

"Did you get my text?" Selene asked. "I should be there in like, two hours."

"Yup! Just in time for the annual Belen Setup at home."

"Don't you mean the annual belen argument?" Selene chuckled. "What are you guys using as the Baby Jesus this year?"

Sari and Sampaguita insisted on taking their grandmother's belen set when they moved to Lipa. The set used to be a point of pride for their grandmother—always bathed in gold lighting, set up with real straw, a little nipa hut she had made special, and a starry sky background with a bright gold star above the hut. The set featured hand painted cows, sheep, three wise men in gilded clothes on camels, and of course Mary and Joseph smiling adoringly at their newborn son.

But three years ago, Sam had broken the Baby Jesus, and every year was about finding the perfect substitute. Last year it was a little doll Sari got from a Happy Meal, another year a piece of cotton, but it was always a huge argument between Sam and Sari about who deserved the place of honor in the belen. Selene had never participated in the decision-making, but always wanted to know who won.

"We're still hearing opening arguments. What brings you to Lipa so early? Are you staying until Christmas?"

She winced, because she knew it sounded clingy.

"Business," Selene clarified. "Important business. Huge business."

Sari bit her fingernail, ignoring the little voice in her head telling her that she shouldn't do that (the voice sounded way too much like Selene).

"I'll see you later, Sari."

"See you, Ate."

Once she hung up, Sari immediately opened up a text thread.

Selene just called, she texted Sam. She's coming!! Did she tell you?

Sam: Yup. Sorry, forgot to mention yesterday, but you were dead asleep after the Christmas party. She kept asking about the Carlton Hotel's Lounge Blend. She hates my plan to fix Lola's house. HA. HA. HA. *holds up sarcasm sign*

"Hay nako," Sari said, biting her bottom lip. "I already did that the other day."

Sari's major contribution to the Tomas Coffee Co. was to manage and maintain the coffee that the family produced, overseeing roasting and packing in the facilities in Sta. Cruz, as well as coming up with signature blends for clients who requested it. The café had never been a major money maker for the company, but it was where Sari's heart had always been. As their advocacy was the promotion of local beans and the fine robusta beans that Sam grew in their farm, Sari was one of the few R graders in the area to be able to blend fine robusta and arabica coffee to make spectacular blends.

The Carlton Hotel had asked Sari to come up with something original for the new Lobby Lounge. Something that fit the tastes of the movers and shakers that met in their lobby, they'd said. So Sari came up with the Carlton—a blend of aromatic arabicas, nutty and smooth, with a syrupy hint made strong and sturdy by Sam's fine robusta, tasting of the woodsy trees Sam interplanted them with. Low in acidity but intense in flavor, it was the perfect fuel for the Carlton's clientele.

But if Selene was sniffing around about it, that meant one of two things—either Sari had called it wrong and the Carlton hated the blend, or something else. Lord only knew what that something else could be, if it was enough to drag her to Lipa.

By the time the afternoon rolled around, any energy she'd managed to get from having secret kissing sessions in the fire escape was gone, eaten away by agitation and nerves. The wind was blowing crazy, skirts and hair flying up, and more than once, a customer came in trying to pat down their hair and take leaves off. Static clung in the air, and she kept getting zapped, and she took it as a bad omen.

"Two caffe lattes, one Americano and a candy cane coffee," her cashier called behind her, supposedly to get the barista's butt in gear to start making the coffee. But, without thinking, Sari stepped in, taking over with a confidence she wished she could feel for other things. Her staff always mentioned that Sari didn't have to do half the things she did in the café itself, that she could feel free to leave them for a day or two if she needed it. But she conveniently chose to ignore that.

Coffee, at least, she could make without thinking and not screw up. All she needed were her senses, attuned so keenly to what she had in front of her that it helped slow her quickly beating heart.

"Two caffe lattes, one Americano and a candy cane coffee for Jay?" she asked, gently placing the takeout cups on the service table without so much as a smile to the customer who picked them up. Sari was about to go up to the coffee lab and toss her phone into the roaster when the café door opened, and she half-expected it to be Gabriel. She whirled, ready with a bright smile on her face when Kira Luz and Sam walked in.

"Oh, it's you guys," she said, turning away from them again to go back behind the counter.

"Ah, I love the hospitality of a café," Sam said, making Kira giggle as they took their usual seats in the café.

Kira and Sam were her most regular of regulars. Kira had opened Gemini Chocolates about a year prior to Sari and Sam taking over their areas of the family business, and they usually got together like this just to support each other and complain at each other. Like a little Girl Boss support group, which was why they were here.

"Sari, you look like you're in a bad mood," Kira announced, leaning over the counter to look deeply into Sari's eyes. "It doesn't suit your café's new floral aesthetic."

"Trust me, Kira, Ate Sari would be last person in the family to develop a floral aesthetic." Sam rolled her eyes.

"No, I'm fine." Sari shook her head, wiping her hands on her apron and smiling at her friends like nothing was wrong. "I'll make your coffee. Kira, the beans today have a chocolatey note, you might like it."

"M'am, I really should—" her barista started, but Sari ignored him and pushed the button on the grinder, moving around the space to make her friends their coffee orders. Kira had the biggest sweet tooth in the world, and her favorite coffee was a caffe mocha that was heavy on the mocha (made with her chocolates, of course), with just a little bit of milk to make it creamier. She made Sam a hot Americano, this time with the darkest roast she had on hand.

But as Sari brought their drinks, she saw Gabriel standing outside his shop, just in her view. Almost like he'd noticed her watching, he turned and smiled at her through the window, giving her a flirty little wink.

Sari blushed. A fierce, hot blush that spread from her cheeks to her toes. Then she realized that Sam and Kira were watching her and she knew she was busted.

"Oh my God, look at you, getting your flirt on with the Baker Boy next door," Kira teased, resting her elbows on the table, and her chin on her hands after Sari set down her drink before she greedily gave her mocha a sip. "Mmmm. I thought you despised him. Just last week we were erasing his specials board to write dirty baking jokes."

"Well, I ran out of jokes, and we really couldn't top 'I'm into roll play.'"

"'I've got big buns, hun,' 'I want you to want me,

I knead you to knead me…'" Sam listed, and stopped when she realized Kira was smiling adoringly at her and Sari was narrowing her eyes at her. "What?"

"Anyway, I…don't despise him," Sari corrected, raising her voice slightly because "Falling in Love at a Coffee Shop" was playing, and wasn't the universe amazing at being ironic? "Does it annoy me that people assume we're courting each other? No. Do I think he should get over himself and order coffee that didn't come in a packet? Yes. Do I also think a lot about sitting in the fire escape with him…sharing…mangoes? Yes."

"Is that a euphemism for something?" Sam's nose wrinkled when she asked.

"No, it's what actually happened." Sari was unwilling to tell them any more than that. "But we're supposed to be talking about other things right now. Like Sam moving away. What I'm supposed to do with my empty room. What Selene could possibly mean by dropping by on such short notice. Kira's issues with Santi."

"Who's Santi?" Sam asked. "Oh, oh, the guy who owns Villa and that really amazing Italian place?"

"Overpriced Italian place, you mean." Kira rolled her eyes. "I swear, if I find out he's a Taurus, I would not be surprised, at all."

"The guy who looks like the Grim Reaper from *Goblin*, yes." Sari grinned, enjoying Kira make a face like she did not completely disagree with Sari's assessment. "He's really nice too."

"He is *not*," Kira insisted, turning to Sam and clearly looking for someone to help her out. "He is standoffish, and a bit rude, and he won't let me eat pesto with regular pasta. At the Christmas Party, he also…"

"He also what?" Sam asked curiously.

"Nothing," Kira stammered, but her cheeks were way too red for there to be nothing. "And Sam, your sister is not dealing well with your moving away."

"She's just going to miss Kylo." Sam waved a hand dismissively, because one should never underestimate a Tomas sister's ability to compartmentalize and push aside their own emotions. "Don't worry, Ate. You can visit him."

"Oh my God." Kira shook her head. "The emotional constipation is clogging up my space. You Tomas sisters need to talk. Your star signs aren't exactly harmonious as it is."

"We're fine," Sam, the Pisces, insisted. "Right, Ate?"

"We're always fine." Sari, the Capricorn, nodded.

Kira shook her head, and just like that, Sari knew something was wrong. Immediately she blamed her parents, just because it was the quickest thing to do. They never thought to encourage Selene, Sari and Sam to talk to each other, because they never talked to each other. They were always gone, never really around to love their girls the way they needed. By the time their grandmother had stepped in, the damage had been done.

And now Sam was leaving, Selene was far away, and Sari was going to be left alone in their grandmother's old house. The fears she'd had before she talked to Gabriel came roaring back with a vengeance.

"Well, what are you *not* fine with?" Kira huffed.

"How about the fact that people don't like staying here?" Sari said, choosing the least of her problems now that she was being forced to think of the bigger ones. How funny that she used to think that Sunday Bakery was her biggest problem. It wasn't a problem at all now, it was…it was nice, having a place like that next door.

"I think sales could be a lot better if people linger, because they'll order more."

"Ate…you know how people stay at a coffee shop to eat?" Sam said, her words chosen gently, and already Sari was bracing herself for whatever point she was going to make.

"Sure." Sari gave a terse little nod.

"And that your food sucks? Your pastries, especially?"

Sari nodded again, although she did it very slowly and reluctantly.

"And given how well you and Gabriel are getting along now, a solution to your issues presents itself?"

"Does it?"

"Do you see where I'm going with this?"

"No," Sari admitted, dropping her forehead onto the table. "This café is slipping away from me, just like everything else in my life."

Kira made a sound that was somewhere in between a buzzer proclaiming a wrong answer and a cow's moo. "That's a lie, and you deserve to admit to yourself that this is what you want. Close your eyes and picture it. Sari, what do you want?"

"I…"

"I don't see you closing your eyes."

"Right." She did just that. Closed her eyes and imagined her café during her favorite time of day. Late afternoons meant that the sun hit her windows just right, filling her open space with warm light. She imagined herself standing at her favorite spot in the café, right in front of the espresso machine, with a perfect view of the entire space that was *hers*. Just that was enough to make her happy, but the daydream wasn't complete quite yet.

In her vision, she was holding a latte, bending down to the pastry case to pick something to eat. It was merienda, after all.

The door opens, the bell rings. Someone walks into the café, a white box with gold lettering balanced perfectly in the person's hand. Maybe "Pasko Na Sinta Ko" is playing, because she loves that song, even if it's the saddest. She looks up, and the warmth of the sun spreads from her fingers to her toes, and she's so happy she's practically floating on air, because Gabriel is standing right in front of her, holding up a box from Sunday Bakery, his smile so warm and his dimples so deep that it makes her feel warm and happy.

"Merry Christmas," she hears him say, as he opens the box for her, revealing a whole brazo de mercedes cake, just for the two of them. And it is that feeling of being loved, of being wanted and desired, that fills her heart with happiness.

"Oh boy," Sari said right away, opening her eyes, shaking her head, her hands, her entire body because she was tense and confused and nervous over her own imagination, and it wasn't fair. "Ohhhh boy."

She liked Gabriel more than she'd thought she did. A lot more.

"She's blushing! By jove, I think she's got it," Sam laughed. "A Christmas miracle!"

"What, what did I get?" Sari asked, suddenly aware that her hands had flown to her face. She quickly lowered them and stuffed them in her pockets.

"Does that mean I can eat *this* with my coffee now?" Kira, her Scorpio rising showing up as she asked, whipping out a white box with gorgeous gold lettering stamped on it. Sari's heart actually skipped a beat. It looked just like the box from her vision.

"Oooh." Sam peered over Kira's shoulder to take a look. "Those are from Sunday Bakery?"

"Gabbers just brought them out, I had to fight someone to get these."

"Boy has a way with sugar, you have you admit," Sam said, nodding, and Sari immediately felt betrayed.

"Boy has been bringing out new menu items like he's trying to impress…somebody." Kira was doing a great job of trying to pull a reaction out of Sari, who simply looked away and pretended to be really focusing on the flavors of her Benguet coffee. "I mean, have you tried the ricotta bibingka? Holy shit, it was *amazing*."

"What flavors are these?" Sam, who always preferred subtle sweetness and drank her coffee black, seemed suddenly interested in the contents of Kira's little box.

Because she was trying very hard to be subtle (and failing), Sari gave the box a quick glance and realized… oh. They were cupcakes. Sari really, really liked cupcakes. Except that her mother had trained her to think that carbs and sugar were not her friends, and if she wanted to keep her body fit, she had no business eating them.

"He doesn't usually make cupcakes, so this is a special Christmas box. Lily is dark chocolate, Daisy is strawberry jam, Mindy is panucha—"

Sari was out of words. One by one, Kira put the cupcakes on plates, placing them all out like gorgeous princesses on parade, catching light and shimmering as they were laid at Sari's feet. Well, her counter.

"Panucha," Kira repeated for Sam. Sari had completely missed Sam asking about the flavor. "You know. Sweet, but really nutty? It makes sense if you've met Mindy."

"No, I mean—"

"Panucha? Round disc of sugar? Peanuts, molasses, muscovado sugar, deliciousness…"

"In cupcake form?"

"Gab said he saw people use it as a topping for ice cream in Taiwan, so he experimented," Kira continued, placing one last, milky white cupcake on the table. This one in particular looked like a pearl one would find inside a clam, and was clearly the jewel of the collection.

"Why would he name the cupcakes after his exes?" Sari asked, perfectly aware that she was nearly nose-to-nose to her table. She couldn't help it, they were just so…pretty.

Now it was Kira's turn to look confused. "Not his exes, dude. His sisters. He's the oldest of nine."

"Oh," Sari said as Sam's jaw dropped. It wasn't that big families were uncommon in the Philippines, definitely not, when the average household had five or six people. It was more because there were very few in their generation that still had *that* many siblings. How could they, in this economy? "He's a kuya."

Sari remembered the look of love and pride on his face when he talked about his family. He'd mentioned needing to escape, and she hadn't understood that, but she supposed she did now.

What else was he not telling her, she wondered.

"The ultimate kuya, really." Kira shrugged, refocusing on the cupcakes. "Anyway, Ivy is salted caramel, Rose is birthday vanilla and Iris is peppermint chocolate. He has two more younger brothers, the twins, but they have their own cake flavor."

"Oh, the half chocolate, half birthday cake!" Sam exclaimed, and even Sari was surprised. Since when did her sister go to Sunday Bakery often enough to just *know* that off the top of her head?

"Can we eat these in here?" Kira asked, indicating the box of cupcakes.

"I guess?" Sari said hesitantly, waiting for the feeling of being threatened to come back the way it had on the day Gabriel first opened his shop. She looked at the cupcakes, and was relieved that she felt nothing but a strong desire to eat them.

"So much for a lifetime ban," Sam laughed.

"See, problem solved. Coffee, cake, perfect combination," Kira said casually, taking a plastic knife and cutting the cupcakes into little quarters so they could all have a taste of each flavor. "Want one?"

"Yes," Sari said quickly, trying her best to act nonchalant, and miserably failing. "What do cupcakes have to do with my problem?"

"Sorry, I can't hear you, my mouth is too full of this *amazing* cupcake," Kira groaned, taking a bite off what Sari remembered as the Daisy, the one with strawberry jam from Good Shepherd in Baguio. More than one customer had come into her shop exclaiming over it. Sari's mouth watered, but she pushed away the desire. Even if she'd all but forgotten why she didn't want it.

Sari turned to Sam, who was too enraptured with the salted caramel Ivy to say anything more than "Mmmm!"

"Guys?" Sari asked the general vicinity, unwilling to show how annoyed she was that her friends were ig-

noring her, refusing to acknowledge that she hated it.
But because she would say nothing about how she felt,
she was promptly ignored as they shared the Mindy,
the panucha cupcake, and became incoherent with ex-
clamations of deliciousness.

"Just pass me one, please." Sari reached and took
the uneaten quarter of Rose, the birthday cake. She
took a bite.

Oh my God.

Selene Tomas herself could come to the café and take
it all away tomorrow, and Sari wouldn't have noticed.
Not while she was eating this cupcake.

Wow.

She didn't know if it was the fact that she'd deprived
herself for the last two years, but she was pretty sure she
was taking a bite of perfection right here. Seeing a cupcake with sprinkles in the cake would have given off the
impression that it was too sugary sweet, but Rose was
not that at all. The soft, moist cake was flavored with
malty cereal milk, but was strong enough to hold up
the vanilla frosting. Sari had no idea what Gabriel did
to the buttercream, but it really did taste like birthday
cake, the kind of cake that you got from a local bakery,
that had frosting that stained your teeth and sugar flowers that weren't good for you, but you loved anyway.

It evoked happy memories, and it actually made her
sigh. She knew exactly what kind of coffee would go
perfectly well with this, could imagine a whole store of
customers enjoying the perfect combination of milky
cake and smooth coffee, sweet frosting and medium
roasted beans.

"Damn."

She wiped her mouth with the napkin and took a sip

of her coffee. Her hand was already reaching for the dark chocolate, but she snatched it back. She didn't have time for this. Her sister was coming this afternoon, and she needed to not be standing around with her friends eating cupcakes.

"I have to…"

"Do you?" Sam asked, mid-bite of the peppermint and chocolate cupcake.

"Yes," Sari insisted, turning and leaving them both. She headed straight upstairs to the coffee lab, but hesitated when she spotted Gabriel's head bobbing around on his side of their shared window. And if Sari was braver, she would walk right into his kitchen and kiss him senseless, admit to herself that she wanted him more than she'd thought, and do more.

In a split-second decision, she turned, walked into the supply closet and closed the door behind her, loud enough that she was sure he heard. She leaned against the door and started to laugh like she couldn't believe what was happening. *You've kissed him. Why are you so surprised that you want him so much?*

Why don't you go over there and do something about it?

Her phone rang, briefly illuminating the contents of the closet. Oh, so *that's* where Sari had left the extra jars for the coffee beans. And the extra mugs. She looked at the text.

Did I just see you go into the supply closet? This is Gab, by the way.

Gabriel? Sari picked up her phone and studied the message, the first he'd ever sent. When had they exchanged numbers? Knowing him (and did she, really?)

he would have come up to her on the guise of "co-ware-house related issues" to ask, but he hadn't.

Sari: How did you get this number?

Gabriel: The Laneways chat group. I just opened a private chat, don't worry. You didn't accidentally give out your number.

Of course, Sari thought, pressing her forehead against the back of the door before she saved his name on her phone as *Dimples*.

No community in the Philippines thrived without a requisite message group these days, and Ate Nessie had one for the Laneways. In the group she shared reminders and upcoming events, greeted the owners on birthdays, holidays and particular saints' days and very occasionally commented on traffic. In turn, the owners shared community concerns, exchanged goods, or collaborated. It was a fun, lively group that Sari usually had to put on Mute.

Sari: Smmdrt.

Gabriel: Is that a typo or are you just happy to see me?

Sari snorted and rolled her eyes.

Sari: I'm standing in my closet, trying to convince my-self not to walk out and kiss you. Your cupcakes are so good. I hate you.

Gabriel: I can always come over there, and you can tell me exactly why my cupcakes are so good.

Sari's jaw dropped, at the same time as butterflies started to riot in her stomach. Was she supposed to pretend that she wasn't flirting with him? Was she supposed to flirt back? How hard? How did she want this to go?

She felt like she should be the one in control of the conversation, even if she wasn't in control of her emotions at the moment. She blamed the sugar, she blamed the cupcakes, but really, she knew it was him. The way he was making her feel.

Oh really? She bit her bottom lip, typing slowly. How are you going to do that?

Gabriel: Well, first I'd have to break down that door.

Sari: Only if you promise to put it back.

Gabriel: Of course. I'm very handy that way.

Sari rolled her eyes. Trust Gabriel to grab the nearest innuendo and wave it around like a toy sword.

Gabriel: Then, I would wrap my arms around you. Touch you everywhere you need it.

Maybe press you against the door, feel your body against mine.

Where would you like me to touch you, Sari?

A frisson of heat shot through Sari's body, pooling in the place that, to use Sam's words, was "getting dusty." She might have gasped, but she'd clapped her hand over her mouth already. Her heart was beating a little too fast in her chest, and her knees felt jiggly and weak. Was it just her or was it suddenly really warm, and dark in this room?

And three gray dots were still showing up on the bottom of her screen. He was still typing.

Gabriel: I can picture it. My hands on you. Warming you up. I bet your skin will be smooth in my hands. I want to give you...

She sucked in a breath.
Pleasure.
"Holy shit," she said out loud, and it almost sounded like a moan to her ears.

Gabriel: Tell me what you want?

I don't really know what I want. Sari's hands were faster than her brain right now, which wasn't surprising given that she worked with her hands. Oh, she knew she seemed cool and confident over text and when Gabriel was looking at her, but that was just a poor attempt at keeping her own emotions in check. Sari was not that cool.

But you could be one of those things.

Three gray dots from him.

There was a knock on the door. Sari jumped approximately fifty feet in the air, even if the closet couldn't have been more than nine feet tall.

"Password?" she asked, her hand over her chest to calm her rapidly working heart.

"Yeah, nice try, Sari. I'm still not going to tell you where the mango farm is," he said, and Sari's laugh bubbled out of her before she could help it. It actually sounded a little strangled, which was definitely not a good thing.

But how did Gabriel get into her coffee lab? Did her desire for him just…open doors now?

"Your fire escape door was propped open," like he'd read her mind, he quickly explained through the still closed door. "Can I come in?"

Sari turned to face the door and pressed her hand against the wood, taking a deep breath. Then she unlocked the door and opened it slowly, enough to reveal Gabriel looking at her, his mouth slightly parted, his breathing rapid, like he'd run here. He looked exactly how she felt—out of her element, but way too excited about the possibilities to worry. He was, clearly, as hot and bothered as she was.

She was into it.

"Hi," he said.

"Hi," she said back, grabbing the front of his shirt and pulling him into the closet with her, plunging them both into darkness. She couldn't see, but she could feel Gabriel's hands when he placed them on her waist. His hands were so hot she thought she heard the hiss of steam rising in the air, like freshly frothed milk. They skimmed and roamed, sneaking under her skirt, gripping her thighs and making her gasp.

"I love that you wear skirts all the time," he said, as his lips claimed the skin on her neck. "Are you warm enough?"

"No."

"Good," he said, and he somehow managed to spin them around and press Sari against the back of the door, his hand hot against her skin as he pulled one leg around his waist. "I believe I made a promise to pleasure you, Sari."

"Stop talking and start doing, then," she said, and wrapped her arms around his neck. She felt the weight of her body shift as Gabriel lifted her up and pressed her back against the door. She immediately felt light-headed and off balance, because oh *wow*. Who would have thought that baking did a body good? Gabriel was strong and warm, and Sari loved touching him, grabbing him, pressing against him. Her skirt was bunched up against the base of her stomach, and she had the room to roll her hips against his leg.

"Oh, fuck," she heard Gabriel mutter darkly, gripping her thighs tighter as his finger brushed up against her underwear. "Wet for me already, Sari?"

"Mhm," was all she managed to say, still moving her hips against his hand as he stroked her over her underwear, teasing and torturing her at the same time, because she wanted more. God, did Sari want more.

"Can I touch you?" Gabriel asked, his voice low as his lips pressed against her neck, kissing the skin there and leaving a little mark. "Sari, please let me touch you."

"Okay," she breathed. "Do it."

The noise she made when his fingers found her clit did not sound like her at all. She never thought she would feel so uninhibited around him, shameless and bold as his magic fingers moved inside her, stroking, feeling, brushing. He seemed to be a little lost, staying on a particular spot and a particular motion until Sari directed him. "Harder. There. Oh, Gabriel, yes, there."

He made her feel like her entire nervous system was a string of Christmas lights, firing at all synapses and making her squeeze tighter, roll her hips harder, ask for more.

"I really like you, dimples." She half panted, half groaned as Gabriel's hand squeezed her breasts through her shirt, and she found a spot on his skin that tasted sweet.

"I want you, Sari," he breathed like he was the one getting an excellent hand job. She didn't think that just hearing his voice like this would be such a turn on, but the way he said it, soft and husky, it was everything. Everything.

It made her squeeze her thighs together as she sucked particularly hard on the nearest spot on his skin. She pressed her fingers against the back of his neck to brace herself and slid her hand between her legs to help him along. Gabriel almost growled, she felt that rumble against her own body. She moved her fingers with the rhythm they were making, almost as if to show Gabriel that this was what she wanted, that this was how she found pleasure. Gabriel gently pushed her fingers aside and took over.

"And?" Sari threw her head back because ohholycrap this was so delicious, and there was nothing to hold on to but Gabriel, so she did, which only made it better. There was a brief moment of madness where Sari actually thought, maybe this one would stay, maybe he could actually stick around…

"And I think," he murmured into her ear. "You are absolutely irresistible."

Sari lost her breath. She gripped hard on the back of his neck, needed him to anchor her, steady her, because this was all so *much*. Gabriel seemed to have a hard time breathing too, his breath hot against her neck. They were actually sweating, the both of them.

He slowly released her other leg, her grip on the back of his neck loosened in favor of just holding him for a few more moments. She pressed her cheek against the space between his neck and shoulder and listened as their breaths sped up and slowed.

"Simbang Gabi," he finally said as reality reasserted itself around them, like it had to catch up to the moment that they just stole. Sari very quickly got a hold of herself. Gabriel kissed her on the cheek, and despite the fact that he'd just spent his time ruining her for other people's kisses, this kiss was the most tender.

"I think I know what to wish for," he said, his voice low and husky as he reached behind her to open the closet door. Then he sauntered out of her lab, and all Sari could see was his back muscles, and the little marks she'd left on the back of his neck.

Chapter Seventeen

"M'am, Sir Gabriel just left," her manager informed
Sari five minutes later. She was back behind her coffee machine after cleaning herself up and willing her
cheeks to stop being so hot. *Eh ano ga?* she thought,
shaking off the feeling. In her estimation, she was doing
a fantastic job of acting like absolutely nothing had happened, even if every cell of her skin was still tingling,
her cheeks still warm and her lips still tingly, even after
re-application of her lipstick and gloss.

"He seemed to be in a real hurry."

Sari was doing her best to hide a grin, but the look
on her manager's face made her think she wasn't doing
a very good job of it.

"He should be," she chuckled.

"M'am, sure ka, you're not dating Sir Gab?"

"Yes, I'm sure," she said, because technically it
wasn't a lie. She hadn't gone on a date with him yet,
so they weren't dating per se. But her staff didn't need
to know that.

"Sure na sure? And your sister just arrived."

"Has she?" Sari singsonged, smiling and thoroughly
rubbing hand sanitizer from the bathroom into her
hands, when she saw Selene sitting in the café.

Selene Tomas was all business in high gloss, the kind of woman who put on eyeshadow and mascara on a daily basis and walked in four-inch heels even in the heart of Lipa City. She was two years older than Sari, and was actually the shortest among them, but the way she carried herself just screamed "responsibility" and "no time for bullshit."

"Is it just me, or are there more people in the Laneways now than there were last year?" she asked one of Sari's staff as Sari took a backward step up the stairs to hide from view.

"The bakery and the café are a huge draw," Sari's store manager explained with a smile. "They've been having a lot of…theatrics lately."

Sari thanked God very silently that her store manager wasn't a gossip, and that her sister seemed to have no idea what she and Gab had been up to in the last one and a half weeks. Selene looked like she was casually surveying the café, and Sari could just tell that she was assessing it, scanning for anything substandard, but Sari felt ready for anything.

"Long black, please." Selene smiled sweetly to Sari's cashier, and immediately Sari knew it was a test. She didn't *have* long black coffee on her menu, mostly because her customers were more familiar with Americanos and lattes.

Her barista shot Sari a panicked look, as if expecting Sari to come in and make the order for her. Sari made a little shooing gesture at her as if to tell her she could do this, because she'd been trained well, and knew the difference between an Americano and a long black. It was all down to the preparation—a long black would mean pouring the espresso into a cup of hot water, instead of the other way around. The key was in preserving the crema of the espresso. Pouring the coffee after the water would preserve that little bit of tawny amber liquid that came from the initial extraction.

Selene assessed the finished cup with her laser sharp gaze. She actually lifted it to closely examine if the crema was there. That was Selene in a nutshell. She knew exactly what she wanted, and wasn't shy about letting other people know.

"You can come out now, Sari," she said, raising her brow over the rim of her cup before she turned and walked to the customer tables and took a seat. "What were you doing back there?"

"I was…checking inventory," Sari explained to her sister, sitting across from her with her shoulders hunched and her fingers laced together so tightly that the tips were almost white.

"Were you really? You look a little…windswept."

"Crazy winds. Global warming, am I right?"

"Uh huh."

Sari flinched.

"Relax, Sar, I won't bite. At least not right now." Selene gave Sari's hands a pointed look, putting her coffee down. "The Carlton group loved your coffee blend. Enough that they want to have it in *all* of their hotel lobbies in the country. I talked to Sam, and she said we should be able to keep up with the demand, especially if we partner up with another farm in Lipa to grow the fine robusta."

"Oh!" Sari exclaimed, genuinely surprised, blinking at her sister. "That's great. About the blends, I mean, I knew they would like it."

"I know." Selene smiled. "Papa did say that you have the gift."

Sari snorted and shook her head. "I don't think I want the gift if Papa said I have it. Where is he nowadays?"

"Last I heard, in Singapore with his newest. Younger than Sam this time."

"And Mom?"

"In a Balinese retreat house re-creating *Eat Pray Love*, but in reverse. They individually send their best Christmas wishes and their regrets that they can't be here for the holidays."

Sari scrunched her nose. "Role models, our parents."

"You still hate them, don't you," Selene noted, and did Sari detect a note of disappointment in her sister's voice? "Have you seen a therapist about your residual anger and disappointment? I have. It's been very helpful."

"I don't need—Selene. Please don't tell me you drove two hours to Lipa to ask me if I have a therapist."

"If you say so." Selene shrugged in that all-knowing, older sister way of hers. "Now this is somewhat confidential, but I need to discuss it with you. You know that big construction site across the Laneways?"

Sari blinked at her sister, not knowing what she was trying to say. The lot across the Laneways contained the rest of the warehouses that used to belong to the Luz family, but according to Kira they'd lost the land in a bidding war against one of the big banks. It had been sitting there, waiting for a buyer…and now they had it in the form of the Lai Group, one of the fastest growing investors in the country. Ate Nessie had announced it on the Laneways chat group as soon as she found out late last month.

"Yes?"

"The Lai Group is opening the biggest mall in South Luzon, and they're offering us a lease."

Sari's jaw dropped at her sister.

"Selene, are you telling me we should abandon the Laneways?" she hissed, not wanting the staff to panic, and she was sure that they were listening. This was a small community, and gossip caught and spread and mixed like ketchup and mayo until it was completely unrecognizable. And it wasn't just that. Selene was talking about taking away the one place in the world Sari called home. She was talking about giving up on a place that was the backdrop of every good moment from the last three years, just because someone else was building a mall monstrosity across the street.

No. No. No, her brain protested. *She can't be asking you to do this.*

"I'm asking you if you think we should sign the lease." Selene took a deeper sip of her coffee like she wasn't crushing everything that Sari considered her home. "They really want us there, bad food and all. Along with the Carlton order, this could be everything we need to put us on the map. Sari, this is the next logical step for us."

Sari tried to ignore the way her heart flipped upside down at her sister's use of the word "us." Was she talking about the company? The family? It was hard to tell, but for the first time in some time, Sari had an instant answer.

"No."

"What?"

"It's a bad idea." Sari shook her head. She didn't know why her fingers suddenly felt cold. "A really shit idea."

"Are we going to discuss this logically, or are we going to argue?" Selene asked, and Sari knew her sister wasn't being bitchy, she was really asking her what she wanted. Selene could go either way. This was how the sisters always resolved conflict, and while Sari appreciated her sister's demeanor, she wasn't sure she was calm enough to discuss this logically.

"I'm trying for logical discussion," Sari sighed. "The best thing to do would be to stick it out here with the other owners. They've treated us really well, they've helped us when we were starting out here. The Luzes especially, they helped us get our first clients. Why would we leave? We still have two years on our lease here, and everyone knows that this is where we are. The mall is going to kill the Laneways."

"We don't know that," Selene argued. "I know the café is doing really well now, but it's not going to be the holidays forever."

Sari shook her head to disagree. She wasn't about to tell her sister that her biggest sale days over the holidays so far had been in the middle of her friendly competition with Gabriel. Her sister did *not* need to know that.

"We've got a good track record here, and more and more people are coming in, looking for something different, something that isn't in a mall," Sari insisted. "When have you ever heard of a whole tour bus of people coming in for a bunch of little shops?"

Selene's bottom lip jutted out as she thought for an argument. Sari's hands shook every time she and her sister spoke like this, and she always wound up crying in the end, but she was determined to keep focused, keep calm, lay out all her arguments and make her sister see her way.

She knew her sister just as well as Selene knew her. She wouldn't have come all this way to ask Sari if her mind was absolutely sold on the move. Sari just needed to say the right thing to convince her otherwise.

"Selene, it's...it's my home. Don't take it away from me now."

Selene opened her mouth.

"At least until the lease is up. Then we can put this to a vote between the three of us," Sari added quickly. Logic always appealed to her sister.

Selene was considering it, taking a sip of her long black and closing her eyes for a moment. Was she considering what to say to put Sari down? Thinking about how to argue back?

Selene tilted her head to the side to watch Sari carefully, as if Sari's face held all the answers she needed. Sari didn't know how her sister did that, but she could see right through her. Like Sari was the most obvious open book. Between their absent father and less-than-interested mother, there were few people in the world she trusted and listened to more than her older sister.

"Okay," she finally said, nodding. "I'll hold the lease."

Selene reached out and squeezed her sister's hand. Sari nearly jumped back at the gesture.

"You're not alone in this, Sari. You know I just want what's best for the company."

Sari opened her mouth. Then closed it. Then opened it again. Of all the things she thought she would hear her older sister say today, it definitely wasn't this.

Selene released Sari's hand and took a sip of her coffee.

"This long black isn't half bad." She shrugged.

Okay, that was the other thing Sari didn't think she would ever hear her sister say.

"So," Selene finally said, smiling. "Baby Jesus. What did you guys end up going with, because the cotton ball baby last year was just sad."

"Sam claims to have found a crochet Baby Jesus that will work, and she wants to keep it there for next year." Sari shook her head and rolled her eyes. "Doesn't she know how important tradition is?"

"It is, but you know you have to be open to new things too." Selene's voice was a little gentle. "Sometimes even traditions have to be made new. Like winning a karaoke contest at the Christmas party with a new partner."

There was a beat of silence while Sari narrowed her eyes at her older sister, who innocently kept sipping her coffee.

"Who told you about that?"

"Sam babbles when she gets nervous." Selene finished her coffee and reached for her wallet, leaving too much money on the counter. "And the moment I set foot in Lipa, Ate Nessie told me my old karaoke partner abandoned me for a boy."

"She didn't."

"It was the perfect blend of chastising for not being here and of spreading gossip, which is her specialty." Sari knew that look on her sister's face. She found all of this hilarious, but was never the type to throw her head back and laugh. "I'll see you girls at home. I'm making dinner."

"You say that like it's a good thing."

"Hush, baby sister, go back to coffee making," Selene said, and lightly patted the top of Sari's head before she stood up with not a single strand of hair out of place. "Sari?"

"Hmm?"

"I know things are changing, with Sam, and this. Are you okay?"

"I'm fine," Sari assured her sister with a nod. "I'm always fine."

Selene wrinkled her nose, but didn't call her out on the lie, choosing instead to nod and leave the café, nothing left behind but a now empty coffee cup.

Chapter Eighteen

December 20

When the Capras family did Christmas, they *did* Christmas. Their house would always be decked end to end with Christmas decorations, and their Christmas tree ornaments had origins older than most of the kids in the house. They had set rules for their Secret Santa exchange, with budgets and wish list spreadsheets. But aside from that, there were the traditional events they had to participate in for December. Their parents' friends, the Dabarkads, always met on December 20, hell or high water. Noche Buena was always with their mother's side of the family, Christmas Dinner with their father's side, and Christmas presents were only allowed to be opened at nine a.m. on Christmas morning.

Gabriel knew all of those traditions, had grown up with them. But among traditional Filipino Christmas traditions his family practiced, the early dawn masses nine days before Christmas just wasn't one of them. Four a.m. was way too early, and while the food for sale was excellent, coordinating an eleven-person family's attendance for nine days straight was too much drama.

But when Sari asked Gab to go with her, he realized

that the timing wasn't as bad as he thought. Mostly because he was already supposed to be at the bakery anyway. What surprised him, however, was a sudden voice call over Messenger from an unexpected sibling.

"Are you even listening to me, Kuya?" an exasperated voice asked from the other end of the line.

"I hang on to your every word, as always, Roselia," he said, using his nickname for her just so she knew he was still paying attention before he yawned.

"Kuya, I wish you would stop calling me by a Pokémon's name."

"Technically," he yawned again. "Roselia is a *kind* of Pokémon. You are totally within your rights to call your Roselia whatever you want, but it's like calling a dog, 'dog,' or Bubbles 'spawn of Satan.'"

"Why are you sleepy? Aren't you always up by six a.m.?"

Six a.m.? Oh. Right. Two-hour time difference.

"It's Friday, Rose. My day off."

She huffed, which made him laugh. Among all his siblings, Rose was the one who called him up most, checked on him, made him feel a little less lonely in his self-exile. Lily didn't count so much, because when she called, it was always just to ask how things were, if he was coming home. Lily was a no-nonsense kind of sister, and sometimes Gab liked that about her. God knows what kind of family they would have been if he had been left as the only responsible one. Daisy called when there were major family developments Gab needed to know about, like when Angelo got first honors or Ivy burned her hand trying to make iced coffee.

Rose called because she enjoyed talking to him, which he appreciated. Gab had considered more than once now telling Rose where he actually was, what he'd accomplished. But not yet. He wasn't quite there yet.

"Kuya, are you really not coming home for Christmas?"

The question made him bite his lip, following a sharp inhale. The pain that he'd been carrying around with him for the last two years lingered. At first it was the pain of missing home. Now, it was the pain of feeling too guilty to go home. It never went away and he missed his family so much that some days he just wanted to get into his car and drive the three hours home and see the chaos of the Capras household.

But then going back to Manila would mean seeing his father, and he was just so tired of having to explain himself to him. The man who'd raised him to be respectful to his sisters, kind to his brothers, who had insisted that as a man, he always had to be *more*. Smarter, richer, more professional and always with the biggest ego in the room. Gab was just never going to be what his father wanted. Until he accepted that, there would be no Secret Santa where everyone knew what everyone was getting before Christmas, no huge present exchange on Christmas morning, no client goodie baskets that they would cook and eat on the same day.

"I'm sorry, Rosie. I can't."

"If this is about Dad, I promise he won't say anything," Rose insisted, pushy as ever, which was one of the reasons why Gab loved her.

"Dad won't be able to help himself," he said, and because he didn't know what else to add, he continued, "I've known him for longer than you have."

"But who's going to make the Christmas cake?"

"Who made it last year?"

"You're going to miss Secret Santa."

"I always send a gift, you know that."

"We miss you. Mom misses you."

"I know," he sighed. Rose made excellent points, but at the end of the day, his mother sided with their father, which meant she didn't support him. "I miss you guys too."

"So come home!"

"Point m'am, I can't afford it yet, and if it means a fight with Dad, I'd rather stay here than ruin everyone's Christmas."

There. Done. Rose knew that when push came to shove, logical arguments were best. She was on the debate team, just like he'd been in another life. This House believes that Gabriel Capras should come home. Rose Capras on the Parliament side, Gabriel on the Opposition. Opening arguments, rebuttals and points made, but conclusion was, there was no way Gabriel was coming home this year. And they both knew it.

"So…are you dating anyone?"

"Wow," he laughed. "And the Whip throws the entire debate around."

"I'm trying to be more sociable!" she exclaimed in the voice that was half exasperation, half desperation, which was Rose's default mode most of the time. "Are you?"

"No," he said finally. "But not for lack of trying."

"Hm. I would think Australia would be your market."

He could tell her now, Gab supposed. He could downplay it, act like it wasn't a big deal. *I'm not in Australia, Rose. I'm in Lipa. Come see me? I miss you guys.* Easy, right?

"I know," he snorted instead. "It's almost like nobody wants to spend Christmas with me."

"Yeah, when everyone's hot and sweaty and just in the mood for love," Rose laughed, and they kept talking for a little while longer, about his work, her studies, the continuing saga of Mindy and her boyfriend Javier being icky and adorable, and Lily moving to a new place in Ortigas. He told Rose about the things he baked, how he named a cupcake after her and she asked, "Am I really as exciting as a birthday cake?"

He pulled into a parking spot, somehow managing to find one in the constant chaos of the San Sebastian Cathedral's plaza.

"Okay. I'm at work. Talk to you later, Roselia," he said, peering up at the soft yellow walls of the Cathedral, the number of people sleepily heading inside. "And go to sleep, it's like four in the morning there."

"I'm going to Simbang Gabi, so it's fine, Kuya. Have a good breakfast for me!"

He said one last goodbye and waited for his little sister to hang up. He should feel guilty, deceiving his family like this, but some things they weren't ready for yet.

A blast of cool air hit him, and his eyes adjusted to the bad lighting of the plaza as he locked his car and walked in the direction of the Cathedral. It was cold, thank God he brought a cardigan with him.

San Sebastian Cathedral was the crown jewel of all the churches in Lipa City. It was big, it was appropriately scary, and there were always people there—street vendors selling goods outside, tricycle drivers waiting for their next passengers, a group practicing a dance number or two in the plaza out front, while faithful parishioners said their prayers inside.

Tonight, on the fifth night of Simbang Gabi, the Cathedral was full of people. Some were here to make their prayers, some were dragged here by older relatives, following tradition, and some, adhering to the old tale that finishing all nine dawn masses entitled you to a big wish, were here looking for a little bit of hope in dark times.

He wondered who he was among those people, wondered what he wanted.

As far as Cathedrals and churches went, Lipa Cathedral was one of the biggest Gabriel had seen. The floors of the church were done in gray patterned tiles, which sleepy children were currently using as an elaborate hopscotch board to distract themselves. Rows of archways made up the main mass area, all painted with frescoes to make them look like they were flanked by Roman arches. Even the ceiling was painted with exacting detail, images of saints interspersed with faux molding giving the church a grand feel. Even from where they were standing at the very back, Gabriel could clearly see the silver glinting off an organ at the front, a pulpit made of the same dark wood and silver as the organ. He could only just get a glimpse of the famous dome from here, although he imagined it was made of the same finely painted molding on the inside.

A marker at the Cathedral entrance explained that it had been around since 1894, and before that, used to be located closer to Taal Lake.

"Gabriel!" Sari's voice rose through the crowd, and bright and beaming, as she made her way to him from one of the side entrances. He tried to kiss her on the lips, but she went for the cheek, and it ended with the both of them blushing at each other like this was the first time they'd met.

He should have just kissed her. He'd certainly been much smoother yesterday.

"Good morning," she told him while the homily went on. They were late. "I'm glad you're here."

"Me too. Do you always attend Simbang Gabi?"

She nodded.

"My grandmother used to insist we go," she whispered. "My parents dumped the three of us kids here in Lipa for the holidays, and Lola didn't know what else to do with us, so we did every Christmas tradition available. Including Simbang Gabi."

"Is she here?"

"Lola? Yes and no. She died about five years ago now."

"I'm sorry."

"It's fine." Sari shrugged, even if he still saw that twinge of sadness in her face, showing a bit of the hole losing her grandmother had left in her heart. "Sam and I inherited her house two blocks away. I always feel like she's around, when I'm here. I was named after her too."

"Sari?"

"Rosario," she clarified. "Pretty much guaranteeing an identity crisis. My name doesn't even start with an S like my sisters! So identity crisis and major middle child syndrome."

"As the oldest, I can't relate," he chuckled. "You and Sam live alone?"

"Yup. Me and Sam in Lola's house. Well," she said, and suddenly he remembered that she was stressing about Sam moving out soon. Damn it. "Soon it'll be just me. Me and my terrifyingly small life, standing still while everyone else is moving on."

"I wouldn't call running a coffee empire small," Gab pointed out to her. "You're not small at all. Not to me."

She opened her mouth, and he wondered if she was going to argue, but then shook her head and decided against it. He couldn't help but feel that this was the first time someone had ever told her that, and he hated the world she lived in that she didn't know that about herself.

"Why do I think I need to tell you these things?" She shook her head. "We've only just met."

"We're neighbors, that gives us a special bond."

Sari snorted, and they both knew it wasn't quite accurate. What was the word for more than neighbors, not enemies, not quite friends but definitely flirting with each other, and more?

"Sam wants to move to the farm." Sari sighed deeply. The church did inspire that kind of honesty, what with all the saints and statues looking at you. "I thought my Simbang Gabi wish would be for her not to move, but it seems like the most un-Ate-like thing to do."

"It does," he agreed, and shrugged when Sari gasped at him. "What? Us older kids are selfish and a little bit entitled. We think we know better, even if we don't. But what our younger siblings never know is that we're mostly acting out of love."

She gave him a sardonic look, and Gabriel liked her best when she was like this. When she knew she had the edge over him, or when she was ready to come back with a quick quip. In moments like that, she was brassy and confident, and he liked pulling that reaction from her.

"I thought you said you couldn't commiserate."

"I'm a man of many facets."

"Sure," she laughed, loud enough for people in front of them to look at them sharply. "It's hard. I'm not Sam's mom, but I *so* feel like it. I just want her to do what I want."

"If your sister is anything like you, she's not going to let anything stop her, certainly not her well-meaning ate."

"And you know this because…?"

"I have eight siblings. None of them ever listened to me, and thank God, because I'm an idiot, most of the time."

It came to the point where the congregation had to hold hands for the Our Father, and Gabriel's and Sari's hands couldn't seem to separate from each other from that time on. *Just like the song*, he thought, hearing the music in his head even as everyone sang something else.

The next thing Gab knew, the mass was over, and everyone streamed out of the church, ready to go back to their beds—but not before having a pre-dawn snack, which was as much of an essential as the actual attendance of Simbang Gabi.

Sari looked like she was as excited about all of this as he was. She crossed her arms over her chest, and he saw her shiver. Without hesitation, he took off his jacket and draped it over her shoulders. She inhaled sharply and looked up at him with wide, wondering eyes.

"Hi." He grinned.

"Hey," she said back.

"So what did you wish for?" she asked him as they headed to the direction of the food stalls, just as bright and awake as Gab was. They walked past the stalls selling shiny turon and hotdogs, past barbecue and smoke, and other vendors trying to capture the crowd's attention before they went back to their warm beds.

"Secret," he scoffed. "You know perfectly well that if I tell you what my wish is, it won't come true."

"That only works for birthdays." Sari rolled her eyes, tugging at his hand as they walked toward the puto bumbong.

"I don't want to risk it," he reasoned, which made her roll her eyes again. It reminded him of the very, very early days of their meeting, when she seemed particularly annoyed by every word that came out of his mouth. It was hard to imagine getting upset with her now.

"You know when I was a kid, I wished it would snow?" Sari looked up at the dark sky, pulling her cardigan closer to her skin.

"In the *Philippines*?"

"Yeah. I had zero concept of how cold it had to be for it to snow. I remember looking up at a sky just like this, fully believing it would snow on Christmas." She was smiling as she looked up at the starry sky, and Gabriel could almost see her, the little Sari, hoping for one teeny tiny snowflake. "It felt cold enough, and I thought that if I wished for it hard enough, snowflakes would start falling from the sky."

Her smile faded then, as if she felt bad for the child that was let down one more time. Gabriel wished he could take that sadness away from her. That for once, someone would come through for her.

She shook it off quickly, and smiled at him.

"Let's eat."

She stopped in front of a stall selling bowls of warm sopas—the kind that was so fancy it had bits of Vienna sausage—but Gab's eye gravitated to something else. Something almost fluorescent pink in the dark of the early morning.

"Oh my God," he said, walking towards the cart like a moth to a flame, completely forgetting that he and Sari were still holding hands. "Pink popcorn."

"Really?" Sari laughed, following him to where a man was selling popcorn from a makeshift stall, a bright yellow lightbulb showing off the shiny pink candy layer on his wares. "Gab, there's pancit! And lomi, and bibingka! You want pink popcorn?"

"Think of the things we could put this on, Sari. I want it on everything," Gab exclaimed excitedly, buying two little paper bags each for them. "My dad would buy a few paper bags for me and my brothers and sisters, and we had to share, of course. You ate and ate and ate, waiting for that lovely morsel of neon pink sugar that gets clumped in the popcorn. And then just when you think you'll never experience it again, it comes back."

A pang hit him with the memory. And it was one of those moments where he thought, *Screw it, why don't we just go home? It's Christmas, it'll be fine.* A moment of weakness, his father would say. But he pushed it aside, kept the smile on his face, because he was determined to let nothing ruin this moment with her.

"You okay?" Sari asked, wrapping an arm around his as if to remind him that she was still there. "You looked like you went somewhere else."

"No, I just—" He took a chunk of popcorn and started to chew. It was warm and sweet, the perfect thing for this time of day.

How odd that the most random thing would remind him of how far away from home he was, how far he was from coming home, really. Standing his ground was great and all, but it did make one very lonely.

If you were home, Dad would tell you off for exclaiming over pink popcorn, the darker corners of his head reminded him, and he remained resolute. Resolute but sad, and much happier that Sari was here with him.

If she noticed that he'd abandoned the rest of his sentence, it didn't show. Gabriel recovered quickly, though.

"I think I need bibingka. And tsokolate. And sleep. Are you hungry? We should eat."

"Or. We could skip the food and head straight to your place."

Gabriel felt his jaw drop to the floor. Seriously, someone had to come along and mop it up, he was so surprised. He didn't think Sari was…that she…but did he…?

"I've got protection."

He couldn't help himself. Gabriel lowered to kiss her, pulling her close and squeezing tight. He felt Sari's warm hands reach up and rake her nails lightly over his scalp, tugging slightly at the curls there.

"Is that where we are already?" he asked.

"Progressing exactly as expected, yes."

"Okay. But can I buy suman and latik first?"

"Make it two."

When he first moved to Lipa, Gabriel would have been content with living in the warehouse. He didn't need much in his life, really, just a bed and bathroom, as long as he had his kitchen. But all of that changed when Kira showed him the little house they had for rent in Bolbok.

Tucked into a subdivision a hop, skip and a jump from the main highway, the little green house was on a slope, under a huge Narra tree that had capiz lights and a swing. It was detached enough from the city to be completely quiet at night, but near enough that he could be in the Laneways in twenty minutes. He loved this about Lipa—the city was as big and busy as any metropolis, but it took very little to find a place to completely escape from it all. Lipa still had its quiet places away from the mad crowds. And here in his quiet little corner of the world, he had Sari Tomas with him, and he couldn't have asked for anything more.

He and Sari burst through the door, walking into his open plan living room, heat radiating off both of them as they kissed like there was no tomorrow. Gabriel found himself holding her tighter, closer, burying his face in the crook of her neck where she was warm. Sari laughed as he exhaled, twirling away from him.

"What?" he asked in confusion.

"Nothing, it's a tickle spot," she explained.

"Oh…really?"

"Gabriel, don't—" she began, but the rest of her sentence was lost as Gab took her in his arms, making her laugh as he kissed her neck. She squirmed, but held on to him anyway, and they both danced backwards and collapsed onto his couch.

"Why does your couch still have plastic on it?" Sari asked, lifting her head to confirm that yes, Gabriel was a loser who had plastic wrap on his couch like he was afraid to tear into it.

"I've never had to fill such a big space by myself before, so I haven't really used this couch," he reasoned. "But the bed's pretty used."

"Oh really?"

Gab only grinned in response, hooking his arms on

the backs of Sari's knees and he lifted her up with zero effort. Sari gasped, but wrapped her arms around his neck.

"What?" he asked.

"I have a book cover that looks exactly like this," she laughed. "Except the heroine's thighs weren't quite as big."

"Oh hush, sweetheart, I love your thick thighs," he said in a British accent, and she just laughed, and laughed, and laughed. He loved that sound, the way it filled the entire house, making it seem a little less empty. Be still his beating heart.

"Lakas ka ga?"

"Aba oo," he winked at her. "Now, milady. To the bedchamber. I'm going to rip the bodice right off of you."

She put her hand over his mouth as she continued laughing. She was actually spasming in his arms.

"Was it something I said?" he asked wryly from underneath her hand. Sari took her hand away from his face and lightly tracked circles with her fingernails on the nape of his neck, twisting and untwisting her fingers into his curls.

"Yes. Remind me to lend you one of my books sometime," she said into his ear, taking a tiny, playful little nibble of his earlobe.

Gab didn't hesitate and walked up the small set of stairs leading up to the bedrooms. His curtains were still open, so he had just enough time to notice that the sky was getting purple. Dawn was about to break.

He put her on the bed and pulled off his shirt.

"Woah woah woah," Sari exclaimed, her eyes wide as saucers as she took in his body. Gabriel never had a reason to be shy about it, and he wasn't. He was the kind of brother who went to the kitchen without a shirt in the summertime. So what if he stood a little straighter, flexed just a little bit? "Your brazo, my God."

"Thank you," he grinned. "Your turn."

She pulled at the hem of her dress, but hesitated.

"Sari?" he asked.

"Just…don't laugh."

She was firm, and suddenly very serious. And damn it, Gabriel was never good at things like that. His siblings knew better than to ask him not to laugh, because he almost always did.

But she lifted her dress over her head anyway, and he could see her hold her breath when the dress was tossed aside. It was so quiet outside that he heard the fabric drop to the floor, heard her suck in her breath. He saw the way her stomach dipped in when she did that, too.

She was beautiful. He loved the shape of her body, the way her skin was soft against his hands. Every little scar, every mark on her, he liked. He ran a hand through his hair, and didn't realize he was biting his lip until he bit too hard.

"Ow," he said.

"Oh stop." She rolled her eyes.

"No. You're beautiful."

"Gabriel, you don't have to—"

"I'm serious," he said, fixing her with a gaze that he hoped showed her how much he wanted her, how much he desired her. "May I?" he asked, reaching out a hand and taking a step forward.

Sari gave him a single nod, and inhaled sharply when he touched her hip. He felt ridges under his fingers as he moved against her skin, and when he looked down, he noticed that dark brown stretch marks traced up Sari's curvy waist, the ones on the sides almost white when he pressed the skin. She had some around her breasts and arms as well.

"Don't look," she told him.

"I want to look," he whispered, pressing his forehead against hers as his hands brushed her stomach.

"Don't hate them."

"They're a part of you. And I would never hate any part of you."

As if to demonstrate his point, Gabriel went down on his knees and placed a kiss on her stomach, tracing the marks with his fingertips.

"I've been told that I shouldn't like this," Sari said, her words slow and possibly carefully chosen as Gabriel continued to kiss her everywhere she gave him access. "That I shouldn't display certain parts of me."

"Whoever told you that is an idiot."

"And you know this how?"

He paused, his lips hovering near her hip. Gabriel looked up at her, saw her pupils wide and her breath getting short.

"Because of the way you kiss me." He trailed his hands from the outside to the insides of her thighs, and he saw goosebumps rise up her arms at his light touch. "I made a promise to pleasure you, Sari, because I knew that you would like it. A *lot*."

"Oh." Sari seemed to relax, and Gabriel brushed his thumbs against the waistband of her underwear.

"May I?" he asked, and he was sure that this was what he wanted. He'd told her that this was what he wanted. He wanted to give her pleasure, make her skin flush and her body twist and writhe.

"Yes," she breathed, and Gabriel's entire body hummed in delight. But he took his time, slowly sliding her underwear down her waist, onto the floor. As if to mimic his moves, Sari reached behind her and snapped off her bra, revealing full, gorgeous breasts, begging for his touch.

He couldn't help it. He laughed.

"What the hell?" Sari asked, taking his pillow and thwacking him upside the head with it. "Bastos!"

"I'm sorry!" he said, putting the pillow aside and leaning over her, kissing her to placate her. "I just saw your boobs and remembered all the wonderful words you can use to describe them."

He lowered his face and kissed the top curve of her right breast, almost like he was apologizing to them. Which he was, a little bit.

"Like?" Sari's perfect eyebrow arched. He tried not to think about how the early morning light was making her skin glow, making her look softer somehow. This was not the time.

"Boobs," he said instead, his voice low and husky as he kissed another spot.

"Breasts."

And another.

"Tits."

He took her right nipple in his mouth and swirled it with his tongue, making Sari moan.

"Dibdib."

"That's chest."

He moved to her left, keeping a hand on her right, coaxing and feeling Sari's skin in his hands. She was blushing fiercely, shamelessly enjoying his ministrations too much to correct him.

"Décolletage."

"That's cleavage," Sari managed to say.

"A thousand apologies, milady. But you're just so…" he said, unable to stop himself from kissing her lips, taking her face in his hands, rubbing himself against her. He cupped one of her breasts with his hands, loving the way his fingers didn't quite cover them, the way her nipples pebbled with a few light touches against the cool morning. They weren't perfect, but they were hers, and that was what turned him on.

"So impatient," Sari finally giggled, her hands moving to the waistband of his jeans, expertly unbuttoning his fly before pulling them down along with his boxers. "Condom?"

"Yes. God yes."

What was it about early morning sex that made him feel like he had all the time in the world? Even with the condom already on, Gabriel was in absolutely no hurry, making good on his promises to Sari, her cries of pleasure cutting through the silence of the dawn.

Her back arched and he slipped his fingers deeper into her, his tongue laving at her clit. She showed him how she liked it, and there was nothing more erotic to him than the sight of her own fingers showing him how to pleasure her. It was better than any sugary, candy treat, and it was all for him.

"Oh my God," Sari gasped, one hand gripping the sheets, the other playing with her nipple. His cock stood at attention at the sounds he elicited from her, and he was so ready for this that he was actually shaking when he nudged her legs open.

"Don't go slow," she gasped, and they both hissed when he first entered her. It was always an adjustment,

the first time with someone, but sweet tension built between them, so delicious and tangible that Gabriel could
probably frost a cake with it.

Sari licked his neck, following it with a tiny suck.

"You taste like sugar," she managed to say before he
sank deeper into her.

"Fuck, you're delicious," he said back, and she raised
her hips in return. Gab didn't stop to breathe, what was
breath when he had to go this fast, this hard?

They moved and shuffled and rocked, and there was
nothing in the air but the sounds of their sighs and
groans, the "yes, yes, yes" from him and the "fuck"s
from her.

And when he came, it was like there was nothing at
all. The whole world fell away in white-hot light, and
he was completely spent. He didn't even know when
Sari got her second orgasm, but he felt all his energy
drain out of him, and sleep finally catch up. He gave
Sari one last kiss, as if to thank her after he was done
thanking God for this.

He noticed her eyes drooping, and he slowly started
to slide from underneath her. He highly doubted a hug
and roll was the best course of action at the moment.

"Where you going?" Sari's words were slightly muf-
fled by her own face, pressed into his chest as it was.

"Can't sleep naked," Gab reasoned. "I'm just going
to put my briefs on really quick."

He saw Sari's shoulder shake, felt her laughter vi-
brating in his body, and he squeezed the skin on her
waist in retaliation.

"Don't laugh, it's a thing. I've had brothers and
roommates most of my life."

"Okay," she conceded, slowly moving to the spot beside him, and Gab leapt off the bed, putting on his boxers before he crept in again. Sari immediately curled around him, her fingers and toes cold, and he shuddered.

"Go to sleep," she said behind closed eyes.

"Yes m'am," he said before he slid his arm under her, pulling her close. She fell asleep on top of him, and he fell asleep just as the roosters started to crow at the morning.

Chapter Nineteen

December 20

As much as Sari loved reading historical romance, she didn't much like romantic comedy movies, mostly because there was always a particular scene that she hated. You know, that scene when the heroine wakes up and finds herself in bed with a complete stranger? There was always screaming, and sheet pulling, and she would have no idea how it happened or why, and oh, wasn't this mystery guy surprisingly ripped?

No, just…no. It was portrayed as cute, almost comical, but it sounded like a terrifying situation to Sari. It didn't sound fun at all, having no idea how you ended up in bed with a stranger and waking up next to them naked. Nope, no thanks.

But this morning, with the sun beating down through her window, and her body and feet warm, she woke up and found she wasn't scared at all. She knew who she was with, what they had done the night before, and she was sure of where they were.

He looked at her and smiled, and her entire heart filled with joy. *There you are*, his gaze seemed to say. *I'm happy you're here.*

Sari wriggled her toes, and Gabriel squirmed underneath her.

"Your feet are cold," he complained, his eyes still closed. Sari wriggled her toes against his warm leg in retaliation, making him squirm again. His squirming was enough to press a bad case of morning wood against her hip.

"And you are *really* awake right now," she teased him, pushing her hip against his erect cock and making him groan.

"May I just say," Gabriel said, his voice still sleep-hewn as they snuggled together in bed. "You went on a date with me."

"I asked *you*," she pointed out.

"Yeah, but still. After asking. And asking. And asking. We're finally on a date. I win."

"Not for long," she laughed, wriggling out of his arms to sit up, and dropping the sheet that was over her chest. Then she kissed him, sweet and deep.

"Oh, sweetheart, you make me want you so bad," Gabriel sighed, his voice still rough with sleep, and Sari kissed him again. And again. She found she quite enjoyed it. Even more so when Gabriel opened his eyes, looking into hers as his hand lazily made its way between her legs. The boy was a fast learner, and by the time Sari had come down from her early morning Os, she was perfectly content to sleep again.

When they were done, and a proper mess was made, Gabriel nuzzled his nose against the spot underneath her ear and said the one thing she was hoping he would say.

"Are you hungry?"

* * *

"Any diet restrictions I should know about?" Gabriel asked over his shoulder as they walked single file from his bedroom to his kitchen. "Allergies?"

She really liked his house. The size and the open layout was perfect for a small family, and that tree swing in the yard was just beautiful. Had Sari had a choice of where to live, she would maybe live in a place like this.

"No allergies. I can eat anything," Sari said, waving a hand in front of him as they walked in. She quite liked his kitchen—it was bright and sunny, and at the front of the house, so it had a view of the driveway, with little purple flowers growing underneath some window boxes. "Where's your coffee?"

Gabriel, who was currently bent over his fridge (providing her with an excellent view of his bubble butt in his boxers), stiffened suddenly and slowly looked over his shoulder at her.

"I…don't have any?"

Sari gasped, like really gasped, like she was in a bad B-grade horror movie.

"Are you serious?"

"Yes?" he asked, retrieving food from cabinets with an ease and casualness that only came with experience. Without batting an eyelash and with the flick of a knife, he started chopping things like he was Cooking Master Boy himself. "I have coffee when I get to the bakery."

"Oh my God." Sari actually grabbed the countertop for support. "You cannot tell me that 3-in-1 is your favorite coffee."

"It's not!" he said right away, keeping his eyes on his chopping. "I just…haven't found anyone who makes my favorite coffee yet."

"Okay, fine." Sari shook her head. "I might as well tell you. In the interest of full disclosure, and so we can get this out of the way. I ate a bit of your cupcakes yesterday. Which may have prompted…all of this."

"Which one?" Now it was Gabriel's turn to gasp, like it was the most important question in the world.

"The birthday cake one."

"Rose, of course," he chuckled, shaking his head as he resumed cooking. "She is going to love that."

There was almost a snort of derision that followed that, but Sari pretended not to notice.

"Your sister is going to love that I was seduced by her cupcake flavor?"

"What? No, I…never mind."

"You're the one who brought this up." She grinned, but dropped the subject anyway. "So, since I've had your cupcake, you have to have my coffee. I have a knack for knowing what people want."

"Hmm, a challenge, I like it." Gab nodded, tossing things into a frying pan. "Okay. We'll go after breakfast, which will be ready in…five minutes. I hope you like tuyo."

"As long as you serve it properly. Rice, tomatoes and patis with calamansi."

"I'll make you a thing that will blow your mind. Hang on."

"For dear life," Sari joked before she left the kitchen to look around the house. Gab had said something about having too much space, and it showed. Aside from the couch with its plastic still on, the two-person dining table with two chairs and his shoes by the door, there wasn't much else to see. Sari wondered how long he'd been living here, if he had any plans to spruce the place up. A framed photo here, a potted plant there. Sunday Bakery was practically plucked out of a carefully curated interior decor Pinterest feed, with neon lights, subway tile walls and mosaic floors. This house seemed extra drab in comparison.

Sari was struck with the realization that her house would look much the same when Sam moved into their grandmother's place at the farm. Sari pulled the bedsheets closer to herself, refusing to entertain the thought even further.

Lipa was a place where you settled down roots, made a living and stayed. Sari had tried Manila, but she couldn't resist this place's siren call. She had come here knowing she would stay. She hadn't been able to imagine leaving.

Seeing how Gabriel set everything up here made her wonder if he felt the same way. Was he planning on staying? Or was he, like most things, temporary?

"Tuyo, sinangag rice with my mom's special tomato mash," Gabriel exclaimed with a flourish, bursting out of his kitchen in just his apron and boxers, holding up the plate of dried and fried herring and a plate of mashed tomatoes drizzled in a little of the pan oil and patis. Then he came back out with rice, both plain and fried with garlic. It was a feast. Sari's stomach immediately grumbled.

"Wow, you certainly know how to make a girl feel special."

"If I knew the way to your heart was through your stomach, I would have pushed you on those sinturis muffins the day we met." Most of Gabriel's plate was already carrying mountains of rice and fish, and he dove right in with his freshly cleaned hands.

"Oh, but wasn't it all so much better this way?" Sari teased, scooping the garlicky rice onto her plate, taking a taste of the tomato. It was perfectly seasoned, and the patis made it salty enough to go well with the fish. "This tomato thing is amazing by the way. I'm stealing it."

"My mom was all about finding ways to get us to eat vegetables," Gab spoke in between bites, and Sari had never seen anyone eat like that. "This is my favorite breakfast. I would have it every day if I wasn't so lazy. My sister Mindy and my mom visited me in Singapore once and the only thing I asked for was tuyo. And tocino. And Vienna sausage. And pancit canton."

"That's all?"

"Mindy complained that her luggage smelled like fish, but it was so worth it."

"Do you miss them?" Sari asked, but immediately regretted it when she saw Gabriel completely stop at the question, like he hadn't expected it at all. He kept his eyes on his food, but was now attacking it with a lot less gusto.

"Yeah," he said, not looking at her as he continued to eat. "I miss them every day, actually."

"So why don't you tell them you're here?" Normally Sari would have a much bigger reaction than this, but she didn't think she had a right to that, especially since this was Gabriel's story to tell, if he wanted to.

"My dad and I are currently having a…disagreement. He thinks baking isn't a lucrative enough career for a man, and until I prove him wrong, I can't talk to him." Gabriel looked ten years younger as he squirmed where he sat, and it broke her heart. Sari, who had never really experienced having parents who cared about you so much that you hated them for it, wasn't quite sure what to say.

"Why doesn't he—"

"He thinks baking is for girls."

She took in a sharp breath with her teeth, because damn. That was messed up. And really, as the expert in Shitty Things Parents Say, she knew there wasn't much she could say to rectify the situation. It was always a hard thing for kids, to find out that their parents—the ones who taught them the difference between right and wrong—could be very wrong, indeed.

"I'm sorry."

"It's fine. Let's not talk about it, okay? I don't want to ruin the morning." He shrugged, and if she had actually used utensils this morning she would have wanted to squeeze his arm. Purely to reassure him, of course. "Eat your rice. We're going to Café Cecilia for coffee."

"I do like a man who knows what he wants." Sari smiled, and the look Gabriel gave her back was so warm and sweet that she felt the need to return it. How unexpected that the boy next door would be the boy that would make her feel this way.

It was wonderful. Honestly Sari never figured she would feel this way about anyone. She was twenty-nine and had been fully with Team No Boyfriend Since Birth. But Gabriel was just so…himself. And he looked at her like he liked her exactly the way she was.

"You're picturing me naked again, aren't you?"

"Oh, shut up."

Chapter Twenty

For reasons that should be obvious, Gabriel was in a fantastic mood. It was always fun, starting something with someone. And it was extra fun because he really liked Sari. She was brilliant and whip smart, cutting when she was in a good mood, quiet when she wasn't. Honestly she could take over the entire world if she wanted to.

For today, she was trying to figure out his coffee order.

"Are you sure you don't need help?"

"Ssssh, sit down and shut up." Sari didn't even look up at him as she busied herself around her lair. Gab rested his elbow on the counter and cupped his chin with his hand to watch her.

He loved watching her behind her coffee machine, moving through the steps like nothing about the process could rattle her. She smiled when she made espresso, hummed when she added milk or water, focused when she dunked the cup into the steam spout thing. He liked watching her in her element, it was incredibly sexy.

She slid a little espresso cup across the countertop toward him.

"Café Cubano for Dimples?" she asked. Gabriel's immediate reaction was to take a picture. Sure, he didn't use social media anymore (it was too much of a hassle, especially with the huge-ass lie he was telling), but the instinct to take pictures was still ingrained in his millennial brain.

"This looks good," he commented, looking at the light amber froth on top, hiding the dark brew below. He'd seen Sari stir brown sugar into this, too. He raised his cup to her and toasted.

"To our next Simbang Gabi adventure," he said. "I already have a plan."

"Oh, really?" Sari asked wryly, taking a sip of her coffee. "Do tell."

"It's a surprise. I don't want to—oh shit," he said, lowering his cup because he'd tried to be cool and sip and talk at the same time. "WOAH. What is this?"

"Cuban coffee? It's interesting, isn't it? You flavor the espresso shot with this frothy, whipped demerara sugar that you make with the first drops of espresso. So it's not just dark, it's really sweet too, like molasses. I figured it was your favorite. And considering we didn't sleep all that much last night…"

"Naughty. And this is amazing. I'll never sleep again." Gab nodded, taking another sip. "But it's not my favorite."

He finished his demitasse serving and felt the zing of caffeine and sugar course through his body, making him stand up and cross the counter, just so he could kiss Sari. He cradled her face in his hands and he loved the way she just melted into him, like demerara sugar in hot espresso.

She sucked on his bottom lip, and nibbled lightly before she pulled away.

"Sorry. You had sugar on your lip," she said, licking the corner of her own lips like she knew it was his favorite part of her.

"Wow, who's bastos now?" he asked, and her face split with laughter. She pressed her forehead against his chest, and Gabriel had never realized how nice it felt to have someone in his arms like this.

"I'm determined to find your favorite," she told him. "Now go. Make people happy with sugar. I like nuts in my cookies, just saying."

"Oh, I had a feeling," he said, brushing her hair away from her face, even if it wasn't really there, just because he had the privilege. "I have an idea that I'm trying out today."

"Will I get to taste it?"

"Only if you're really, really good." He tapped the tip of her nose and pulled away.

"Ugh, you guys are disgustingly adorable, and I can't even hate you for it because I'm so happy for you," Sam interrupted as she walked into the coffee lab with her black mini-horse following dutifully next to her. "Ate, your barista was asking about the Cecilia blend you wanted to use?"

"Right!" Sari jolted up from where she and Gabriel were huddled together, and she knew exactly where she was going to get whatever Sam needed. "Work. Coffee. Things."

"Mm, I like all those things," Gab agreed.

"Sweet baby Jesus," Sam said out loud while looking at the ceiling. "Lola, look at your apo, so malandi."

"I thought you were the one who wanted her to walk naked around the house? You didn't say which house," Gab felt the need to add, which only made Sari gasp and blush furiously while Sam gaped at him like she couldn't decide if she liked him or hated his guts. Gabriel laughed. He had the strongest feeling that Sam would get along well with his siblings, but cut the thought off almost immediately. There would be no siblings meeting, no teasing, no Dabarkads gathering where they would be asked when they were getting married. No.

"What have I done?" Sam shook her head, pretending to collapse on the daybed. Gab found himself watching Sari work for a while, and had the sublime pleasure of seeing her in her element. She talked to her sister without missing a beat in the barista's usual dance with the espresso machine. Her hands knew exactly where to go, and she was smiling, and exactly where she was meant to be. And for someone who so rarely shared herself with other people, seeing her in her inner sanctum felt like the utmost privilege.

The lab was neat as a pin, which was very much like her. But it was warm and homey still, especially with the daybed and the floor-to-ceiling bookshelves. This was a room that was definitely lived in, and the kind of room one settled in.

This was her place. She didn't look like she wanted to leave it.

A pang hit Gabriel's chest as he imagined not being here anymore. Who would talk to her at the fire escape? Who would dance with her through their shared windows?

Not yet, he reminded himself. *The mall deal hasn't happened yet.*

"You were the one who wanted me to have naked dance parties at home, Sam." Sari sipped her coffee as if completely innocent in this scenario. Already Gabriel was looking forward to all the shenanigans that they were going to get themselves into—into, out of, through.

"I'm going. Dog, Sam, Sari." Gabriel nodded to Kylo, who blinked at him in response. "Merry Christmas."

"I can't believe you greeted the dog first," Sam protested.

"I'm seeing your sister later, and the dog isn't allowed in my bakery," he said, giving Sari a little wave before he decided to take a new route and walk down the steps to go through the café to get outside. He could swear he heard the two sisters exclaiming over each other behind him as he descended the steps of the coffee lab and walked out the door.

There were exactly ten steps between Sari's doorstep and his. He counted them out today, his smile getting bigger and bigger with each step. Did he have his hands in his pockets while he was whistling? Why yes, he did.

Hello, kilig, my name is Gabriel. So this is what you feel like.

"Psst, hijo," Ate Nessie greeted him after he went back downstairs and joined her at their usual bench. "Did I just see you coming out of Café Cecilia?"

"I plead innocent until proven guilty."

"Oks, pretty boy." She rolled her eyes. Such tenacity and judgement from such a wise woman, but Gabriel thought it best not to tell her that. "Are you still coming to help me set up aré?" She pulled a box out of her pocket, waving it at him. It took Gabriel a moment, but he realized it was a cell phone, still in its packaging. Ate Nessie had been one of the big winners of the night at the Christmas raffle, winning a high-end phone that one of Kira's clients had generously gifted to be given away. Unfortunately, Ate Nessie didn't know how to set it up, and was ignoring the bidding war currently ongoing for it.

"Of course. I told you, it's a date." He crossed his legs as he sat next to her, pulling bonete out of the paper bag between them. Steam rose from the inside of the bag, and he took a deep sniff of the bread. It smelled like fat. Delicious, filling, fat. "Mmm."

"You have a visitor, by the way." Ate Nessie pursed her lips and used them to point in the direction of the front of the bakery. Gabriel followed the path her mouth made and realized that a lone figure was peering into the bakery window. Gabriel paused and tilted his head to the side.

"Santi?"

"Gabriel." Santi turned to Gabriel with a barely-there smile. Santi's hands were still in his pockets, and Gab would have been convinced by the illusion of utmost propriety and too-stiff neatness if he didn't have a bit of pizza flour on his neck. It seemed impolite to mention it, so he decided not to. "I need to discuss something with you."

"Is that a flower in your pocket, or are you just happy to see me?"

He looked confused. "Is that a dirty joke?"

"Never mind. You wanted to talk?"

Santi shifted uncomfortably where he stood, his gaze sweeping the Laneways like he was making sure nobody saw them together. Gabriel tried not to point out that his gaze lingered a hair too long on Kira's shop. Santi coughed to clear his throat and glanced at Ate Nessie.

"Maybe we can talk somewhere a little more private?"

"Ala eh," Ate Nessie rolled her eyes. "That's my cue to leave, I guess. Gabriel, I will be back so you can set up my cell phone. Do not let Santi eat any of the bonete."

"Oks. I'll guard them with my life." Gab nodded, cradling the bag in his arms as Ate Nessie narrowed her eyes in Santi's direction and left the bench.

"You know she's going to tell everyone we're having secret discussions," Gab whispered, opening the door to the bakery for him. Santi coughed again and entered the shop, which was empty for now. It usually was at eight in the morning, then nine a.m. hit and people would come streaming in. "You really need to see to that cough, Sants."

"I'm not sick, it just helps make a point sometimes." Santi slid into one of the seats, and he looked hilariously out of place in Gabriel's bakery, especially in his crisp pants and gingham shirt.

"Coffee?" Gabriel asked. "I only have 3-in-1."

He winced. "That's fine."

Readers, it was not fine. Santi got his coffee from Tomas Coffee Co., and it was very not fine. Gabriel's eyebrow shot up. He was aware of very few things about Anton Santillan, one of which was that Santi was the most particular guy in the planet. He ordered his restaurant's desserts from Gabriel because according to Santi, Gabriel's tiramisu and cannoli were "adequate." He was the only place in Lipa that had their own exclusive blend by the Tomas Coffee Co. because the ones they sold commercially were "passable."

He just didn't seem like a 3-in-1 kind of guy, was what Gabriel was saying.

"Is everything okay? I can't tell if you're spooked or excited." Gabriel frowned as he settled back into his seat, Santi cradling his coffee and Gabriel with a bowl of shredded star apple with evaporated milk that Faye had given him when he came in, the bonete already safely set aside to be warmed up later.

Santi wrinkled his nose at the bowl.

"What is that?"

"Star apple," Gab said in between bites, his mouth full of the milky, grainy purple flesh of the fruit. The milk took away some of the tang of the sap, leaving only the fruit's sweetness. "Talk."

"Right," Santi's nose was still wrinkled, even more so after he took a tiny sip of coffee. "I just came from a meeting with the Lai Group. They want Sunday Bakery. Apparently your little prank war with Sari got a lot of attention on social media, so they're ready to make us a lease offer. Their first choice deferred the lease, so we're getting the prime spot."

Gabriel nearly dropped his star apple and his spoon, but his mouth hung open anyway. For all of Santi's propriety and fussiness, Gabriel totally respected him. Santi had almost single-handedly restored his family's crumbling hotel near Alaminos Road, turning it into one of the most exclusive wedding venues south of Manila. Food from La Spezia, his restaurant, was talked about by anyone who was anyone in the Philippine food scene and always made "best of" lists from *Best Eats* to *Lifestyle Asia*.

But most importantly, Santi was really supportive of Gabriel, and was the reason why Gab was able to open the bakery. And the thing was, Santi hadn't exactly kept his movements about the Lai Group a secret. Gabriel had just…decided not to think about it.

"Oh," Gab reacted, trying to seem cool, when inside, he didn't know if he should celebrate or storm off in a huff.

Wasn't this everything that you wanted? he asked himself. *Wasn't this the whole reason why you came to Lipa? Why are you hesitating?*

"They love the idea of Sunday Bakery," Santi continued, oblivious to Gab's turmoil. "They're offering us prime location at a cheap price, but only if we sign exclusively with their mall chains, and promise to expand to three stores in the next three years. Sending them the sinturis muffins was the perfect touch. So much so that one of the partners approached me and asked if we were interested in entering a joint venture for the expansions. He thinks you're the Christina Tosi of the Philippines, and wants to market the bakery that way, with you at the helm of it."

The compliment landed in Gab's chest and made his ego swell and grow. But the rest of it? Gab took a bite of his star apple, and the fruit tasted like ash in his mouth. Ever since he'd first pursued baking, his father had told him he wasn't going to make this a career, it wasn't viable, it wasn't for him.

Well, Gabriel had just proved him wrong. And he was really proud of himself for it. It felt amazing that this huge mall wanted him, wanted to partner with him. But he kept remembering the fire escape, the window he shared with Sari, and he just…he didn't know.

"They can announce next week if we say yes," Santi continued, subtly pushing away his coffee cup, preferring to tap his fingers against his thigh instead. "Are you in?"

Gabriel brushed invisible crumbs off his lap. His mother used to tell him that he always had crumbs on his lap, food on his mouth. Like he was trying to consume the entire world as fast as possible. And here he was, right at the cusp of getting everything he sought out to get.

This was what he'd come to Lipa for, what he and Santi had worked for. Gabriel had given up his family for this, and he was so close to getting it. It was going to be fine. This was what he wanted. He deserved this.

He nodded.

"I'm in."

"Really?"

"Really. Let's do this. I'm ready. You're ready. Are you ready?"

"Yes, of course." Santi looked mildly offended at the accusation, but didn't say anything else. "I'm going to hold off the announcement, just until the end of the holidays. I don't want this news buried. I want it out, and loud. Put it up on a tarpaulin loud."

"That's fine. Things are pretty busy here at the moment."

"Sure." Santi nodded. "And you're resolute."

"I'm what?"

"Resolute. Determined. Unwavering."

"I know what resolute means, Santi. I just don't think I've ever heard anyone say it out loud," Gabriel chuckled. "But yes. This was the way it was always going to be."

"Good. I'll let them know." Santi agreed, putting his coffee cup down after a single sip. "I think you've made an excellent choice, Gabriel. Welcome to the big leagues."

Santi actually smiled.

Chapter Twenty-One

December 22

The two Tomas sisters currently lived less than five minutes away from Lipa Cathedral. Gabriel didn't know who L. Tomas Street was named after, but he was sure it wasn't a coincidence that the family happened to live here too. It reminded Gabriel of his sibika classes, where he was told about how the richest of families lived closest to the church and the plaza. Had this been the colonial period of the Philippines, the Tomases would be pretty high up the food chain.

Sari was already waiting for him when he arrived, sitting in a moonlit patio in her usual white shirt, with a thin cardigan and a gorgeous green skirt that billowed around her. Her hair was pulled away from her face, and she wore red lipstick that drew attention straight to her lips. If he took a photo, she would look listless and bored, like a goddess stuck in a family meeting on Olympus. The only sign he got of her nerves was her foot tapping against the side of the table.

"Hey," he said, and she looked up, as if she didn't see him park his car in their driveway, as if she hadn't seen him be let in, or jog up the small set of stairs to the house's doorway. "Good morning."

"Good morning," she said back, and any nerves or fears she had seemed to melt away as she smiled.

"Yes, good morning," a third voice added, and Gabriel nearly jumped when he realized that someone was already standing behind him. The woman had a severity where Sari had softness, but was soft where Sari's hard edges were. She was also carrying a yoga mat under one arm, was dressed in tight leggings and a sports bra in spite of the pre-dawn chill.

"Selene Tomas." She held her free hand out to Gabriel to shake. Her grip was…firm, to say the least. "Are you a florist?"

"What?"

Selene pursed her lips in the direction of the abundance of flowers he was cradling with one arm.

"These? They're for you," he said, picking up a bunch of Queen Anne's lace flowers and handing it to Selene, who looked as confused and bewildered as Sari. "Then I have these," Gabriel continued, taking another bunch of bright orange mums, "for Sam."

"I'll take those," Selene said, taking the flowers and adding them to her pile. "And those?"

"For Sari," he finished, handing the last and biggest of the bouquets to Sari, a bunch of big pink peonies, still closed and waiting for a little sunshine and water to grow. Sari accepted the bouquet, staring at him like she had no idea who he was. Their hands brushed against each other on the exchange, and he managed to rub the back of her hand with his finger, just to assure her that *yeah, girl, this is happening.*

Behind him, Selene snorted and covered it up by clearing her throat.

"Are you attending Simbang Gabi at the Cathedral?" She asked them.

"Oh, I was thinking of going somewhere else tonight," Gabriel said, ignoring the look of surprise on Sari's face. "Just for something different."

"Well you're spoiled for choice here, I guess. She has to be in the café by nine," she announced. "Use a condom, please."

"We always do," Sari and Gab said together, making Selene roll her eyes before she went into the house, presumably because she had done enough sun salutations to pull the sun up from the sky like Apollo and his chariot.

"I've never seen my sister so impressed. Did you come up with this on your own?" Sari asked, picking lightly at the pink petals and smiling at him. Normally the question would strike Gab as rude, or condescending, but there was nothing Sari could ask from him at this point that he could deny. He was trying to make a good impression, after all.

"No. I stole it from the Viscount Babington, who stole it from the Duke of Hallmere."

She blinked at him.

"You…you read the Babington series?"

"My mother did. For a lot of my childhood I would come home early and she was at home with a new baby. She would put us all down for an afternoon nap by reading from the books—skipping over the dirty parts," Gabriel explained, shifting uncomfortably because he'd never told anyone this before. He'd never had a reason to before. He used to love listening to his mom read the books—most of the time having no idea what was going on, but his mother loved playing up the voices, using different tones and accents to entertain herself and her children.

"Huh. Which brother would you say you are?" Sari asked.

"Allistair, of course," he snorted as they walked to the gate. Gab's car was parked in front of the sidewalk. "He's the oldest."

"I think you're more of a Carter, the third brother. Eats a lot, travels to avoid his problems. But you don't have a problem with your temper."

"Give it a couple more years," he chuckled as they settled in. Once he was sure Sari had her seat belt on, he fiddled with the GPS on his phone and started their quick drive. "But I do like Carter. When he makes that declaration in front of everyone to defend Penny? It's the stuff of great romances."

Was it just him, or was this the biggest smile he'd ever seen from Sari?

They were still early when they arrived at the church of his choice. A little way away from the main thorough-fare of Lipa was Carmel Church, a sprawling complex that, upon entering, gave off serious Spanish piazza vibes, with the shapes of the buildings and the greenery growing there. Every wall was painted a fresh, lemony yellow that glowed even in the dark before the dawn. The entrance to the church was made of three portico arches underneath a rose window, and any embellish-ment to the building was painted a stark white. There were no vendors here, just people coming in for the mass. It felt more serene, quieter. Gabriel pulled the car into the parking slot and killed the engine, letting the night settle in between them.

"I like Carmel," Sari told him, looking around as they stayed sitting in his car, their seats both slightly reclined. Neither of them seemed ready to head to the church for Simbang Gabi. "Did you hear about the miracles that happened here?"

He shook his head.

"They say rose petals fell from the sky," she told him.

"Do you believe that?"

"About as much as I believe attending all nine Simbang Gabi masses grants me a wish." Sari laughed weakly, and Gabriel noticed she was nibbling at her bottom lip, staring at something on the console between them.

"You can hold it if you want," Gab said, flexing his hand, curling and uncurling his fingers like he was showing off to her. "I'm giving you permission. Come on, Sari. You know you want to."

She snorted and looked away just as Gabriel was doing spirit fingers for her. And just when he thought she was getting sick of him, with her head still turned away, Sari reached for his hand and squeezed it.

Gabriel wanted to jump out of the car and send the good Lord and the Virgin Mary his ever loving thanks for this moment. But that would have meant letting go of her hand.

"Are you still not going to tell me what you wished for?" she asked him suddenly.

"You don't see me asking you what you wished for," he argued, and she seemed content with that answer. He wondered how she would react if he told her about the mall deal for Sunday Bakery. Surely she would be happy for him, right? It was a good thing. And she cared about him, and possibly wanted good things for him.

But for the life of him, he didn't know why he didn't tell her then and there.

"Let's stay here for a while," Sari told him.

He could have stayed here with her forever.

"Are you really not seeing your family for Christmas?"

Until of course, she asked him questions like that.

"It's hard to explain how exhausting it is to be around them sometimes," he sighed, and he wondered how long he'd been carrying that particular thought around, because oldest brothers weren't supposed to think things like that. "My sisters would all rather have their teeth pulled than admit they're wrong, my brothers are so young I can only understand about half of what they're talking about—"

"Youths," Sari snorted like she'd long suffered a similar fate, and he chuckled softly because it was too accurate.

"Then my mom will fuss about everything, refuse any help to the point of stressing herself out, which will of course, eventually anger my dad. And of course there's Bubbles."

"Bubbles?"

"Bubbles. Part cat, part spawn of Satan and locked in an epic battle between himself and my shoelaces. And it's just me, he never does that to anyone else. I can't leave sneakers just lying around the house unless I want them to be completely shredded by the time I get to them."

"That sounds awful. But that's not why you're not going home."

"Funny, Kira never said anything about Capricorns going straight for the kill."

Sari squeezed his hand. "Is it your dad?"

"Of course it's my dad." Gabriel dropped his head back against his seat, exhaling a breath he hadn't realized he had in him. "He has such outdated views of what it means to be a man. And I didn't really notice."

"What do you mean? Because he didn't like what you ended up doing?"

"Yeah. The girls he encouraged to do anything they wanted, to work on things that would make them happy. He's harder on us boys, making sure we stay 'in line,' we know what it means to be 'a real man.' He would hate the fact that I have neon lights on my shop wall, that I serve pink cupcakes and wear pins on my jackets." He looked down at his little enamel pin, a dangly one with a pug and a star. *But not for long,* he thought. Soon his father would actually be proud of him, be happy for his son's success.

"I like your stupid pin," Sari clarified, and he turned his head just in time to see her watching him. "But continue."

"And my sisters are all stubborn enough to take that as a reason to rebel against my dad and become the scariest, strongest women I know."

"Good for them."

"I know. Lily's thirteen months younger than me, and I really think she's the oldest. Daisy's one year younger than her, and she takes care of everyone with the scary sort of efficiency that works on us. And Mindy is…well. She's a force of nature. She can do anything she sets her mind to. She and Sam should never meet." He couldn't help the little smile on his face, just imagining Sam and Mindy conspiring in a corner to take over the world.

"Then there's the younger kids. Ivy loves all French things, but I have a feeling she's growing out of it. Rose always feels like the middle child, but she's really the sweetest. Then Iris, who loves being the youngest girl. Old enough to bully the twins, but young enough to still get all the perks. Then the twins, Angelo and Mikael. My parents named them after the archangels but they might as well be Bubbles' accomplices for all the things they've managed to pull."

Gabriel pressed his lips together. He did that whenever he threw up too much, and right now he felt like he'd done just that.

"Sounds like you miss them."

"I do," he sighed. "I can't help it. I'll always be the kuya."

"So why stay away? If you're hoping your dad will change, I can tell you from experience that he won't." Sari squeezed his hand. "You can't change anyone. It's not your job. The best you can do is decide if you can still be there for them. If you still love them."

He knew she was right. And he knew that she knew more about this than he did. It wasn't going to do any good, keeping this rift between himself and his father open and gaping.

"I know," he sighed, putting her hand on his lap so he could trace circles on her palm. "I just... I need time away to wrap my head around this new reality I have to live with. I will never be man enough for my father, and I shouldn't care."

"We choose the kind of people we become," Sari said gently, her gaze suddenly far away. The church bells were ringing, and the mass was about to begin. "I think you love your family more than you hate what your father thinks of you."

"Let's get out of here," Gabriel proposed. "Are you hungry?"

"Always."

One of the reasons Gabriel had decided that Lipa would be a good place to settle in was because of the food. Here, everyone had their bulalo place of choice, a Filipino food restaurant of choice, and a favorite secret lomi spot. When he moved here, Gabriel took his time to find his own, and now he made sure Sari knew that she was the first person he'd ever taken there.

They pulled up in front of Rose's 24-hour carinderia, a little spot on the side of the road in front of his subdivision. It looked slapdash and put together at the last minute, as if the person who added this extension forgot about the project halfway through and left. But they had lots of seating, al fresco ambience and, according to them, served "probably the best lomi," and that had been enough for Gabriel to try the place.

Sari was actually rubbing her hands together in glee. Finally, something they both agreed on.

"I'm going to get extra chicharon on mine," she announced as they walked up to the shop and took their seats.

"Extra chicharon, and red onions," he agreed.

Moments later, large bowls of thick yellow noodles and equally thick pork-based soup appeared in front of them. The lomi almost stuffed to the brim with sinful things like pork belly, kikiam, squid balls, fish balls, pork liver and a generous sprinkling of crispy chicharon on top. It was always warm, and the flavorful amber colored soup always hit the right amount of saltiness. Sprinkled with patis, the soy sauce and egg took it over the top.

It was, in short, a bowl of heaven, and the perfect thing to eat this early in the morning.

"This is pretty good," Sari announced as they both slurped their soup noisily, ordering a 1.5 litre of Coke just because it matched the lomi perfectly, nevermind that it was four in the morning.

"You say that like you've found a better lomi hut."

"I have," Sari insisted. "It's in this old bahay na bato on the same street as Carmel, it's dark and slightly creepy, but I swear the lomi is the best."

"And yet I can see you're already halfway through your bowl." Gabriel tapped a little ground pepper into his, just because he liked to feel fancy. "Hmph."

"Give it time, little grasshopper, you will learn to not love the first lomi place you walk into." Sari scooped up a little bit of liver from her bowl and held it up to him. "Here. Peace offering."

Gabriel looked at the pieces of meat hovering above her bowl.

"You hate liver, don't you?"

"I noticed you ate yours right away, so I figured you liked it. It's the perfect solution." She smiled innocently at him. Gabriel pretended to be tired and exasperated, but she deposited his liver bits into his bowl after Gab gave her a nod.

"Hell's teeth, woman, you will be the death of me," he said in his best approximation of the Queen's English.

She gave him the most adorable confused look he'd

ever seen, but then she didn't say anything for a full minute, and Gabriel thought that this was it. He'd given up all of his cool cards and there was nothing left. And could the earth swallow him up right *now*?

"Can we bake something?" Sari asked instead.

Now that, he could do and still look cool.

"You're hijacking this date," he lightly accused her as they walked back to his car. "But yes. We can. I have a whole kitchen and a sprinkle cabinet."

"I think we both know that I've already seen your sprinkle cabinet," Sari giggled, wrapping her arm around his waist. *The way to Sari's heart is through her stomach.* Once her fingers found his skin, though, his entire body shuddered. The girl had the coldest hands and feet he'd ever encountered.

"Sari, it's twenty-three degrees outside." He said this the way he would say *you silly goose* right after.

Then, in admittedly one of his favorite moves, he took the edge of his jacket and tucked Sari underneath with him, letting the warmth of his skin envelop her. Sari snuggled closer to him, and he couldn't help but wrap her closer around him.

"Where to, m'am?" he asked.

"Sex, then cookies," she said, then she blinked. "Wow. Sentences I never thought I would say."

"If it helps, I think you're onto something," Gabriel laughed. "My place or yours?"

"Yours. I like your bed."

"As you wish."

Sari took the wheel this time, and the quiet was giving way to the noise of the dawn. The sky was a brilliant blue, a promise of the bright day to come. There weren't a lot of people out, anyone who was supposed to be in bed was probably still there.

It was a nice time to drive, this early in the morning. The streets would be free and winding, and it was so cold that it was better to keep the windows open. Gabriel managed to dig up his copy of *One Christmas* from his dashboard and was now blasting "*Kumukuti-kutitap*" on the unsuspecting passers-by. But everyone was used to a little noise now and then, especially here, where every street corner seemed to have a karaoke machine set up for the holidays.

"I like your house, did I tell you that?" Sari asked as they pulled into his driveway. Evidently, he'd forgotten to turn off the capiz lights under the acacia tree outside, and it made the tree swing look like something out of a fairytale.

"Thanks. I like it too," Gabriel said, and Sari just wrapped her arms around him. She was either really cold, or a snuggler, either of which he didn't mind so much.

They sat at the swing, and he liked that her feet didn't quite reach the ground. Gabriel used his feet to get the swing to sway them gently, but forgot to keep the momentum going when Sari curled into him and kissed him.

"I could kiss you all day," he said, chasing a longer taste of her bottom lip, kissing the corners of her lips quickly. "Your lips are delicious."

"Just my lips?"

"Sarcasm, Sari? Really," Gabriel asked, throwing an arm around the back of the swing, while the other played with the tips of her hair, which was blowing in all directions thanks to the swing.

"I just expected more from someone who found me irresistible."

He laughed, mostly because he liked that Sari was as bastos as he was, and kissed her again. The swing had slowed its movements now, and it was much easier for him to press his hand to her cheek. Sari lightly took his wrist and made his hand move down, down the side of her neck, to her shoulder, where her sweater was starting to fall.

"May I?" he managed to ask between kisses, and Sari's hand moved his to the collar of the sweater. Gabriel pulled down the sleeve with excruciating slowness, exposing the creamy morena skin on her collarbone. Sari tilted her head back to give him more access to the swathe of skin. He bent forward and licked the dip of her collarbone, lightly sucking on the exposed spot.

"You mean a lot to me," he said so softly that he almost wished she wouldn't hear it. "You know that, right?"

He lowered the sweater even more, and found the base of her throat, leaving a little mark there. Sari groaned and ran her hand through his hair, tugging slightly at his curls, letting her nails scrape his scalp.

"I know."

They found condoms in the bedside drawer, right where he left them. Thank God, because he had wondered if he had any left.

"Don't worry, I have spares in my bag," Sari said slyly, pulling his arms so he stood straight, his hands moving down to grip his favorite parts of her. He left soft kisses, deep kisses, kisses that were slow as the morning.

They were creatures of the dawn, the rest of the

world half asleep and half awake, while they were oh so alive. Here in the early morning, nothing could touch them, or change. Not yet, anyway.

"Sari," he said, his voice rough and husky as her hips rolled against his.

She pushed him backward on the bed, and Gabriel rolled them over so he was on top. Her breathing rose as his hands slid down, lifting her skirt and tracing a path to her inner thighs.

"Sari," he started again.

"No." She shook her head, placing both her hands over his mouth to stop him talking. "Don't say anything."

"Why not?" Although it came out sounding more like "wrrrnnnt?"

"You say the most bastos things, and I can't really focus on anything else when you start talking dirty," Sari complained, lowering her hands like she was surrendering.

Gabriel laughed so hard she had to poke his waist to get him to focus.

"I am…not sorry," he confessed, shrugging.

"See, this is my problem, you have the sweetest face, but the things you choose to say out of that mouth…" She shook her head, catching him in a kiss, as if to punish him for the naughtiness that Gabriel wanted to tell her.

"Forgive me, Sari. But I can't help it. You are fucking irresistible. I think you are sexy. I want to come inside you, to make you moan and groan until you can't take any more."

"Ugh." Gabriel wasn't sure if that was a moan of

pleasure or a groan of exasperation, and he loved it. "Put your money where your mouth is, Dimples."

He did like a challenge. He and Sari took off each other's clothes. He had a little mental map of what went where—it was the responsible adult in him—but who took what off, he didn't know anymore. And he didn't care, not when he had this absolute goddess on his bed.

"I want to try something," Gabriel announced. God, this woman was making his brain go haywire. "Trust me?"

"Is that a question, or a request?"

He started to reposition the both of them, and he couldn't help but see the spark of curiosity lighting up Sari's darkened eyes as she followed his lead. He lay down, and with one arm, pulled her up so she was sitting on his chest, her thighs so close to his cheeks. Her eyes grew impossibly wider, her breath already coming in quick gasps. Even Gabriel had to admit, he was excited.

"Hands on the headboard," he told her, pressing his lips together and using them to point to the headboard behind him.

"What?"

"Safety first."

He could see she was nervous, but she complied, her eyes on fire with lust and anticipation. She licked that sexy bottom lip, and Gabriel could. Not. Wait. He knew how to pleasure her, she'd taught him how. He lifted his head and gripped her thighs before he licked.

Sari's hips bucked into his face, and he liked it. The guys from New York used to say that going down on their partners was a chore, but to Gabriel, when you had a woman as delicious as Sari, it was no chore at all.

"Oh my God," she breathed as he found her clit and laved his tongue around it. "Wait, wait…"

He stopped. He could almost feel Sari clench at the loss of him.

"We can't. My thighs…"

"To die in your thighs is a heavenly way to die," he said, running his hands over the backs of her legs and squeezing her butt. "We can stop if you want. What do you want, Sari?"

She hesitated for a moment. Then, to Gabriel's disappointment, she let go of the headboard, slinking down and not-accidentally rubbing her thigh against his now very heavy erection. Gab groaned, suddenly he needed more friction. More contact. Sari's hand was *right there*.

"Ah ah ah," she said, kissing him, and he knew she could taste herself on him. She sucked his bottom lip. "We have all the time in the world for new things, Gabriel. Right now I just want you. I can't believe you're here."

He shifted so he was leaning over her now—so close he could count the eyelashes that almost touched the tops of her cheeks, could notice a tiny little scar under her right eye. Dawn was taking its time today, but he could see the lights dancing in her eyes. And it wasn't just lust. Lust was there, still hot and burning, but there was also happiness. The disbelief. The I-can't-believe-you're-here-and-I-like-it. All in her eyes.

"I can't believe I'm here either," he told her, giving in to the urge to kiss her irresistible, rosebud lips again. "Fuck, you're beautiful."

She raised her hips, and Gabriel's entire body stiffened as his erection rubbed against her hip.

"Put a glove on and let's get this show on the road,

shall we?" she asked. He wasn't going to last very long, he knew.

He bolted away from Sari, so fast that he could have outrun a cheetah in those two seconds, and grabbed a Tropical Hot Dalandan Delight, opening it and slowly slipping it on. Sari felt around his penis, as if checking his handiwork.

"Mmm," she said.

"Again, you're pretty bastos too," he helpfully informed her, taking her hands and lifting them over his head, using the headboard to keep them both steady. She loomed above him, her breasts within distance of his lips, and he slid inside.

Sari set a punishing pace for both of them, and it took everything in Gabriel to keep up with her. He lifted his hips, looped his leg over hers, gripped her hands tighter as she writhed and danced above him.

And when he finished, he nearly smashed his head into hers, the release way more intense than he imagined.

"Oh my God," Sari gasped, collapsing over his chest, her thighs squeezing him as Gabriel felt all his strength leave him. She slowly slid off him, making sure that the condom was off and everything was fine.

He slipped on his briefs and joined her in bed, wrapping his arms around her. He put a hand on her cheek and used the crook of his elbow to lift her forehead so he could kiss it.

"You kiss nice," she told him, smiling. "Can we bake cookies now?"

"Ten minutes," he yawned.

"Five."

They stayed for an hour.

* * *

The Laneways was quiet when they arrived—usually Gabriel and Sari were the only two people there that early in the morning, baking goodies or roasting beans for the day. In the daytime, both Café Cecilia and Sunday Bakery were bustling and busy, with people coming in and out constantly. Truth be told, Gabriel had never seen their places like this, quiet and with all the lights closed.

He noticed that a lot of things were the same—clearly neither of them ascribed to feng shui, with all the plants they had inside. Both places were airy and modern, the kind that let a lot of light in. But where Gabriel liked clean white subway tiles and an accent neon light wall, Sari preferred natural wood tables, cool toned walls and brown paper bags of coffee as decor.

Gabriel stopped in front of his shop door and paused.

"What?" Sari whispered, and he had a brief moment when he imagined that they were about to pull off an elaborate heist, which was exciting and hilarious at the same time.

"This is the first time you're coming into my bakery," he said in equally hushed tones, even if there was nobody else around to hear them. Deliveries weren't coming in until six, so they had enough time to make cookies. "This feels momentous."

"Just open the door." Sari grinned at him, and he turned the key. It was like opening the door into his own heart, and Sari was walking into it. She turned, and her skirt swooshed around her legs, and the smile on her face was so bright he wanted to remember it forever.

"What are we baking?" Sari asked as they went upstairs to the kitchen.

"I think I have ingredients for your favorite cookie," he said, pointedly trying not to look at Sari's reaction to seeing the inside of his bakery for the first time.

"Oh really? Do pray tell, what is *my* favorite cookie flavor?"

They walked in, and per usual, seeing the clean bakery waiting for him made him happy. For someone who always knew his place in his life—the oldest brother, the most responsible, the most reliable—this bakery was the place that felt most like home. It was a rare feeling, knowing he was at the right place at the right time, with the right person. How could he not bake cookies to celebrate?

"One of the best selling cookies in the shop is the Sosy Tita," he explained, going around the kitchen and grabbing ingredients and tools like he did this every day (and he did, but he was usually alone). "It's based off the legend of the Neiman Marcus cookie—"

"Where the woman bought the recipe and thought it was two dollars fifty, but it was actually two hundred fifty," Sari said, nodding. "Which never would have happened here, by the way."

"I know. It's all confusing," Gabriel chuckled, walking over to his apron rack and looping it over his head. "But anyway, when you think of that story, doesn't it sound exactly like the richest tita you know?"

"Ah, Sosy Tita makes sense now," she agreed, coming over so she could pull the apron up over his head. "Take this off, please."

Gabriel couldn't help it, he grinned. "Baby, I would love to, but I'm still a little tired, and it's not very sanitary."

"Get your head out of the gutter, baby." Sari rolled

her eyes and put the apron over her own head, tying it behind her back before Gabriel handed her a bandana to wrap around her head. "I want to bake. I didn't mean you were going to help me. Just tell me what to do."

Then she looked expectantly at him, with her apron on and her hair pulled back with a banana yellow bandana. Gabriel couldn't help it, he took a photo with his phone.

"Sari," he said, kissing her to placate her. "You know how I would never presume to come into your coffee lab and tell you how to make coffee?"

"Yes."

"So you see why I bake the cookies, right?"

"Fine," she shrugged, turning to the sink to wash her hands. "But tell me what to do. I'll help hand you things."

According to his idol Christina Tosi, the secret to the perfect cookie was to cream everything together so well that the batter was almost fluffy. Baking was a science, and cookies in particular turned out perfect because you took the time to blend each ingredient perfectly with the next, so much so that your dough shouldn't drop even when you placed it over your head.

"You're confusing cookie dough with Blizzards," Sari unhelpfully informed him, eating chopped walnuts that she'd deposited into her hands while Gabriel stood in front of his mixer. She had chocolate on her cheek and sugar on her neck and Gabriel had just realized that she was the worst baking assistant he'd ever had.

He bent forward and brushed the chocolate off her lip with his thumb before he sucked it.

"I thought you said you were tired?" Sari teased, and he shrugged innocently.

But she did pass him the ingredients when he needed them, and he had to admit, she was way more precise than he was when it came to measuring things. In short, they made a pretty good team.

"I could talk forever about double-rising-agent recipes, and using glucose over regular sugar, but I know what I'm talking about. Here," he said, turning off the mixer because the batter was perfect. "Taste."

He held his finger out to her, laden with cookie dough. Sari blinked at the offering before she looked up at his face and sucked the dough off, her teeth scraping his finger slightly.

Holy shit.

"Bastos," he managed to say, and Sari shrugged like she couldn't help it. Then her face changed. He'd seen it enough in his favorite anime, that second when the characters' faces go wide, accompanied by a little ping! sound before they floated away on magical food clouds and explained exactly why what they tasted was so good.

"It's so…fluffy," she said. "Fluffy and rich. I've never had cookie dough like this."

"See? Science," Gabriel declared, swiping a bit of cookie dough for himself. The recipe called for walnuts, oats, grated chocolate and his personal addition—potato chips. He'd come up with it after his mother came home with a box of chocolate-covered potato chips from Japan.

"I bow down to you. And you're right, this is my favorite." Sari nodded, taking more of the cookie dough, this time actually rolling it into a little ball before she ate it. "This really makes you happy, doesn't it?"

All of the breath was sucked out of Gabriel at that

moment. It seemed like such a simple question, but to have her asking him? It meant the world. It was worth all the burns and cuts he got in culinary school, the long hours he spent standing in a professional commissary literally just waiting for butter to soften, and the little snorts and derisive laughs he got from people, from his own father, when he baked brazo de mercedes for his mom, or cupcakes for his siblings.

"How much are you willing to bet that this dough never makes it to the oven?"

He was happy, and he deserved everything he got. And he wanted to share it with this girl, this clever girl who was stubborn, funny and just so damn amazing he was surprised that she liked him. He wanted her to be the first person in the world to know he'd done it. He was going to make his father happy, and he was going to get to go home.

"Sari, I'm opening a store at the Lai Mall."

And just like that, all the joy and the happiness of the moment stilled, like they had stepped into a different dimension, where time ceased to exist. There was only this space, their breathing, and Sari's face.

A face that he couldn't quite read. She didn't look thrilled or surprised, it was more…shock. Sari had a spoon of dough in her hands, and she put it aside to stare at him and just…blink.

"You're leaving," was the first thing she said.

His world crashed around him slowly. Like a deflating souffle, losing air slowly until it could no longer support its own weight. She was disappointed. And *hurt*. He couldn't understand why she wasn't happy with him. He wouldn't be able to take it if Sari got upset with him for getting the thing he came here for.

She bit down on her lip, and looked away before he could properly understand the emotions on her face. When she turned to him, her emotions seemed to see-saw from anger to…disappointment. He didn't expect her to be disappointed. "…oh my God."

"You don't seem happy about it," he said, and he knew he was pushing her buttons a bit, but he needed to understand. Why was she so disappointed? "Sari, it's a great opportunity, and I can't say no. I keep telling you, my dad—"

"I know, I get it," she said, even if she was shaking her head. She was slipping away from him, Gabriel realized, and he didn't know why. "No, I get it, I get it. He has to know how good you are at this." He wished he could just grab her and hold her close, and wished he wasn't breaking her heart. "Congratulations."

She took the bandana off, the apron off, and was fumbling around the kitchen like she didn't know where she was, but needed to know right away.

"Sari…"

"I have to go. I'm happy for you, Gabriel, I really am." She was already halfway out the door. "You totally deserve this. Save me a cookie?"

"Sari, come back, let's talk about this," Gabriel said, following her downstairs.

"There's nothing to talk about!" she shouted, and the ferocity of her tone took him aback. She shook her head, and he could see her walls rising higher than Fort Santiago, blocking him off from the parts of her he loved the most. "You're *leaving*. And I am not going to be one of those girls who makes you put your career on hold just so we can make out in closets and pretend we like each other."

"Hey," now it was Gabriel's turn to be a little fierce, gently taking her wrist to keep her from leaving. "Don't say it like that. You're making this sound cheap."

"This shouldn't mean anything," Sari said, moving her hands between the two of them. "Because if it does, then it means you went out with me knowing that you were going to desert the Laneways. Malls have done nothing but kill small businesses like ours. Like *mine*. I thought you'd settled here, that you were laying down roots like I have. I'm sorry that I was so wrong about you."

Gabriel had been a debater in high school and in college. He'd been trained to keep calm and keep his manner cool. He knew how to respond when someone was trying to tear him down point for point, and he knew exactly how to use his words.

But words failed him today.

He let go of Sari's wrist and slid his hands over her cheeks. Her eyes were glassy, and even in the darkness of the store, he could see they were brimming with tears she was holding back by sheer force of will. He waited for her to give him a tiny, shaky nod before he seared her lips with a kiss.

His hips jerked when Sari's cold fingers slid under his shirt, but she was holding on to him tightly. She kissed him back, almost as if she was trying to wrestle control from him, and he let her. He let her take the lead, but never let her go.

In the distance, they heard the roosters from nearby start to crow, greeting the new day. All of Gabriel's strength left his body, and he pulled away to see that Sari looked…absolutely miserable. He backed off immediately.

"I'm sorry," he said, and he didn't know how they were so happy just moments ago in the bakery. She was in pain, he could see it on her face, and it was all his fault. "I didn't…"

She shook her head and kissed him again, her nails scraping his scalp as she kissed him hard, like it was the last they would see of each other.

Why did it have to be?

"I can't stay with someone who's determined to help my home fail. And you knew I felt so fucking *alone*, and you—"

"Why does it have to be one or the other?" he argued, following after her. "You know how much I gave up for this, and I thought you would be *proud*—" He stopped himself quickly. It wasn't Sari's approval he was after. "I just thought you would be happy for me. I thought you understood why this would be important!"

"I guess that makes us both wrong, because I thought you understood that I wanted you to stay!" she roared back at him. "That everyone in my life is trying to leave me—"

"Nobody is trying to leave you, Sari! Your sisters are still here, and I'm still going to be here!"

Tears sprung in her eyes, and Gab recoiled. It was a horrible moment, to realize you were the reason for someone else's tears. He wondered if his father had ever felt this way when he and his mother fought. He wanted to take it back, it would be fine, his hurt didn't matter. But he couldn't. His emotions were valid too. And he never meant to make her feel like he would abandon her. He thought they could make it work.

"I thought you wanted me," he told her.

"Unlike you, I can't do it at the expense of my home,"

she said, and now Gabriel was hit with the shock of Sari breaking *his* heart. He didn't know what to say after that. He couldn't.

Seeing her chance to leave, Sari turned and walked away from him. Gab didn't have the heart to make her come back, or convince her why that was wrong. He just watched her close the door behind her, walk the ten steps back to her shop.

He stood there in the middle of his empty shop for a long time. For the first time, it didn't make him as happy as it used to.

Chapter Twenty-Two

December 23

"Where are you going?" Sam asked, after Sari showed up to Sta. Cruz in a blind rage a little later that same morning. The drive would have usually taken her fifteen minutes from the Cathedral, past Hotel Villa and down Alaminos Road until she reached the gates by the highway. She'd let her anger stew and simmer the last couple of hours, throwing herself in her work and refusing to look at the window. To Gabriel's credit, he didn't try to talk to her or convince her to talk to him, which only proved her point—he was leaving her.

And as always, Sari refused to be anything but fine about it.

"I missed Simbang Gabi," she said out loud, because it was already 9 a.m., and she'd felt too horrible and rotten to get up and go to Simbang Gabi that day. Innocent churchgoers and food sellers did not deserve her anger or frustration.

"That's okay, I'm sure Lola Rosario won't be too mad at you for it," Sam said gently, leading her sister through the door of the house. The restoration looked like it was going really well. Sari hadn't been to this house, even during the process of Sam's move, but that didn't mean she didn't appreciate it. "You do lose your wish, though."

Sari paused before she shook her head. "I think I've had enough of wishes."

As Sam had described, Sari could hear the rustling of the bamboo trees her grandfather had planted just outside. The inside of the house was nice, open and airy, all white concrete walls and hardwood floors from the Narra trees in the property. Sam's decor was sparse, and there were more rooms than she was certainly able to handle, but it was so worth it for the back garden the house opened up to, currently still a mess of grass and old dead trees.

Sari knew it was going to be beautiful when Sam finished it up.

Selene and Sam were supposed to be going around the farmhouse, making a list of all the work that still had to be done before the house was 100% livable. But Selene was asleep on the couch in the living room when Sari had burst in, asking for a beach bag.

"Ate?" Sam asked as she and Kylo followed Sari to the second floor of the house, the both of them barefoot as they'd left their slippers at the base of the stairs. Sari took the bag she had on her and overturned the contents on the perfectly made four poster bed. "What happened? I'm sorry I forgot to text you again last night, I was so wiped out here…"

"It's not you. I just need to get away from here."

"Why?"

"Does it really matter why? I need to go," Sari said, taking the huge tote bag Sam handed her. It was a bay-ong made of straw, with a soft cloth lining inside and pompoms attached to the outside. Cute, and totally clashed with Sari's mood, but she was in no shape to be picky. "I can't find my swimsuit, so I'm going to borrow yours. Have you unpacked it yet?"

"Yeah, it's in the upper drawer of the aparador." She pointed, and Sari pulled out a stool that she spotted nearby and used that to get to the top drawer of the closet, rifling through Sam's stuff before she found the bathing suit.

"This is my bathing suit," Sari grumbled, holding the suit in her fist and shaking it at her sister.

"An honest mistake." Sam waved her off. "But where are you going?"

"Wallet, keys, phone, lip balm, tissues, wipes, sunglasses," Sari murmured, once again giving herself a pat on the back for always carrying around too much. "I can buy sunblock in a convenience store. Can I borrow a towel? A mat?"

"Towels in the bathroom, and I'm pretty sure there's a banig in the bodega. You're going swimming?"

"I'm going to Laiya," Sari announced, her destination decided about a second before Sam finished asking her question.

"Okay," Sam said, following her sister as she retrieved the items she was borrowing. "Why?"

Sari paused in front of the bed and inhaled sharply.

"Gabriel and I just broke up."

"After three days?"

Holy crap. It had only been *three days*? It didn't feel right, even if all she needed to do was consult her calendar to know it was true. How could she possibly feel so strongly for someone she'd been with for that short of a time? Since when did Sari live her life like she was in a nineties rom-com? It wasn't even her preferred genre!

"Fine. I guess we were never really together in the first place," she huffed and stuffed a towel into a tote bag Sam had lying around. "But he's leaving, just like you are, like Selene and Lola and Mom and Dad did, and can I just have *one day* to myself so I can process it?"

Sam paused from where Sari was packing and tentatively reached out to her, but Sari shrugged her hand off. She refused to look at her sister, refused to register the hurt or the confusion on her face. She wanted out. Out of this, out of everything. And where did you go when the place you loved most in the world didn't feel safe?

The beach. Or at least that was what Sari thought.

"Fine." Sam's arms were already crossed over her chest as she and Sari descended the steps of the rest house, putting house slippers back on. "Go already. Take my car. Take Kylo."

"What?" Sari snapped. "I am not taking your gigantic horse—"

"Sari," Sam's voice was serious and a little bit angry, enough to make Sari startle and stop. "Take Kylo."

Very suddenly before her eyes, her baby sister turned into an adult, one with more wisdom and practicality than Sari would ever have. Given the features she'd inherited, Sam looked the least like their grandmother, but seeing her reminded Sari of their lola so much that her heart ached. Lola would have been proud. "You will take my keys, take Kylo, and take all the time you need. Just fill the tank when you get back."

Then, before Sari could say anything else, or refuse

her younger sister, Sam threw her arms around Sari, hugging her tight.

Minutes later, with Kylo already snoozing in the backseat, Sari opened her windows and drove as fast as she was legally allowed to the beach. It was December 23, and the entire road from Lipa to Rosario to San Juan and to Laiya was open to her. And there was not a single Christmas song to be heard.

"You have *got* to be kidding me," she told the receptionist, after she and Kylo arrived two hours later. "That's your *day* rate?"

"Christmas is a very popular time for visitors." The receptionist gave her a strained smile and Sari immediately narrowed her eyes. Next to her, Kylo stood and placed his paws on the table, panting slightly at the woman behind the desk, who jumped at the sight of the gigantic dog and his slobbery tongue drooling on her desk. "It comes with a cabana, a free drink and meals, madame."

"That's miss, to you," Sari said, and reluctantly handed her the cash. "One day pass, please. And whatever it is you charge for pets."

"I'll have someone take you to a cabana right away."

"Come on, Kylo," Sari said, gently tugging on the dog's collar to get him off the table before they headed out to the beach.

Geographically, Lipa was much closer to Taal Lake than it was to Laiya. The honor of best beach went to Lobo for its diving spots, and with Mindoro a quick ro-ro away, there were much more spectacular places to go. But Laiya was easy to drive to, easy to get in to, and when there weren't a lot of people, it could be exactly what someone needed when they wanted to get away.

There weren't many people now. It was still a work day, after all, but in the distance, the staff was clearly setting up for an office party, complete with the requisite karaoke machine. It was a little blip in the otherwise calm, serene horizon. If she had a boat and set out at lightning speed, she would be in Marinduque within the hour, Mindoro in even less time.

Sari and Kylo sat together under the umbrella set up for them, Kylo drinking greedily from a bowl of water while Sari nursed a bottle of San Mig Light and a bowl of saging saba con hielo while looking out at the sea. She was playing chill French music on her phone, the kind with a woman singing to a guitar and a double bass.

The sound of the waves was calming, and the salty tang in the air helped clear her foggy brain. Here there was no café to worry about, no sisters who never stuck around or wanted to move away, no Gabriels who were trying to leave her.

"We should have done this ages ago," she told Kylo, who came over to press his nose against her shoulder, as if making her move over before he dropped his gigantic body on the cool sand next to her. Sari absentmindedly started to scratch the big black dog's ears.

It was a beautiful scene, but Sari had to admit…it was horribly lonely. Even with Kylo by her side.

"Well, you're just going to have to suck it up and get used to this," she said out loud, not caring that tears had sprung in her eyes at that one sentence. Damn it. Where was coffee when she needed it?

Kylo grumbled and snuggled closer to Sari. She

sighed as her thoughts turned to the soon-to-be-empty house by the Cathedral. She could see herself walking around the house, growing older and more alone, just like her grandmother had. Lola Rosario was independent through and through, but never really let anyone into her life. She had three granddaughters she never really shared her life and her problems with, a son who couldn't care less about her, and a husband who had died too soon.

That's not exactly true though, is it? Sari reminded herself. *Lola Rosario had Lolo Marco until he passed. She shared her coffee and traditions with you. She shared her farm with Sam. She shared the business with Selene.*

She was never really alone.

And neither are you.

"Fine," Sari told Kylo, pressing her nose against his side while she scratched his belly. "I'm going to miss you. But you'll love living in the farm. Just…don't chase after the pigs. Or the chickens. Take care of Sam. Although we both know you're already doing a really good job of that."

Kylo turned and licked a huge stripe on Sari's cheek. She said nothing, but wiped it off with the towel. Then she whipped out her phone and dialed Selene's number.

"Ready to talk?" she asked, like she'd been expecting this call. Trust her older sister to know best about her. Sari sighed.

"Yes," she said, and she heard the sounds of shuffling, Selene calling for Sam to stop trying to clean the shelves wrong and to come here.

"Oh, is this an emotional, heart to heart sisterly meeting?" Sam's voice was amused as she came on. "I don't think we've ever done this before."

"Sari needs to talk to us," Selene said, using a perfectly neutral tone she used whenever she was trying to mediate fights between them. "Sari?"

"I miss you, Ate," Sari said finally, feeling a little odd talking about her feelings through her phone, but being unable to see her sisters' faces helped a lot. "I miss you when I don't know what to do, and that's a lot of the time."

"You can always call me, you know," Selene said, sounding a little hurt. "I'm never too busy for you or Sam."

"Yes, but sometimes I just want you to be my sister, you know?" Sam interjected, saying the exact thing Sari felt. "Like you don't have to be the boss all the time. I like knowing that you like to change up your nail polish, or that sushi is your comfort food."

"I didn't even notice that," Sari admitted.

"Oh," Selene said, like what Sam said had truly surprised her. And Selene Tomas no longer enjoyed being caught off guard. "Um. I feel kind of insecure about my nail polish addiction. It's…a lot."

"Ay, Ate, have you seen my collection of lipsticks? This is a shame-free, judgement-free zone," Sam said. "Right, Sari?"

"Right," Sari said, and let that be the jumping off point for her to say what was on her mind. "Sam, I… I'm still a little torn up about you leaving. I know I act like it's all fine."

"Sure," she heard Selene chuckle in the background.

"But I'm going to miss you. And I kind of hate that you left me in the house." Sari played with sand in her free hand while she tried to sort out her feelings. "It felt like you were leaving me because you hated me. Who's going to kill all the ipis now?"

"You think I'm brave enough to kill the ipis?" Sam laughed on the other end of the line. "Ate, I only do it because it's one of the few things I get to do for you. You and Ate Selene take such good care of me, I want to try to do it myself, so you guys have time for yourselves. I'm sorry I made you feel abandoned. But I'm still here! I will never leave you, and I will never really hate you, even if you want to push me away. I'll kick down all your walls if I have to. For you too, Ate Selene."

"I don't have—" Sari started to say, but didn't continue the sentence. She supposed that because Sam was only twelve when their parents separated, she was the one who got to live her life with a little less baggage than Selene and Sari.

"I left the house because I don't want you to worry about me anymore. But my God, Ate. I'm not leaving you!" Sam's voice was a little shaky, and Sari felt her eyes suddenly get hot with tears. It felt oddly cathartic to cry, not because she was angry, but because her life was changing, and still she had her sisters at her side, cheering her on, as she cheered them on too.

"Sari," Selene's voice, which, did Sari detect a little wobble from her? "Take all the time you need there at the beach. Sam and I will be here when you come back. And when you're ready…"

"Tell us exactly what that jerk Gab did so we can come up with a plan to take him down!" Sam yelled from the background. Sari laughed through her tears and agreed.

"I'll bring back buko pie," she promised, knowing it was Selene's particular favorite.

No sooner had Sari dried her tears and put her phone away, it started to ring, this time displaying an unregistered number. Suppliers, clients and interested customers all had access to Sari's phone number, so she didn't think twice about picking up.

"Hello?"

"Is...is this Sari Tomas?"

"Yes," she said suspiciously. "Sino sila?"

"You're Sari Tomas," the voice said again. "You... you're the one in the video?"

"Video?" Sari was totally confused now. In a world where social media presence was key, she wasn't shy to admit that the only time she was online was when she was managing the socials for Café Cecilia, so while she was technically adept, she didn't really check out what was going viral, who was getting married, who was getting engaged. For obvious reasons, it wasn't really her thing.

"The viral video of the lyre band flashmob in Lipa. That's you, isn't it?"

Sari's jaw dropped so low she was surprised it hadn't hit the sand yet. There were just so many questions. Who took the video? Who posted it? *Where* did they post it, and how on earth did this person manage to find Sari's number?

"Who gave you my number?" seemed to be the best place to start.

"Well, point one, anyone who saw the video can see the name of your café in the background," the person said like this was no big deal. "Point two, I Googled the name and found the café's number. After a phone call and asking your staff about you, they gave me your number. So…ta-dah."

Sari slapped her palm to her forehead. She was going to *kill* her staff when she got back to Lipa. Or re-train them. One or the other.

"Okay, well. Yes, that was me. Who are you and what can I do for you?"

"My name is Rose Capras, and I'm looking for my brother."

Sari nearly dropped the phone on the sand, but her gasp was enough to make Kylo look up at her curiously. Sari scratched the big black dog's ear until he relaxed again.

"You're vanilla birthday cake," she remembered.

"Yes, he did mention I was being immortalized in cupcake flavor," Rose sighed, and Sari wasn't sure if that was exasperation or relief in her voice. "Sorry, I'm really sorry about just calling you like this. But…you do know my brother, don't you? I recognized him in the video."

"Yeah, I know him. He's the guy in the video," she confirmed, collapsing backward into the beach chair.

"I knew it!" a voice exclaimed from the background of the other end of the call, and Rose immediately shushed whoever it was. "Sorry about that. Is it true he opened a bakery there?"

"He did," Sari said, picking up her saging con hielo and taking a huge bite. The bananas had been drenched in syrup just long enough that it still tasted like banana, but was made better for the sweetness. Yes, Sari was totally trying to distract herself from this conversation, because this wasn't her conversation to have. If she was petty, she would just text Rose her brother's number and be done with it.

But no. Sari wasn't petty. She was just…lonely.

"Your brother is really good at baking," she said instead on an exhale. "He makes people happy with what he does. And he misses his family a lot."

"Sure." Rose sounded annoyed, or at least Sari thought she did. "All evidence points to the contrary. He lied to us for a year."

"Sometimes it's easier to lie than to tell other people how we really feel. Or to run when we feel like we're backed into a corner," Sari said, and yes, she was aware that she was a hypocrite. Kylo didn't have to look at her like that.

"That sounds really stupid," Rose huffed.

"Well, no offense, but your brother is an idiot," Sari snorted, shaking her head. "But he's also here. Trying to be worthy of your dad."

"Dad again," Rose grumbled like she'd heard this argument a thousand times over. "Papa is never going to change. Kuya's just going to have to suck it up and accept that."

"I know."

"Okay," Rose said, and that was the surest thing Sari had heard her say. Based on their phone conversation so far, she had a feeling that Rose Capras wasn't always sure of herself. But you grew out of that, usually. "Can we…can we come there?"

"Probably a good idea to call him first."

"Probably."

"But you can text me here if you need anything," Sari said, just because she believed in solidarity among sisters with stubborn older siblings. And she wasn't about to subject Gabriel's family to a wild goose chase to Lipa without someone pointing the way.

Even if Gabriel was leaving her.

There was a shuffle on the other end of the line. Sari could hear arguments and hissing before someone took over the call.

"Miss Sari…" a voice she didn't recognize asked. She wondered which of the siblings this was. She usually got confused when Gab showed her a photo. But it was safe to assume it wasn't part of the older batch of kids.

"Oh God, just Sari, please."

"Ate Sari, then. This is Iris. Number seven, if you're confused. People usually are."

"Ah. Peppermint chocolate," she realized. Iris was the youngest of the girls, and (Gabriel had been happy to say) everyone's secret favorite. "I'm not confused. What can I do for you, Iris?"

"Can I ask…are you and my brother…?"

Sari braced herself. But thankfully Rose seemed to save her from answering the question by telling her little sister off (*"obviously* they're together!"). Iris was undaunted, though, and tried to argue that the video was unclear, and Gab's status was still set to single.

It was a full minute before Rose wrestled back control of the phone.

"Sorry about that," Rose said. "But I'll let you know when we get there. Thank you so much, Ate Sari."

"You're welcome, Rose. You too, Iris."

"Bye, Ate Sari!"

Then they hung up. Sari took one look at the calm beach, the utter peace of the waves and the sun beating down on the sand. Her dessert bowl was empty, her beer was gone, and her dog was asleep.

She stood up and stretched her arms, digging her cold toes into the warm sand. After a quick look to make sure no-one was watching, Sari pulled her shirt off over her head, revealing a modest but still sexy bikini. A teeny, tiny part of her wished Gabriel was here right now to see her and eat his heart out.

But he was about to have bigger problems.

"Watch my stuff," she told Kylo, who used her bag as a pillow and fell asleep before Sari walked toward the water. Who was going to stop her?

The caption "getting my vitamin sea" was a corny cliche because it was true. There was no better way to clear your head than to dunk your head under the salty water, floating with the waves as the sun kissed your skin.

This was when Sari had her big revelation.

When she and her sisters were younger, easier to bring around, their father used to take them to the beach. Sari knew, even early on, that the beach trips were his way of avoiding their mother, but she loved them anyway.

On those trips, her father taught her how to swim by holding her in deeper water before he let go of her and told her to relax.

Sari, of course, nearly drowned every time, until he picked her up by the armpits.

"You've gotta keep kicking, kiddo. The water isn't as deep as you think."

That was how Sari learned how to swim. Even when she was left by herself, as long as she kept kicking, kept her mind clear and had moments like this, she would be fine.

"I'm tired of kicking," she told the sky, spreading her

arms out over the water. Then she closed her eyes and gave in to the tide, letting it gently rock her. The water wasn't as deep as she thought it would be.

Sari was in a better mood when she drove back to Lipa, speeding down the highway with her windows open and her hair getting an instant blowdry by the wind. Kylo stuck his head out the window and howled, as if singing along to "*Christmas in Our Hearts.*"

Her phone rang again. Really, if Sari was ever going to actually run away from her responsibilities, she should learn to at least be on airplane mode.

She knew she couldn't, obviously, she was a sister and a business owner and couldn't afford to be on airplane mode, but a girl could dream.

Incoming Call: Dimples

Well, Sari wasn't about to answer. She had absolutely no reason to talk to him, they had barely been together long enough to leave any belongings with each other (unless their hearts counted, *ba dump tss*), or leave anything of importance to one another.

At the end of the day, she felt rubbed and raw, and any further provocation wasn't going to help. There were only so many times her heart could break, and with Gabriel Capras, it would take very little for him to crush it fully.

So it was better not to talk.

After letting it ring for a while, he called again. Still, she refused to answer, because it was a driving hazard. Because he had nothing to say right now that she was ready to hear. Because she was tired.

The ringing stopped. Then it started again.

"Hoy, why are you calling me, dimples?" she yelled at her phone, and by some weird flux of technology, it answered her.

Calling Dimples on speakerphone.

"Putang—"

"Sari," Gabriel answered on the second ring, and Sari jumped, because his voice was urgent and just a little bit loud. "What the hell?"

"Gabriel, I can't talk to you right now."

"Oh, really! You don't want to talk to me? You—"

Sari pushed the End button to hang up. Not her finest moment, but just hearing his voice made her pulse race and her heart break all over again. He was leaving, just like everyone always did. Sari might have already accepted that she was going to be alone, and she was going to be fine. There was nothing more they could do about it.

Kira Luz is calling, her phone rang, and Sari managed to answer, putting it on speakerphone again.

"Kira?"

"Sari, don't hang up, this is important," Gabriel's voice insisted, and Sari actually growled.

"You dirty bastard. You dirty, sneaking, underhanded, dastardly little…"

"I may be a bastard, but I slept on it, and now I have my fight back, and we need to talk about this."

"I think we already said everything that we needed to say."

"It's been eight hours, and I can't bake cookies for shit. Our dough is still in the freezer."

Sari bit her bottom lip at the use of *our*. There was no more *our*. As of eight hours ago he'd made it clear that this was nothing more than a little flap and throttle. Kiss and tickle. Whatever. And Sari had made sure it would stay that way. So she swiped at Gabriel instead.

"My presence has nothing to do with your baking," she huffed. "You've been doing this long before I came into the picture, and you're too good to let your skill slip just because I wanted out of this."

Hell or high water, rain or shine, Sari could pull an espresso or roast beans. It was one of the things she prided herself on. She found it hard to believe that Gabriel could just forget how to do the thing that made him the most happy.

"The point is, I understand that you don't want me. You don't want to listen to me, or care about what I have to say. Fine. What I…"

No, you dummy. I want you so much. That's the problem. I love you, and I can't bear to see you go is my problem. I hate you because you turned out exactly like everyone else. Sari inhaled sharply, and her breath was shaky. Sweat broke out at her palms, but she kept her hands on the wheel. Sari had been bottling up everything for too long now. So long that her own emotions were spilling out.

"…my sisters!"

"What?" She'd almost forgotten that Gabriel was still on the other end of the line.

"Rose and Iris are here," Gabriel said finally, his voice calm, but even from the other end of a phone line she could tell he was agitated. "They cut school and got on a bus to Lipa, then took a tricycle to the Laneways."

"Oh," Sari said, doing her best to focus on what he was saying. "And?"

"Rose doesn't even walk to Jollibee outside her school, Iris has never ridden a tricycle in her life and they came here. I don't even know how they figured any of this out on their own…"

"Aren't they both in college now?"

"You told them where I was."

Sari had always wondered what her reaction would be if someone accused her of doing something monumentally stupid. Apparently she did not take to it very well.

"You think I'm petty enough to call up your sisters, tell them you've been lying to them for the last year and make them come here to confront you?" She huffed. "Give me some credit."

In the back of her mind, she understood his frustration. If his sisters were anything like Sam, doing something as reckless as that, even if it was for her, would have had her hopping mad too. But Sari was in too deep into this yelling match with Gabriel now, and they were both acting like complete fools. It only served to point out that they were both too petty and too childish to be together, if they argued like this. Hell, this whole thing had started because of a prank war!

Well, no. This whole thing had started with a cookie. A cookie that a customer brought into her shop. Her brain went back to that moment in the kitchen, him in his element and her snacking on walnuts and chocolate, just watching him. She pressed her lips together. If she thought about it hard enough she could still taste the cookie dough. The chocolate, the nuts, the chips… it should all be too much, but it worked well together.

The cookies would have tasted like love. Damn it.

"Rose and Iris came here for you." She forced herself to focus on the conversation. "Do you know how lucky you are that in this entire universe, two kids cared enough to come to you? Did something they'd never done before, because they love you and missed you? You have a whole family that wants you around! I would kill to have someone do that for me!"

The last sentence made tears burst in her eyes, and she gasped, shocked at the sudden flow. It wasn't that she felt bad for herself. Oh no. She was just so…mad. At him, at what he was trying to push away, at herself, for doing the same to him.

Sari pulled up in front of a small roadside pasalubong center that promised the best buko pie in Batangas. The vendor looked like he was about to approach, but by then Sari was full-on crying, and it made him step back.

Emotions were pulling her down in their riptide, rollicking and rolling, tossing her in every direction. But oddly enough, they were emotions that Sari was familiar with, ones she'd fought against for so long.

Then she took a deep, shaky breath, and kicked against the tide.

"We can't all have people who always want to be around us, who want us to be around. So go home for Christmas, open your new shop, get everything you've ever wanted and everything you deserve. Don't be afraid."

"Stop it," there was barely a second of silence before he leapt in. "Sari, stop acting like you're being this… this martyr for me when you're the one who's scared! I told you, things don't have to change that much. I can still be here. You're the one who is too scared to admit that you *want* to make me stay. You be selfish! Fight me on this! Demand more because you deserve it!"

She didn't know how to respond to that. Honestly, she didn't, because nobody had ever told her that before.

"You don't believe me, that's fine. Push me away. Like you always will."

She sucked in a breath, because that *hurt*. She'd closed her own life off for so long that to have someone see right through her was absolutely horrible.

Her fingers hovered over her phone, tempted to end this conversation. But damn, that would just be proving his point, wouldn't it? On a scale of one to ten, how petty could she be?

"Sari?"

"I'm fine," she snapped, pulling tissue from the box she kept on the dashboard and blotting it against her eyes and her runny nose. "Or I will be. But this is not your concern right now. Your sisters are in your bakery, finding out about this whole secret life you had, and I'm sure they're worried. Rose called me. I didn't know that they were planning on coming alone. She and Iris sounded worried about you. So be the kuya and talk to her."

Then she hung up. There was only so much her heart could take right now.

Without missing a beat, she rolled down her window and smiled at the small group of onlookers that had now gathered at the passenger side window. For a brief moment, her brain told her to be alert, this was dangerous. You never knew what could happen.

"M'am, are you all right?" A woman who wore her hair in a bun exactly like her grandmother used to had approached the car, approached Sari like she was a wounded animal.

"I just got off the phone with my ex," the truth spilled out, and really, she shouldn't have said that.

"Get this girl a glass of water!" the woman said to nobody in particular, and the crowd scattered. Moments later, Sari was sipping water while Kylo poked his head out the open window and barked at the passers-by, as if to ask her why they were stopped in the middle of nowhere.

"Thank you," she said after she finished greedily drinking the contents of the glass.

"Of course, hija. It's Christmas, after all."

Sari looked at the stall and watched the way their makeshift drinking straw and soda can parols danced in the breeze. She smiled, and turned to the woman. She pursed her lips in the direction of the buko pie.

"How much for ten boxes?"

Chapter Twenty-Three

December 23

Gabriel glared down at his two sisters, the both of them giving him furtive glances as they continued to munch on their paninis from La Spezia and tablea made by Café Cecilia with chocolate from Kira's. They were sitting in the spot in his bakery near the window, therefore giving the entire neighborhood a full view of Gabriel's big reunion with his family.

Reunion or haranguing? Gabriel was still trying to decide.

Don't get him wrong, he was thrilled to see Rose and Iris again. He was actually surprised they figured it out—he would have thought Mindy would beat them to the punch. But they couldn't think that what they did was right, or smart. Nobody had known where they were, what they were doing, where they were going, and he was seeing red at the thought of them possibly getting hurt.

Which was why his first instinct was to find someone to blame. And he'd blamed Sari. And now she was never going to talk to him again. Shit.

He sighed deeply and collapsed into the chair between them, picking up a panini and eating. Ivy opened up her backpack and placed a jar with a piece of tape on it that said Belinda on the table. Gabriel recognized it immediately.

"You brought my starter," he said, almost cradling the thing in his arms. He already had one going upstairs, but Belinda was just a little more funky. "She's still active."

"Yeah, you think we would knowingly kill your little pet?" Rose asked. "Give us some credit, Kuya?"

"Are you going to call Ate Lily or Ate Daisy?" Iris said in a tiny voice. If Gabriel didn't know any better, he would think she said it like that intentionally to get him to side with her. Ah, the magic of the youngest kids. "Because they know, don't they? They always know. And you guys keep everything from us."

"I haven't decided yet," he grumbled in between bites. "And of course they know. Because I was responsible enough to tell someone where *I* was going."

"Yeah, but Ate Rose and I didn't lie, so…"

"You shouldn't have yelled at Ate Sari," Rose jumped in, more confident than Gab had ever heard her. "It's not her fault we found you."

"I know."

"And you shouldn't have lied about where you are," she added, because she was on a roll, and far be it from Gab to stop her when Rose was on a roll. "It's not my job to explain Dad's feelings to try to justify them, but you can be just as irrational as he is. And, I like to think that he says these things because he cares for you, you know? Why else would I be able to get a history degree, of all things?"

"Because you love history and research, and you

couldn't have been anything else," Gab pointed out, and it was the truth. Rose was one of the smartest people he knew, able to bring up facts and absorb things at the drop of a hat, which was what made her a much better member of the debate team than he had ever been.

"And you love baking, and you couldn't have been anything else," Rose insisted, smiling. Gab fought the sudden urge to hug her, because she was so smart. *When did the little kids get so smart?*

"Speaking of baking," Iris said, lowering her cup of tsokolate. "Kuya, can we *please* have some of those pain au chocolat? Or the cookies? Or the cupcakes? Or that cake, oh my God. Is that mango?"

Gab leaned back against his chair and crossed his arms over his chest, glaring at his littlest sister.

"Or…not?" she asked.

"Go ahead. But just *one.*"

"You're starting to sound like Mom and Dad. And Ate Lily. And Ate Daisy. I have too many authority figures in my life," Iris complained, getting up from her seat and marching to the counter, where Ransom was watching their reunion with great interest. "It's probably why I've never had a girlfriend yet!"

Gab turned to Rose, and waited. He could sense that his sister had more to say.

"Kuya, are you really not dating Ate Sari?" Rose asked. Gabriel breathed through the shock the question sent to his heart, and the pain that still lingered there. "I mean, I saw the video. I don't know a lot about love, but that was so sweet."

"She is sweet, isn't she," Gabriel sighed. Thinking about Sari three weeks ago had been frustrating. Two weeks ago it was with equal parts affection and kilig.

Now it was just…hurt. That someone who he thought understood him, didn't get him at all. "I don't know, Rose. I thought she was going to be supportive of my plans, but she kind of flipped on me."

"You can't always expect an exact reaction from someone, Kuya. I mean, look at what happened with Dad, and with us. You thought we were just going to sit back and let you do things alone?" she asked, and Gabriel remembered that at Rose's age, he'd insisted to his father that he was going to make a living out of baking. Had he been that…young? Woah. He also remembered what Sari said, about having people who loved him and came here for him. What she didn't seem to realize was she had those people too. And he wanted to show her that.

"I guess not," he said, grinning at his sister. "I mean, I did miss you guys testing my bakes."

"And I miss your cupcakes!" Ivy exclaimed from behind the counter, holding one in each hand. Oh boy. She was going to be a sugar-run nightmare for the drive back to Manila.

"Are you coming home with us, Kuya?" Rose asked, smiling expectantly like she'd read his mind.

"Yeah," he said, reaching out to tug her ear. "I'm coming home."

Chapter Twenty-Four

December 24, Noche Buena

Christmas Eve was Sari's favorite night of the year. The festivities were in full swing all around the Philippines. Karaoke machines came alive, lights came on, lechon was roasted and shared, boxes of pie distributed to her staff and suppliers. The Misa de Gallo had the Cathedral almost bursting with people, some in ordinary, everyday clothes, some dressed up in their Sunday best, all huddled with their families and loved ones to celebrate the last mass the midnight before Christmas. Sari, Sam and Selene had attended together, choosing the least terrifying statue to stand near, bringing huge hand fans to stave off the heat that came from the crowd.

After mass and a short walk back to the house, the three Tomas sisters watched a special report that Sam streamed on her phone, showing residents and tourists in Baguio all bundled up in scarves and beanies, reporting a new low of twelve degrees Celsius.

"It's happening," Sam insisted, pointing at the screen, still in full makeup while wearing pajama pants and a tank top. "Global warming! The next thing we know we're getting snow for Christmas!"

"Now *that* I would like to see," Sari said, taking a huge bite of her pan de sal stuffed with quezo de bola and cured fiesta ham as she slid into the empty space on the couch between her sisters. All three of them were dressed in silk bed robes from Lola Rosario, so special they only used them for Christmas. They had fuzzy slippers on and were eating as much as they could. In the corner, the belen was practically glowing, with the Baby Jesus, a chocolate bunny, nestled in his manger.

Just another classic Christmas in the Tomas house.

"Trust me, you don't," Selene jumped in, taking a bite off the buko pie in her hand. Noche Buena in the Tomas house was traditionally a utensil-free affair, because Lola Rosario hadn't had the heart to ask her maids to wash dishes on Christmas Eve. Nowadays, it was mostly because the sisters were lazy. But it was always about the silk robes and pajamas while you stuffed yourself with Christmas food.

"Take the buko pie away from me, I love it too much."

"Of course Ate Selene likes the least sweet dessert," Sam joked, returning to the living room with a bowl of sopas, macaroni, hot dog slices, shredded chicken and all. "And I notice someone is hoarding the brazo de mercedes."

"Hoy, it's Christmas, no judgements." Sari waved her sticky spoon at Sam. She couldn't help it, brazo was one of her favorite desserts. She thought it was brilliant, making a fluffy meringue roll from the egg whites and using the yolks to make a custard filling. Nothing wasted. Not to mention it was always sweet and dissolved like clouds in her mouth.

Her mother used to tell her that sugar clung to your thighs and never went away. Well, Sari had tried to stay away from sugar for two years, and her thighs were still pretty damn big. So no time like the present.

And if the brazo de mercedes reminded her of Gabriel, well, she was really good at pushing that particular thought aside.

"Exchange gifts!" Sam announced, leaping up from her spot on the floor to head for the Christmas tree.

"We don't exchange gifts until midnight," Selene reminded her, walking over to the food table to pick up a slice of ham from the platter and eat it. Lola Rosario was probably turning in her grave at the sight of her granddaughters eating without toothpicks, at least.

"New tradition! The three of us exchange gifts now, and we can open all of these other gifts in an hour or two. And as previously discussed, I claim all the gift baskets with food. I need food."

"What you need is a roommate, so you don't go stir crazy." Sari was now cradling her second brazo slice. "And so they can make sure the house doesn't fall to total ruin."

Sam gasped a little too dramatically. "I am a strong, independent woman who doesn't need a man to pick up after her!"

"Nobody was taking about a man-roommate. Do you remember hearing me talk about a man-roommate?" Sari asked Selene, who shrugged innocently. "But okay, let's exchange gifts. My gift to you is a trash can, because you can never have too many trash cans."

She pointed to the Christmas tree, where at the very back, three pretty trash bins in the shape of three different dogs were waiting for Sam. Her little sister squealed and jumped up, hugging Sari before she took the cans and made Kylo sit next to them.

"I love it! Oh my God, I can't tell the difference," Sam said, snapping a thousand photos. "And don't worry, Ate. I'll be here every weekend. And I'm in your shop so often, it'll be like nothing changed."

"Things have changed though," Sari insisted, shaking her head. She turned to Selene, who was looking at her like she was waiting for Sari to say something more. "But I know it'll be fine. We'll be fine."

The bright, beaming smile on Sam's face had more sparkle than a Christmas tree. She hugged her sister again, and looped Selene into the hug. Who would have thought a phone call by the beach did wonders for one's emotional health?

"I might as well tell you both too," Selene said, her chin still resting on top of Sam's chest. "My gift to you, Sam, is actually joint with Sari's. And mine. Sort of."

"Huh?"

"I got the three of us tickets to Paris for this April," she announced. "I planned a whole route from France to Italy where we end up in Rome, but…if there's anything you guys want to change, I can be…flexible."

Sam winced. "Oof, Ate, you sound like you just took a bullet."

"Wait, you're saying we're taking a vacation, just the three of us?" Sari asked, reaching a hand up to cover Sam's mouth. Selene smiled and nodded.

"Merry Christmas, Sari."

"Ate Selene got Ghost of Christmas Past, Present and Future-d!" Sam managed to wriggle her mouth free of Sari's hand.

"…what?" Selene asked her.

"What? Wasn't that what the movie was called?"

* * *

After Noche Buena, it was already well past two in the morning. The sisters popped open a bottle of wine and rang in Christmas with a bang and a semi-impromptu Greatest Hits of Christmas dance party. Soon enough, the noise died down, the neighbors were still going strong on the karaoke, and Sari found herself wandering out to the balcony, nursing a cup of barako and just one more slice of brazo. Oh well. The rest of the year was there to make up for the holidays anyway.

She curled her feet under her, listening to the Cathedral bells celebrating the birth of Jesus, and took a sip of coffee. Barako was sharp and acidic when you drank it, but it had a way of warming you from the top of your head to the tip of your toes, like a very sudden, very fierce hug.

Sari smiled.

Her phone chimed.

Rose Capras (@CapRoselia) is now following you!

Intrigued, Sari tapped Rose's photo, and videos from Capras Christmas came on-screen. Clearly the Caprases turned Christmas into a huge affair, the background showed off bright twinkle lights, a much bigger tree that Sari had ever owned, and infinitely more presents. There was a lot of noise, a lot of screaming and singing, and a black cat running around. They were playing the same songs Sari and her sisters had just been dancing to.

"Merry Christmas!" Rose's face appeared on camera, and behind her, three faces that looked like carbon copies of her pressed together and repeated the sentiment.

"Kuya Gab, Kuya Gab!" The camera moved and

pointed to Gabriel, who was eating…a brazo de mercedes. That he probably made himself. "What did you
wish for when you did Simbang Gabi?"

"And does she happen to make really good coffee?"
a voice, not Rose's, asked, and even from the camera,
Sari could see Gabriel's face turn totally red.

"Son, you've been holding out on us again," a deep
booming voice laughed, and Sari saw a hand clap on
Gabriel's shoulder as he smiled at someone off-camera.

"Daaaad…"

The video cut off, and Sari was pulled completely
out of it, like she'd forgotten that she wasn't with the
Caprases in their bright, happy house in Alabang. She
sipped her coffee again, and Selene emerged from inside the house, pulling her silk bathrobe closer to her
body. Her hair was a little mussed from when Sam tried
to braid it, and she was actually barefoot. It was a rare
sighting of Selene Tomas with all of her guards down.

"I love Lola Rosario for giving us these, but they're
worthless against the cold," Selene grumbled, sitting on
the coffee table next to Sari and taking a bit of her cake.

"Hey!" Sari protested. "What has gotten into you,
Ate?"

"I'm not sure." Selene shrugged, leaning back on
her hands as they rested behind her on the coffee table.
"Peace, joy, goodwill to man? I've always felt more relaxed when I'm here in Lipa. Which is probably why I
so rarely come here."

"Oh. I never knew that."

"Lots of things you don't know about me yet," Selene chuckled before she lifted a leg and lightly kicked
Sari's loose robe. "But I did promise I would try a little
more. You ready to talk about the baker boy?"

"The baker boy is moving on with his life. I'm all right."

"Is 'all right' special Time Lord code for 'really not all right at all'?"

"What?"

"Ignore that. But Sari. You're miserable. You've been acting like the world is going to come crashing down on your shoulders since the moment Christmas started. And I can see you trying to make things better. But some days it just doesn't work, does it?"

Her voice was so gentle and kind. Sari had always thought that while her grandmother clothed her and fed her, Selene was the one who'd raised her, and truly loved her. Selene was the voice in her head. Her conscience, her slightly scary guide.

And if Selene was telling her something was wrong... well, she had to be right.

"I just feel like everyone's moving on without me," Sari said, and her shoulders actually heaved at the weight that the sentence lifted off of her. How long had she been holding on to this? "First it was Mom and Dad, then Lola, then you, then Sam. And now Gabriel. I wasn't supposed to like him this much, or need him this much, Ate. And I'm really happy that he gets what he wants. Even if I'm not a part of it, but I miss him. I might even love him, and that's terrifying, because he could leave me, and devastate me."

"Does it have to be like that, though?" Selene asked her, kicking her robe again. "Gabriel isn't moving to another continent, he's going to be across the street. And if you're worried about the Laneways, then we'll deal with it when it comes. Life is always going to change up, Sari. You and I know that more than most people.

But if you give him the chance, I'm sure Gab will do everything he can to stay with you." She squeezed Sari's hand. "And I know I'm not a therapist, and I might not know everything, but Sari… I still think you should see one."

"I know," Sari agreed. Not because she needed fixing. She just needed a little help. A new perspective.

"And…if there's anything we've learned, the three of us, it's that people can still stick around no matter what the crazy circumstance. That relationships take work that you have to be willing to put in. We're Tomases, and we are anything but cowards."

"You're calling me a coward?"

"Yes! It's called falling in love because you trust that the other person can catch you." Selene grinned at her sister. "And yes, I got that from one of your historical romance books. But isn't that why you love them so much? Because the heroines are all strong enough to go after what they want, and damn the consequences, damn society?"

"I'm not a historical romance heroine though," Sari grumbled, pulling her knees up and resting her chin on top of them.

"No. You're Sari. You're one of my two favorite sisters, and I think you could fix this if you wanted to." Selene took one swallow of her coffee and kissed the side of Sari's temple. "Now go to sleep. Santa Claus won't come if you stay up."

"If you think that's going to work on me, then… fine," Sari sighed, getting up from her spot, taking her plates and coffee cup back into the house. She didn't know what to do, still. But maybe a good night's rest and a little Christmas magic would help.

Chapter Twenty-Five

December 25, Manila

"Gabriel, I think we need to talk."

Gab looked up from the breakfast table where Iris was trying to show everyone a video of a meme that he still didn't quite understand. As with a lot of events that involved the Capras family, Christmas morning was a loud affair. Everyone was still in their pajamas at eleven in the morning, having a lazy brunch of leftovers from the night before. But this morning, there was the addition of butter that Gabriel had made with unpasteurized milk from Blossom Farms (his siblings had been so confused when he explained that you could easily *make* butter) bread that he'd made just that morning with some of his old starter, and quezo de bola cheesecake already in the refrigerator.

The man couldn't sleep, but hey, at least his siblings were happy and very well fed.

Carrying a cup of coffee for both of them, Gab followed his father to the patio, where his father sat in the chair he sat in every afternoon to play Candy Crush. Hunter Capras was a man of work and routine, and you could always know where to find him depending on what time of day it was.

Inside he heard Mindy saying, "Oooh Kuya is in trou-ble!" while Lily and Daisy shushed her. Which always prompted Mindy complaining about why she was suffering from middle child syndrome when she was clearly part of the big kids group (she was not).

"Dad?" Gab asked, sitting across from his father. The scent of freshly brewed barako made Gab's stomach twist. He still missed Sari. Clearly baking his pain away wasn't going to work this time.

"I know we don't usually talk about things." His father frowned, putting his phone down, which only meant Gab was in big trouble. "But we need to talk about this last year."

"I got a mall deal too, Dad," Gabriel said, because this was exactly what his father wanted to be proud of. "They're opening a big one next to where my shop is, and they want us to open a store there. Then three branches in three years."

Hunter's face was inscrutable, but it softened slightly with a smile. "That's great, son," he told him, which was a lot more of a subtle reaction than Gab was expecting. "Are you happy?"

"I…guess so." Gabriel shrugged. "This is what you wanted for me, isn't it?"

"Me?" Hunter asked, clearly surprised, and Gabriel really, really wasn't enjoying where this conversation was going. "All I want for you is to be happy and settled. Comfortable with your life. Even if it's not in Manila. Your mom and I were just hurt you didn't want us to be part of your life."

"But you said…" He couldn't believe this. After all

of this time, after everything he'd given up, *now* his father chilled out and decided he could do whatever he wanted? Gabriel found himself standing, his pulse racing, his heart hurting. "Dad, you *said*…"

"I know what I said." Hunter frowned slightly. Everyone commented how much Gab looked like his mother, with the dimples and curly hair and all, but Gabriel oddly recognized a bit of himself in his father, in his stubbornness, his unwillingness to admit that he'd been wrong. "But you're old enough that you can decide on what you truly want for yourself. If that's a big store with three branches, great. If it's what you're able to do now, then that's fine too. You should be able to define for yourself what you need. You're not a kid anymore, Gabriel."

He felt his heart sink in his chest, even as hope blossomed to replace it. All this time, he'd buried himself in the weight of his father's expectations, and he was *just* getting that he didn't need them at all. Daisy and Lily and even Rose were right—Hunter was never going to change. But it didn't change how Gabriel loved his father. In the most complex way possible. But the choices Gab made were his, and his alone. And he knew the choice he had to make now.

He wanted to stay.

He wanted to stay in the Laneways with Sari and Ate Nessie, Kira and Ransom and Faye, wanted to be part of the community there. He still had a year on his lease, he could use one more. That didn't mean he wasn't open to expanding his business later on, because he still did. But not yet. For now, he wanted to stay in the place that felt like home.

If he was younger, he would yell at his father for this.

Make him understand even a little bit what Gabriel gave up trying to please him. But he didn't want to do that anymore. His father was trying his best, just as they all were, and didn't need to be saddled with more guilt than his son was already feeling.

I'll end up fighting on him with everything, Gabriel thought, shaking his head. *Thank God I have Mom and the siblings.*

"Dad," Gabriel said, giving his father a quick hug. "I want everyone to drive up to Lipa for my bakery's grand opening. I'll put you guys up at this cool hotel in the city. I think you'll like the weather there."

Hunter patted Gabriel's hand, and squeezed for a second. "I'm sure your mom and I will like it. Are you going somewhere?"

"I have to talk to my business partner." Gab shook his head. "Shit. Santi is going to *kill* me."

Unless Sari kills me first, he added to himself before he headed back into the house, where predictably, all eight of his siblings were surprisingly quiet at the dining table. He clapped his hands together.

"All right, who wants to help me win back the love of my life," he announced, and every one of them gave him an enthusiastic cheer.

Chapter Twenty-Six

December 26

The café was open promptly on December 26. It was also the first day that Sam was officially sleeping at the farm, and the day Selene was driving back to Manila. Oddly enough, Sari was fine about it all. Selene had insisted on setting up a private chat with just the three of them, with the only rule being that they couldn't discuss work.

Help!! There's a giant spider in the bathroom!!! Was the first message in the group from Sam. *Even Kylo is totally terrified!*

Sari was at the store at the earliest possible time, roasting beans for the day. Then she picked up her usual order of fresh milk from Blossom Farms (ignoring the pang that hit her in the chest as she passed Gabriel's subdivision). Life moved on, and while the Christmas spirit was still going strong in her, there was an unmistakable tug of wistfulness in Sari's chest.

She missed him. She missed him in every baked sweet she ate over the holidays, missed him in the scent of butter and sugar in the air. She missed him whenever her neighbors across the street put on *"Sinta"* on the karaoke machine, which so happened to be once every hour.

Then her shop opened, and it eased the tension in her chest a little. Life goes on, and change was always going to happen. Sari was behind the counter, whipping up candy cane coffee after candy cane coffee. Her customers were in a celebratory mood, clearly, and she was drinking it all in.

"Hey, we saw all the billboards for the new mall," Mrs. Ventura, one of her regulars, said as Sari placed her takeaway coffee on her amiga's usual table. The Mrs. Vs had been coming to her café ever since she opened, and had been loyal customers of her grandmother before her. Kira liked to joke that she wanted to be just like them when she grew older. "And Sunday Bakery was there in big block letters! Qué horror."

"He is a traitor to the Laneways!" Mrs. Vargas declared, thumping her poor table with the heel of her hand. "What a typical man. Handsome in the face, kind eyes, but will rip your heart out from you when you least expect it. And I bought mango cakes from him, too, for my Noche Buena!"

"What do we do, hija? Start a protest against the mall? Make someone write an article? Find someone in city hall? Do we know his grandmother?"

"No, no." Sari shook her head, wiping her hands on her apron and trying not to look her customers in the eye. Her chest felt a little tight, and she rubbed at the spot. "We're fine, titas. As long as we have customers like you, the Laneways is going to be fine. Gabriel can do whatever he wants. And if you think we're just going to let the Laneways go down without a fight, then we'd be really bad business owners."

Oh. Oddly enough, Sari completely believed that now. Selene's words had reassured her that things were always going to change, and she was going to have to adapt. Sure it sucked that she was going to have to see Sunday Bakery across from her, but Gabriel really did deserve that kind of success, if that was what he wanted.

She had everything she needed around her, and knew that the people who truly loved her would be there when she needed them most. Her small life was a happy one, and she would be happy with who came and went.

The Mrs. Vs were exchanging looks and waggling eyebrows at each other. Sari knew that the titas were silently communicating by the power of their perfectly threaded eyebrows and didn't really feel like interrupting.

"Sari?" Mrs. Vargas asked.

"Hmmm?"

"Have you ever considered getting a different commissary for your pastries? I love your coffee, hija, but, you know. New Year, new supplier?"

Sari blinked at Mrs. Vargas. It was the first time she'd ever expressed any sort of dissatisfaction with Sari, and she'd said it so kindly. Sari smiled and refilled her cup of barako.

"I'll think about it, Tita V."

"Hala, Tita V daw!" Mrs. Vargas laughed, because it was a joke Sari had always used around the Mrs. Vs. "Hay nako, Sari. I know your New Year's resolution, na. New food supplier, and then a boyfriend! You still have time. You're young, and beautiful, and there is still a lot of time to diet!"

Sari sighed deeply and ignored the little burn on her weight. It was pretty hard to think there was anything

wrong with her body now. Not when she could lift bags
of coffee beans to her lab and after being called a goddess in bed by the baker boy next door.

"I'll get your bill, titas," she said, turning on her heel
and walking back behind the counter, where Kira was
watching the two old women twitter with laughter and
continue people watching.

"One would think their New Year's resolution would
be to be less catty," Kira despaired, taking a sip of her
coffee. She'd come in as soon as the shop had opened,
declaring she needed to escape her family for today.
"You okay?"

"Oh, I'm fine." Sari shrugged. "Just thinking about
what they said."

"Sari, you can't let a couple of titas convince you to
change anything about yourself—"

"No, I was thinking more along the lines of the
food," Sari interrupted her, wiping down the counter
after a customer left. "They're right. It's ridiculous that
I keep serving bad food, and bad pastries when I know
where to source really good ones locally. Do you think
Santi would ever agree to sell me some of his paninis
and pasta?"

Kira's immediate reaction was to roll her eyes so
exaggeratedly that there was a brief second where Sari
thought her irises would completely roll off the top of
her head. "First of all, how would I know how Anton
Santillan thinks?"

"Well—"

"Don't answer that. Second of all, I am a little offended that you would think that I know how Anton
Santillan thinks."

"But—"

"No, don't answer that either." Kira dropped her head on the table for one second, and Sari gave her an indulgent smile. When Kira finally realized how she truly felt about Santi, it was going to knock her off her feet in the best way possible.

Sari should know. She'd fallen in love with the baker boy next door after nine nights.

"I wouldn't count on him saying yes right off the bat, but I know Santi respects you, or whatever." Kira waved her hands in front of her face. "I'm sure if you talk to him, you can come up with a deal for food."

"Why do you hate Santi so much?"

"I don't hate him," Kira huffed. "He's just…such a Virgo, you know?"

"I have to say, I don't."

"It's tricky, because Geminis and Virgos are both ruled by Mercury, but are sort of opposite signs…"

For the rest of the afternoon, Sari spent the day working, talking over her shoulder as Kira hung around for the rest of the day. Kira continued to explain to her why astrologically, a relationship would never work out between her and Santi, and why a relationship between a Libra like, say, Gabriel and a Capricorn like Sari would be difficult, but oh so worth the work.

"Do you think the Laneways is in trouble?" Sari asked Kira, who frowned and swirled her spoon in her second mocha of the day. She was also nibbling on a piece of 70% dark chocolate that she always seemed to have in her pocket. "With the mall and all?"

"Well, I consulted with a businessman," Kira said, and pointedly looked away when Sari's eyebrow rose so high she was sure it touched the ceiling. "What!"

"Kira…are you sure you and Santi aren't actually

friends?" Sari asked curiously. "Because you seem to talk about him a lot. We've been failing the Bechdel test for our last couple of conversations now."

"Hoy bes, no!" Kira looked absolutely incensed, even though Sari could clearly see that her friend was blushing. "I can't be friends with Santi!"

"But he's your consult about this mall thing, isn't he?"

Sari continued to tease Kira for a little bit, and Kira was making a really bold attempt at acting like she wasn't being affected. They talked about the Laneways, their plans to keep things going. They talked about the things they got for Christmas, potential plans for the New Year, and came up with a plan to make a special chocolate and coffee pairing set for Valentine's Day, even if it was months away.

By the time Sari was ready to close up that evening, she realized Kira was still there.

"You stayed," she said, blinking at her friend.

"I did." Kira smiled. "I knew you would drive yourself up the wall thinking about Sam, and the move and whatever is going on between you and Gabriel. So I thought I could help get you out of your own head."

"Thanks, Kira." Sari wrapped her arms around her friend in a tight hug. "You're the best."

"I am," Kira sighed, and loosened her grip on Sari to look guiltily at her. "But I have to admit… I was under orders."

Sari's brows knitted together in confusion. "Sam asked you to stay?"

"No…"

"Selene? I thought you were scared of her."

"Oh, I still am. It was Gabriel, actually. He was just leaving Manila, and I had to make you stay until he got here. And he said he just arrived."

Chapter Twenty-Seven

"So," Kira said, holding up her phone like she was making a big deal of replying to Gabriel's message. "What should I tell him?"

What indeed. Sari's heart was beating a little too quickly for her to think properly. But already she wanted so badly to hold him in her arms. To kiss him, and tell him that they were going to be fine.

"I'll be upstairs," Sari said, and if pressed to repeat what she had just said, she would find it impossible. She didn't exactly know what her heart was doing. Beating still, probably, but in an erratic kind of way. In a way that made her palms sweat and her knees weak. "You go ahead."

She needed to make coffee. Her grandmother always told her gifts made hard conversations just a little easier.

How could she not see it before? Well, because he drank coffee that came in a sachet, that's why. But she'd figured it out, exactly what he would want. Something a little childish, but deliciously dark and sweet.

"Sari?" Kira asked, reaching over to touch Sari's wrist. "You sure?"

"Yes," Sari replied, and her cheeks were already hurting because she was smiling so much. "I'm sure."

Sari wiped her palms on her apron and left the rest of her cleaning to the staff, practically running upstairs to the lab, floating on air, so excited that she missed a step and banged her knees on the stairs.

"OW."

"Oh my God, are you okay?" Warm hands touched her, and Sari looked up just in time to see Gabriel's concerned face, checking for cuts, for bleeding, bruising, anything. He held up three fingers.

"Quick, how many fingers am I holding up?"

"I'm fine." Sari shrugged him off, but it was a struggle to get up those stairs with a straight face, her knee was on fire. "Ate Nessie told me you were in Manila."

"Well, I do run a business in Lipa," he said, closing the door behind him and following her to the counter, where Sari was overcome with the urge to make coffee. She was already firing up her Slayer and grinding her beans, excited because she had figured it out. Gabriel's favorite. "My family wants to come over to the house for New Year, so I thought I would bake ahead."

"You went home," Sari said. "How was it?"

"Rocky as hell at first," Gabriel admitted. "There were tears. Mostly from me."

"You're such a softie."

"I missed you, Sari," he said gently. Sari smiled back at him, because she felt like she was in *Groundhog Day*. She'd lived this moment before, and could live it again over and over, and each time, her heart would skip a beat, and she would completely forget that her knee was throbbing because she was so happy to see him. "But I'm not sorry I pursued the mall deal. Or, well, that Santi pursued the mall deal. He is *very* good at his job."

"I agree." Sari nodded. She walked over to her

roasted beans for the day and picked up the darkest of the beans, tiny little things that shone like bits of onyx, until she put them in the grinder for a quick, coarse grind.

"You agree?" Gabriel asked, as if completely confused. "What do you mean?"

"I mean, I'm sorry I tried to stop you from getting what you wanted," Sari told him, her brows furrowing as her happiness gave way to a bit of guilt. "And that I didn't properly tell you how I felt about it. I should work on talking about how I feel more."

"I know, but you did tell me," Gabriel insisted. "I was the one who didn't listen, when I should have."

"I should have trusted that you were going to stay with me if you wanted to. But I really was worried about the Laneways."

"Don't be!" Gabriel shook his head, practically jumping out of his seat. "I called Santi yesterday."

"Oh."

"I wanted to choose you, Sari. I wanted to show you that I wanted to stay."

"Oh, Gab, you didn't…"

"Santi told me about the Lai Group's plans," he continued, and Sari could see he was practically thrumming with excitement, before he turned on his heel and walked to the direction of the fire escape, opening the door and propping it up with a chair. A cool breeze swept into the room.

Then he disappeared for a brief moment to open the fire escape door to the bakery, and kept it open too. He retrieved something from his kitchen and walked back to Sari like he'd never been gone in the first place. "City hall was worried about competition between the mall and the Laneways, so they agreed to fund the building of a bridge between the entrance of the Laneways and the mall. As long as the Luzes agree, and I imagine they will, the Laneways and the mall can stay together."

He placed a white box with bright, gold lettering stamped on it on the counter next to him, a red ribbon wrapped around the box like a gift. Sari was sure she could smell dark brown sugar, walnuts and chocolate. And she was pretty sure it was coming from that box. But Gabriel was saying so many things she could barely focus.

"That's all well and good, but I still convinced Santi to defer our move for at least two years," Gabriel said, quickly untying the box like he couldn't wait to show her what was inside. "I want more time with you, Sari. I want to be here. I'm staying. But not forever."

She released the coffee from the chamber, and the coarsely ground beans smelled incredible even from where she was standing. Gabriel tilted his head curiously at the coffee as Sari tamped it into the espresso machine.

Sari opened her mouth. Then closed it again. She'd never expected Gabriel would be willing to choose her over his career, the career he worked so hard for. Nor did she want him to. But she realized that what he'd given her was a compromise. A way to choose her, and a way to choose his dreams.

"I'm sorry I made you feel like you were being abandoned," he said. "I was only thinking about myself when I told you. And I shouldn't have done that. But Sari, you have to know. I don't want to leave you. I'm happy here in Lipa, happy here in the Laneways. But I really want this expansion for Sunday Bakery."

"And that's okay," she said, and she surprised herself with how fast she said that, how sure she was about that answer. Some things the heart just knew it wanted, and Sari wanted Gabriel like she knew she wanted to keep this place running. Like she knew that things were going to work out. "Not that you need my permission. But it will be okay. And you're sure you want this? To stay here for a little longer, I mean?"

"Yes," he said, and he sounded half-relieved. "I spent the last four years wandering the world, wanting to find a place of my own, the place where I belonged, so to speak. And that bakery is everything I ever wanted for myself, regardless of what my father thinks, even if he already said he was happy for me…"

"You guys talked, that's good." She nodded without looking up from what she was doing. In her peripheral vision, she noted that Gabriel was taking one step toward her, then backing away again.

"The bakery is my work. But I belong with you. I'm here to stay. I want to work this out with you, and make a home here. Finally take the plastic off of my couch. I can't imagine a morning without bonete and coffee, or hearing church bells when I drive home. But most of all, I can't imagine being here without you. You're home to me now."

"Oh." Sari stopped mid-movement, in the middle of making a double shot of espresso. Her mind became blank, and she forgot what she was doing. Her heart was beating in her chest, bursting with so much joy that she could barely hold it in.

"The only thing I wished for at Simbang Gabi," Gabriel continued, chuckling and showing off those damn dimples that made Sari weak in the knees every time she looked at them. "Was to be with you."

Then he opened the box, just as Sari placed a glass on the counter in front of him.

Gabriel watched as she poured the espresso into the condensed milk, the dark liquid turning a light caramel as she stirred.

"I don't want to be left behind," she admitted to him.

"I won't let that happen," he said, his fingers briefly touching hers. He was already standing close. "I'm sorry I did that to you."

"And I really, really like you. Scarily enough, I might even love you."

"Same."

"That's it? I tell you I think I'm in love with you, and all you can say is same?" Sari laughed.

"Same…and these are our cookies."

They were massive, bigger than Sari would have thought, in uniform size. The grated chocolate had melted, creating a lovely marbling on the cookie, with walnuts and oats occasionally poking out. Would the cookie be crisp? Fudgy? Soft? Sari didn't know. But she already knew they were going to be absolutely delicious.

Gabriel took his spot back behind the counter. She wished she knew what to tell him, because she didn't have the words. Was she just supposed to throw herself into his arms and cry, and believe that everything was going to work itself out, because it was Christmas?

There were more words to be said between them, more conversations to have about this. It turned out that they communicated best when they were both being rational adults. But he'd already asked her the important question. She was willing. Oh God, she was *so* willing. But was she ready?

"Well?" he asked, and she thought she'd imagined the way his voice caught just a little. He'd said it so softly she wondered if she was meant to hear it.

She looked down at the coffee she'd made for him. A bit had spilled over the rim of the glass, so she swiped it with her finger and took a taste.

Sari didn't know what would happen next, if this was going to be the happily ever after she wanted for herself. In the books she read, happy endings meant marriage and dozens of children. In the movies she watched, the camera pulled close on the two highly paid heads and let them kiss before pulling away like the story had never happened in the first place. What was her happy ending supposed to look like?

She didn't know. Neither of them could make sure promises of what tomorrow was going to be.

She could, however, make coffee. And she could sit here with him and eat cookies together.

"I've been trying to think of what your favorite coffee was," she said to him finally, sliding the glass in his direction. "I thought all you wanted was something sweet. But you're a little dark too. So Vietnamese coffee with dark roast robusta beans it is."

Gabriel's face grew into the biggest, brightest smile in the world. It was a smile that could make an ice queen's heart melt, and make any scrooge give in to the spirit of Christmas.

Sari sat next to him and pulled the box of cookies to herself. It was still a little warm. He took a sip of the coffee.

"It's perfect," he announced, his eyes never leaving hers.

She took a bite of her cookie. The chocolate was warm and dark, but the rest of the cookie still stood out, bursting into her mouth with sugar and walnut.

"Thank you for staying," she said finally, smiling. Then, because she was never one to have words, she reached her hand out for his. Gabriel squeezed her fingers, and it felt like home. "I'm glad you're here."

"Me too," he said, putting his coffee aside, and kissing her.

"We're going to be so bad for each other," she told him, with zero feeling behind the words. "We're both stubborn, petty and dedicated to our jobs. I need to see something before I believe it, and you're famously indecisive."

"We're also very loyal, and are willing to put in the work of understanding each other's emotions, and communicating," he pointed out. "Kira says Earth signs are really good at making Air signs feel grounded. And might I point out, I'm a Taurus rising, so…"

"And we're just going to trust the stars on this?"

"Not the stars," Gabriel said, his dimples now on full display. "Us."

And in the background, "Pasko Na, Sinta Ko" played. Such a sad song, but Sari thought it suited the moment. All Sari needed right now was the snow. There were other things they still needed to sort out, apologies she needed to make, deals with him to strike. But they were going to be okay. She was sure of it.

"I wished for you too," she told him before she finally placed her hands on his cheeks, and kissed him.

Epilogue

December 31, Media Noche

Filipinos choose to end their four-month-long Christmas season with a bang. Therefore, New Year's Eve was just as an important night as Christmas Eve. On this night, Catholics flocked to church to pray for hope in the upcoming year. Then they retreated to their homes with masses of food, as was custom in any holiday celebration in the Philippines.

But before all of that, there was the entire day the family spent prepping for the occasion. The Caprases did holidays in style, after all, and just because they were celebrating it in Lipa for the first time, didn't mean they were going to take it down a notch.

The boys had gone grocery shopping. This was mostly to get them out of the house while the girls did the rest of the preparation for Media Noche. While Gabriel was a kitchen whiz, both the twins and Hunter Capras could not be trusted in the kitchen or with grocery shopping, so he joined the group setting out of the house as the voice of reason.

"We're doomed," Mindy groaned as Gabriel unlocked his car. "We'll have chips and cereal for Media Noche and there won't be any milk."

"That was one time!" Angelo protested from the backseat.

"Have fun!" Sari said, and Gabriel could see her pressing her lips together so she didn't laugh out loud. For their first New Year's Eve together, Gabriel had accidentally left Sari in his house with his six sisters. A fact that he did not realize until after their shopping trip, when he and the twins were loading the groceries in the car.

Gabriel: I'msorryI'msorryI'msosososorry

Sari: Mindy saved a video of you dancing to Justin Bieber on her phone. I'm fine here.

Gabriel: Oh GOD. Let me preface by saying that I was six.

Sari: Six...teen, more like.

Gabriel broke most, if not all driving rules on the way back to his house. His brothers were only too glad to play rollercoaster, while his father gave him a wry look as they took a shortcut.

"In a hurry, son?"

"My sisters are ruining my love life," he said desperately.

"I don't think I've ever seen you this excited to spend time with the family," Hunter Capras said, and Gabriel knew that was part teasing, but also partly true. It was a complaint that they used to lodge at him all the time— always too busy, always out, never there, never at home.

But now? Ironically, it took moving to Lipa to make him love the time he had with his family more.

"She must be really special."

"She is," Gabriel agreed. "But it's everything, Dad. I get to bake and make people happy with my food. I get to be close to Sari. And you guys are welcome here anytime."

"I'll take you up on your offer. Your mother wants to visit all the churches."

They got home just in time for Gabriel to still hold on to a tiny scrap of his dignity. Apparently Mindy had saved his Captain Underpants video for last, and therefore Sari never got to see it.

"You say that like I can't send her the video," Mindy cackled, holding her phone close to her chest.

"I have the video too!" Ivy chimed.

"Me too!" added Angelo.

"Me too!" Mikael joined in.

"Oh, will you look at that, now I have it too," Sam, who had arrived with Selene ten minutes before, grinned with nothing but pure evil. Gabriel was basically screwed.

The Media Noche dinner was a rousing success. The girls had laid out three large rented tables underneath the Narra tree, with place settings for everyone. Their mother ordered the biggest bilao of pancit palabok from Amber's, and just the sight of the noodles and the shrimp made Gabriel's mouth water. She also got pork barbecue from the same place, because nothing went better with palabok than barbecue. To complement the savory dishes, the Tomas sisters brought pichi-pichi from their favorite shop in the city, half topped with cheese, the other half with dried coconut, depending on the preference. There was steaming hot tsokolate from Gemini Chocolates, and to top off the meal itself, Gabriel brought out a huge vat of sopas—with extra hot dog slices this time, as requested by his siblings.

For dessert, he made ice cream with the ube jam he'd gotten from a seller in Baguio and served it with Stick-O, which they sometimes used as an ice cream spoon. Then there was a selection of biscuits in lemon, pandan and butter to go with the tarragon tea, tsokolate or barako.

But his favorite part of the meal was the brazo de mercedes—made just because he wanted to, and just because he knew it was Sari's favorite.

"I'm dead," Mindy groaned, dropping face-first onto his couch with a biscuit in one hand and pichi-pichi on the other. "I forgot what your baking tastes like and now I hate you."

"If nobody wants the last slice of brazo…" Sari edged close to the serving plate, fork ready to slice.

"Ew, Ate, why would you eat pichi-pichi with coconut? Cheese is the way to go," Ivy argued, waving around her own cheese-laden piece.

"Cheese is only good for ice cream and spaghetti. Fact," Lily announced, sitting ever so regally on the end of the couch near Daisy's head, still working on her bowl of sopas. Selene, nursing a cup of tarragon tea and a stick of Stick-O, nodded sagely in agreement.

"It can't be a fact just because you say it is!" Mikael argued, his mouth practically purple with ice cream.

Over by the brazo area, Gabriel stood next to Sari, poking her lightly on her side.

"Hey," he said gently, and she looked up. She had a little sugar syrup on the corner of her lip, but otherwise she was perfect and beautiful, and he was so lucky to be loved by her. "How's the brazo?"

"Can I please have this in my shop too?" she asked. "It will work *so well* with the barako. And those biscuits? If we can get mini versions I can serve them for dine-in orders."

"Anything you want." He smiled, because of course she was thinking of her café at a time like this. It was one of the things they'd decided to work on—Gabriel was going to make a small line of pastries just for Café Cecilia, and Sari was going to make him a specialty blend in exchange. They'd heard the entire Laneways breathe a sigh of relief when they finally came to the same solution everyone else had thought of the moment they heard of the rivalry.

"Save your New Year's kiss for me?" he murmured into her ear.

"Convince me." She turned her head toward him and giggled, licking her spoon.

Once the New Year's dinner was cleared, it was the Tomas sisters' turn to entertain when the fireworks came out. Now, Gabriel's experience with fireworks was limited—he'd seen them, sure, but they were usually accompanied by music and lights and a goodnight from the theme park where he saw them. Apparently, Selene, Sari and Sam had different ideas.

"You look like you're about to blow up a bank," he said, his eyes wide at the bouquets of fireworks they carried in their arms, taken from the back of Sam's truck.

"This is all standard New Year's stuff," Sam insisted before she and one of her drivers headed off to the base of the driveway to set up.

"Ooh, what is all of this?" Iris asked as she and her siblings tentatively approached. Selene laid everything out in neat, separate piles for easy access and brought out a little matchbook from her pocket.

"It's everything you need to ring in the New Year," Sari informed the wide-eyed Caprases. "We have sparklers, or baby fireworks, as Sam likes to call them, lusis or the Harry Potter wands that actually shoot sparks, then the usual fountains, Catherine wheels, cake fireworks…"

"Cake?" Gab's eyebrow shot up.

"You know," Sari said. "Boom! Wheee! Pak! Wooow."

She'd punctuated this with hand gestures that were less than useful.

"That was unhelpful."

"You'll know when you see it," she insisted, before she pointed at an ominous-looking belt of brown triangles held together on a string. "Then there's that."

"Dynamite?" Angelo whispered.

"Sinturon ni Judas," Selene said ominously. Did Gabriel just imagine the little cackle she made after that? "If you're going to ward off evil spirits for the New Year, you might as well go all out."

"This is a little excessive, don't you think?" Gabriel asked, looking aghast at all the explosive devices that were now sitting in his driveway. It wasn't hard to imagine one of his siblings accidentally setting the cat on fire.

"This is standard stuff! The neighbors will get crazier, I'm sure," Sari insisted, tapping him on the chest, picking up a pack of lusis. "Make sure you have a mask later, the smoke will be intense. Now who wants to light up the lusis?"

For the hour coming up to midnight, the older kids kept busy helping the younger ones not start fires with the fireworks. Sam had taken charge of the big fireworks, and would occasionally light up the sky with green and red showers of sparks, fireworks that made noise as they shot up to the sky, and fountains. The neighbors had apparently gotten the memo too, because when the neighbors across the street weren't lighting something up, the Tomas/Capras contingent was, and if it wasn't them, it was the house to the left of Gabriel's rented place. Lipa had quickly become a city of sparks and noise, and it was like nothing he had ever experienced before.

Then his mother set up a pair of huge speakers, and music was playing to accompany the scene. In Gabriel's head, it was a lot better than any theme park scene he could have watched.

Holding a sparkler, he checked the time. Two minutes to midnight.

"I got it," he told Sari, approaching her as she held up a huge lusis, making shapes in the dark as Mindy took a photo on her instant camera.

"Hey, safety first, dimples!" She giggled, as three of his siblings snorted at the mention of his little nickname.

"Sorry," he said, tossing his used sparkler in the bin Selene provided before he approached her again. "It's about a minute to midnight. And I just wanted to say. You made this year…amazing. I love you."

Sari looked like she was about to drop the lusis, so he took it in hand with hers, slipping his other hand around her waist. Almost like destiny (or a really well-timed coincidence), *"Hooked on a Feeling"* played, and Sari started to laugh.

"Oh look, they're playing our song," she said, and they started to sway together. She looked up at Gabriel, content and happy, and his heart swelled too. "Happy New Year, dimples."

"Happy New Year, sweetheart."

They might have kissed about thirty seconds early, but from the way the fireworks were bursting around them, their families exclaiming close by, it was just as perfect.

* * * * *

Reviews are an invaluable tool when it comes to spreading the word about great reads. Please consider leaving an honest review for this or any of Carina Press's other titles that you've read on your favorite retailer or review site.

To find out more about Carla de Guzman or the #romanceclass community, please visit www.romanceclassbooks.com

Author Note

Some of my previous readers might have recognized most of the Capras family from my previous title, *Chasing Mindy*. I hope you also enjoyed the story of the oldest Kuya Gabriel as much as you liked Mindy's.

If anyone has a recipe for the Red Ribbon mango cake (you know, the one with the perfect mango dome in the middle?) I would love if you could send it to me, and I can make my sister bake it with my mom's mangoes, and I will be happy forever. Might I also say that Neiman Marcus cookies are the best cookies in the world. Please don't try to change my mind.

Sadly, the Laneways does not actually exist in Lipa, but was inspired by an alley in Little Bourke St. in Melbourne. Melbourne, however, does not have bonete, pan de sal or sansrival, what a conflict!

Also, disclaimer, I am not a fan of lomi. But I really love tuyo in the morning.

This book was written in 2018, and the world has changed so much since then. And while we're still trying to figure out what the future is going to look like, this is what I can offer for now.

#romanceclass is a community of Filipino writers, readers and creators of romance in English. *Sweet on*

You would not be the book it is without all the other titles in the catalog. I highly encourage you to check them out. Let me know if you want a rec, too!

Acknowledgments

I have been wanting to write a book about a baker for a long time. Blame it on The Great British Bake Off and my absolute love of a brazo de mercedes and Becky's Kitchen's Swiss Chocolate Cake. Mmm. But it didn't really come together to me until October 9, 2018, when Chachic invited me to be a saling-kit to her, Honey and Kat on a coffee session at the Giving Café. Someone joked about writing a barista MC, and Sari and Gab just sort of came to life right after that.

Thank you to Raoul, who very patiently answered my questions, and also for roasting my mom's coffee beans. The house has never had such good coffee.

The photo on the cover features the lovely and uber talented Rachel Coates and Jef Flores! Thank you Chi Yu Rodriguez, the emotional photographer behind #romanceclasscovers, the kilig you bring is on another level, kaloka.

To Stephanie Doig from Carina Press, who understood how important the voice of this book was to me, and answered all my impatient questions.

To Ninang Layla, who always has my back, and I like to think my entire writing career is thanks to her careful hand and listening ear. And for saying yes to all my panic-messages to her.

To the #romanceclass community, I dedicate this book to you. I wrote it just imagining what you guys would find sweet, nakakakilig, and funny and happy, and I hope that I was able to do that. Thank you for allowing me to be myself, and to find the thing that my heart enjoys doing!

To the Original Rosario, my Mom, who made all her farm dreams (and more) come true. May all your baby cows be girl baby cows. And to Dad, who planted all of the bamboo, and made me climb down a river and up a cliff one Holy Week. Thank you for not complaining (more than you already do) about how much I love a good café. I'm so happy you guys found a little home away from home in Lipa. And to my siblings! I hope you never read this. Or if you do, you don't tell me that you did.

Special shout-out to Gabbie (Gab, Gabbie, get it?) who explained to me how chocolate can explode, and how sourdough starts don't start.

And to Ma Cel, the original Cecilia. Lipa always reminds me of you, and all the Christmases and New Years we celebrated with you.

To Tito Johnny and Tito Quitos, who made Lipa special.

About the Author

Carla de Guzman is a Capricorn with a Libra moon and a Virgo rising, and she loves spending her midnights at her desk, writing contemporary romance. She loves to travel, and writes the love stories that those travels have inspired. She's currently on a quest to see as many Impressionist paintings as she can, and is always in search of the perfect pain au chocolat.

Follow along on her adventures on Instagram and Twitter (@carlakdeguzman) or on her website, www.carladeguzman.com.